GAME THEORY

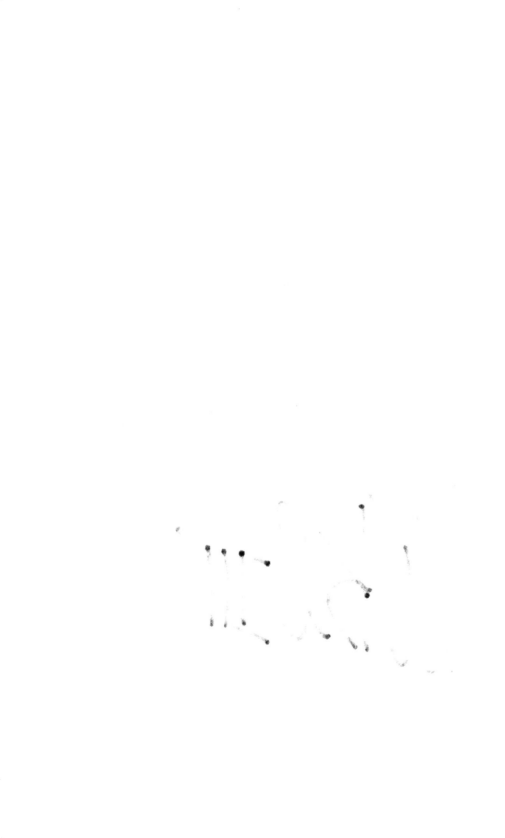

GAME THEORY

William Lange

Published by Pacific Arts Publishing

Publisher's Note: This is a work of fiction. Names, characters, places, and incidents are a product of the author's imagination. Locales and public names are sometimes used for atmospheric purposes. Any resemblance to actual people, living or dead, or to businesses, companies, events, institutions, or locales is completely coincidental.

Game Theory/ William Lange –First Edition
ISBN: 0999437003
ISBN: 9780999437001
Library of Congress Control Number: 2018930906
Pacific Arts Publishing, San Diego, CA

FOR PEYTON

Contents

PROLOGUE: A Delivery

He hated the work. His arms and back were wooden from lifting heavy boxes. His legs and feet were cement blocks from waiting for elevators, climbing endless stairs, trudging long halls and then hurrying back to the van. He had already delivered over two hundred packages, and he still wasn't finished for the day. *They say it's always like this during the holidays,* he thought. *I just have to get through it.*

Even if it hadn't been so busy, it would have been a difficult day. Heavy clouds had swept over the city early, and by midmorning, a drenching rain had started to fall. Then the temperature plummeted, and the rain froze and covered the streets with thick, black ice. Accidents popped up everywhere. In minutes, getting from one building to the next had become nearly impossible. But now—*finally*—he was down to his last delivery of the day. *After this one,* he thought, *I can return the van to dispatch and go home.*

He breathed a deep sigh of relief.

The van flashed its warning lights, starting the auto park sequence that would tuck it into the DELIVERIES ONLY parking space in front of the building. He used the moment to mind-click into the company's scheduling center to update his records. When he clicked out, the van was parked. He turned up the collar of his heavy jacket, jumped out, and opened the cargo doors. His last delivery was there, sitting in the middle of the van. It was a big package, wrapped in brown paper and marked for delivery to the penthouse apartment. He craned his neck to look up at his destination on the building's top floor, but the clouds and rain blocked his view. An icy raindrop stung his eye. He shook off the pain and started for the main doors.

As he approached the entrance, he was surprised to see there wasn't a doorman on duty. He expected one, even at this late hour. The residence was one of Chicago's most exclusive places to live and buildings like these were always guarded. His surprise grew even further when he stepped into the building and found the atrium deserted and the security desk abandoned. He wondered why, but a powerful thought overcame him and told him it wasn't his problem. He put his head down, gripped the package and walked toward the elevators. His heels clicked on the marble floor, echoing in the empty lobby.

The trip to the top floor was fast; the numbers on the digital display blurring as they raced upward. The elevator opened across from the penthouse. He stepped out to allow the sensors to alert the occupants he was there.

He didn't have to wait long. The apartment door became transparent, revealing a woman standing in front of him. He wanted to reach out and touch her, but he knew he couldn't. It was a security feature he had seen a handful of times in the most expensive residences. It allowed the caller and occupant to see each other from behind the protection of a locked door. A nice feature, so long as you could afford it. Few people could.

The woman behind the door was beautiful: green eyes flecked with copper, full red lips, and long auburn hair cascading in waves to her shoulders. He hadn't expected it. A pang of guilt hit him. His emotions had swung back and forth like a pendulum all day and he had struggled to understand them. But now that she was standing in front of him, everything was clear.

"Yes?" the woman asked.

"UX Express," he replied. "Got a package for . . .uh, Lupe Vincente. Needs a signature."

The woman hesitated. “Awfully late, isn’t it?”

“You’re telling me, lady,” he said. “The regular guy missed it yesterday. My super found it and sent it out, so here I am.” He looked out from behind the big box and smiled, flashing his soft brown eyes; he knew he had to gain her confidence and get into her apartment to complete his job. “I was s’pposed to be home hours ago,” he added, fixing his face into a sympathetic mask. “But I could come back tomorrow.”

“Oh no, that’s silly,” the woman replied. “Please, come in.”

Without hesitation, he shifted the package to free his left hand and followed her into the apartment. As the door closed behind him, he reached behind his back to touch the knife in his pocket.

It will do the job perfectly, he thought.

1

A Perfect World

*"Reality is merely an illusion,
albeit a very persistent one."*

Albert Einstein

SUNDAY, DECEMBER 7
12:03 a.m.

Jack Waldron stood in the marble hallway between the bathroom and bedroom, watching her. Fresh from the shower, soaking wet and naked except for the white terrycloth bath towel tucked around his waist, he ignored the puddle of water growing beneath his feet to focus his attention on her. He couldn't pull his eyes away from her. He loved watching her, whatever she was doing.

She was sitting on the far side of the bedroom, brushing her hair with an old-fashioned wooden hairbrush. A thin red negligee draped from her shoulders and exposed her freckled back. He watched her as she moved the brush through her long auburn hair, mesmerized by the way the muscles in her back rippled with each short, impatient stroke.

Her eyes had darted in his direction when he stepped into the room, but now she was pretending not to notice him. He smiled, thinking she was playing with him, but his smile faded fast when he noticed her pouted lips and the strain around her eyes. He knew the look. She was angry. He didn't have to ask her why. She was always angry when he had to leave. *It's the way she is,* he thought. *There's nothing I can do about it. Nothing unless I change her.*

He could change her if he wanted. It would be easy to do. He had considered it many times. But he loved her the way she was, flaws and all. He knew he would never do it.

He tucked the towel tighter around his waist and started across the bedroom toward her.

The bedroom was big, and furnished in the spare, modernist style that had become popular in recent years. Pollock, de Kooning, Miró—twentieth-century expressionist masters she loved, and he tolerated—hung on sectional walls and brought the room to life. Two couches, end tables, and lamps formed a sitting area in the center of the room, and on the room's perimeter, floor-to-ceiling windows curved in front of an expansive patio. The towering glass panes provided a sweeping panorama of the city and Lake Michigan. Tonight, as always, the view was spectacular: the city's lights sparkled, and a bright moon cast a shimmering path across the dark waters of the lake.

As he crossed the room, a warm wind wafted in through the open patio door. The breeze carried her scent to him, flooding him with memories of their lovemaking. He could feel the press of her lips, the pull of her hands on his back, the urgent push of her body against his. He felt himself growing aroused but forced the feeling away. *Not now. Now I have to leave.*

Besides, he knew he would be back. He always came back. He couldn't help it.

When he reached her, he stood behind her and extended his arms to caress her shoulders. "Have I told you today how beautiful you are?" he said.

She locked her eyes with his in the mirror and reached up to flick his hands away. "Not going to work this time, Jack." She started to brush her hair again.

"Rebecca," he said, exasperated, "you don't have to be like this."

The brush stopped moving. She glared into the mirror, slammed the brush on the dressing table, and stood to face him. She was tall and could look him in the eyes with just a slight upward glance. "How am I supposed to be?" she asked. "Am I supposed to be okay with you coming and going whenever you please?"

"It's not like that, and you know it."

"Yeah, sure, here it comes."

"Look, Rebecca, face it. You left me. And now, when all I want to do is to come here and enjoy this—whatever the hell this is—you make me feel like a piece of crap."

"I didn't leave you, Jack," she shot back, "*she* did. And besides, it's not that simple, and you know that better than anybody." She inched closer, wrapping her arms around his waist, pulling him tight. Her warm body pressed against his, her hot breath tickled his cheek. Her green eyes, flecked with tiny bits of copper, poured into his. "Why can't you stay here with us?" she asked, wetting her lips with her tongue.

She's not making it easy. She never did. "You know why," he said. "I have a life. I have responsibilities."

"But I miss you, Jack. And Sarah misses you, too. It makes me sad when she wakes up and you're not here." Their daughter Sarah was a fun-loving, pigtailed, five-year-old version of her mother. Just the mention of her name tugged at his heart.

"I know," he said. "Don't remind me."

"You won't be sorry," Rebecca said, her tone brightening. "We can take her to the lake and watch the boats. She loves that, and so do you." She nibbled his left ear and ran her fingers through his hair. He felt the blood in his veins pump and his resolve melt, but then, a pulsing blue light filled the room.

Alert. No choice now.

He pulled her arms away from him and stepped back. "I have to go," he said with finality.

Sadness flooded her green eyes. "Be careful," she said through a weak smile, "and hurry back. We'll be waiting."

Jack formed the thought *exit* in his mind. When he did, the room dissolved around him into a kaleidoscope of multicolored pixels, spinning, twirling, and melting into nothing.

2

Stranger in the Mirror

12:09 A.M.

When he emerged from his Game, Jack was staring at his left foot. It was propped up on a cluttered coffee table, his shoe tucked tightly between a half-empty bottle of whiskey and a half-eaten slice of pizza. He found himself fascinated by the shoe's appearance—scuffed, scratched, and desperately in need of a shine. He wondered why he hadn't noticed it before and done something about it. But as the real world slowly crept into focus, he remembered why. He didn't give a shit what his shoes looked like, and he certainly didn't give a shit what anyone else thought about them, either.

And with that thought, Jack knew he was coming back.

The clock on the wall, a mechanical relic passed down from one tenant to the next, told him he had been in the Game for seven hours. It was no wonder that he was so slow and confused. Coming out of a Game was harder than going in. Going in was easy, just a moment's disorientation that quickly went away. But coming out was different. The scientists had an explanation, something to do with the way the body produced a neurochemical cocktail to adjust to the depersonalization disorder experienced inside a virtual reality environment. The longer you were in a Game, they said, the more chemicals the body made and the longer it took for the body to clear them. It was like a hangover. They also had a name for it—Neurochemical Saturation Syndrome—but it was a name everyone ignored. Because the Game's interface was through the brain's occipital lobe, everyone just called it "lobed."

Right now, Jack was really fucking lobed.

He looked around his third-floor apartment. Cramped and claustrophobic, it was just three rooms and a utility kitchen. The pockmarked walls begged for paint. The scratched and scuffed floors cried out for repair. A single smudge-covered window peered out onto his crumbling neighborhood on Chicago's south side. Tonight, an icy rain pelted the window and froze into rivulets that blurred the flashing signs, holograms and neon lights of the bars, eateries, and storefronts on the street below. He shivered, vowing to complain again to the choleric Pakistani apartment manager about the clunky steam radiator that sat impotently banging and sputtering against the far wall. He burrowed deeper into his stained couch, trying to get warm.

The room was almost empty, just a few pieces of dilapidated furniture sprinkled here and there. He wasn't following modernist design; he just couldn't afford to buy more. The divorce three years ago had left him broke and broken. He spent most of his salary on whiskey and black- market Game credits. The whiskey helped him cope with the real world; the Game credits let him escape it. Nothing else mattered much.

He sat up straight, pulling his leg back from the coffee table, jiggling it and knocking over the silver photo frame. He leaned forward, picked up the frame, and stood it back upright on the table. The frame held a live motion photo of Rebecca and their daughter, Sarah, taken years before. Sarah smiled and waved at the camera. He gripped the bottle of whiskey and took a big swig, waiting for the pain to go away. It was taking more whiskey these days, but he didn't care. He stood up and walked to the bathroom, snapping on the fluorescent light above the mirror. He watched his image flicker and sputter into view.

He didn't know the person in the mirror. He remembered his other self—the man in the Game. That man was sober and tough. That man knew where he had been and where he was going. But that man—the man he used to be before the guilt and the nightmares—disappeared long ago.

The man he was looking at was unrecognizable. His eyes were unfocused and dull from too much whiskey, his skin pale from too many hours spent in the Game. He was painfully thin, wasting away from skipping meals, out of shape and weak from ignoring the training routine he had followed for years. His black hair was unkempt and unwashed. He needed a shower and a shave. The man in the mirror didn't care where he was going. He had stopped caring long ago.

He even had the scar to prove it.

He traced the deep gouge on his right cheek with his finger—a two-inch scar irregular in size and shape. It marred his handsome face. A good surgeon could make it less noticeable, but he had decided long ago that he wouldn't fix it. He chose to leave it behind when he played the Game because the scar had no place in it. The Game mirrored the life he had once lived with Rebecca and Sarah, and the scar had come after that life ended. But here in the real world he found the scar useful. It reminded him of his rage and of the revenge he would someday extract.

He remembered that he had an alert.

He splashed water on his face, dried with a stained towel and headed into the living room. He took another swig of whiskey, then tapped the plastic link that circled his right ear and stretched an extension arm to the back of his neck. The touch turned on his external mind-link to the WorldNet.

The effect was immediate. To an outside observer it might look as if Jack was simply staring off into space, but not to Jack: Jack was using his mind to move through the vast WorldNet at the speed of thought to retrieve his messages. The scientists called it Neural Interface Interaction, but everyone else called it "mind-clicking" or just "clicking." When he clicked his alert icon, a message appeared: "CODE 187: TOWER PARK 3, PENTHOUSE APARTMENT; OFFICERS ON SCENE."

What the fuck? Jack thought.

He froze, unable to process what he was seeing. His brain raced. His heart pounded. He recognized the address. *Code 187. Homicide.* He hoped it didn't mean what he thought it might mean.

It couldn't mean that. Or could it?

When Jack could move, he moved fast. He raced to the front door, wriggled into his shoulder holster, and tucked his service weapon into it. He pulled on his heavy coat, grabbed his gold Unitex Chicago Police Department detective's badge from the side table, shoved it into his pocket, and started down the stairs.

When he rounded the corner of the stairwell, the door to his apartment was still open.

3

Blue Smoke

12:47 a.m.

Detective Eddie Rodriguez was pissed off. Dressed in a rumpled gray suit, black raincoat, and black fedora—clothes he'd thrown on when he got the call—Eddie was steaming mad at the bad luck that placed his name at the top of the call sheet and put him here in the middle of the night. He hated waiting for the idiot medical examiners to finish their work. *Those assholes already know who committed the crime,* he thought. *Everything they're doing is just bullshit.*

Bullshit. Bullshit. Bullshit.

The more he thought about it, the more his anger grew.

He lit a number-four nootropic and took a long, impatient drag, exhaling a cloud of luminous blue smoke. He watched the smoke twirl and twist in the climate-controlled air, waiting for the cigarette's energy-enhancing effect to hit him. If someone wanted to complain about the cigarette and preserving the integrity of the scene of the crime, that was fine with him; he would tell them to fuck off and work faster next time. Besides, there was already plenty of evidence for the prosecutor. Everybody knew that, too.

Eddie dropped his gaze to look at the murdered woman lying on the floor in front of him. "Man, she was *fi–i–ine,*" he murmured, dragging the word out into a long three-syllable construction. When he had stretched it as far as he could, he added his own short epitaph: "What a fucking waste."

"Yeah, but she doan luk so gud mow."

The garbled words came from Eddie's partner, Detective Duane Chapman. A six-foot five tower of jellyrolls squeezed into a cheap blue suit, Duane stood next to Eddie polishing off a chocolate bar. He gave Eddie a broad, dumb grin through a mouth ringed by smears of chocolate.

"What the fuck, Duane?"

Eddie shook his head. He hated Duane and complained to anyone who would listen to the reasons why he didn't deserve "dumbass Duane" as a partner. If Duane's father hadn't been a captain, Eddie complained, there was no way he would have even made the force. And that Duane made detective in less than three years . . . well, that was just department politics. Eddie thought about his own slow, painful climb up the ranks and vowed that someday he would pummel Duane even more senseless than he was already.

Eddie glared at Duane, twisting his pockmarked, ferret like face into an angry mask. Duane caught the glare and nervously cleared his throat; he had seen Eddie's rage explode before and wanted no part of it now. "I said," Duane articulated carefully, "she doesn't look so good now."

Eddie stared at Duane for another long moment. When he turned away to focus his attention on the body, Duane let out a long sigh of relief.

She was face down on the carpet, naked except for the torn remnants of yellow panties still clinging to one of her bruised legs. Stabbed a dozen times from her lower back to her neck, her wounds were deep and covered in dark blood that had taken on the consistency of wet pudding. A knife stained with blood was stuck deep in her back, and stood out in stark contrast to her pale, freckled skin. Her fingers still clawed the carpet in a testament to the pain she must have felt when the knife plunged into her repeatedly.

Looking at the body didn't faze Eddie; it was just part of another night's work. "Yeah, well," Eddie grudgingly opined, "the rich bitch deserved it."

"Why?" Duane asked. "What'd she do?"

"She was lovers with that one over there." Eddie nodded in the direction of a woman on the other side of the room.

The woman Eddie nodded at was Latina, attractive, and past middle age. How far past was anyone's guess, but it was easy to see she was one of the lucky ones—a woman with the fine, balanced features and good genes that defied aging. Her skin was dusky and unblemished, and her toned body showed hours spent in the gym. Her short, dark hair and athletic form gave her a "tomboy" look, but it didn't stop the men in the room from looking at her the way men look at a sexy woman. Dressed in a dove gray designer suit, she wore just one piece of jewelry—a gold charm bracelet that dangled from her left wrist. Her expensive designer shoes, in a color that matched her suit, sat clumped together on the floor next to the sofa. Sobbing uncontrollably, she was curled up into a fetal position on a sofa while a uniformed female officer sat next to her trying to comfort her.

"Who? What?"

Eddie shook his head again. He decided that dealing with Duane was like dealing with a child; he would have to go even slower than usual for Duane to comprehend. "Do you see that woman there," Eddie said, articulating each word, "the one crying? She's Lupe Vincente, the number two big shot at the company." Eddie placed special emphasis on *big shot*, spitting it out with bile.

"Yeah, I see her, so?"

"You know who she is, don't you?"

"Yeah, I know. So?"

"So, she was living with this one." Eddie nodded at the woman's body on the floor, his disdain written on his face. No one else cared about sexual preferences anymore, but Eddie did: the first girl Eddie had dated dumped him for a woman. The incident had made him the laughingstock of his high school class. Even though it was nearly twenty-five years ago, it still pissed him off.

"Oh."

Eddie stared as Duane peeled back the wrapper on another chocolate bar and appraised it with hungry eyes before taking a bite. "What?" Duane said.

"They were together, Duane." Eddie studied Duane's face for a trace of understanding but saw none. "Gay, Duane. G-A-Y." Eddie spit out each letter slowly and carefully.

Duane's eyes darted to Lupe, the body, and back to Eddie. A broad smile of understanding swept over his face. "No shit?"

Eddie shook his head in disbelief. "Yeah, Duane, no shit." He took a deep breath and exhaled. "You know, Duane…"

Loud shouts erupted near the front door, but the police officers at the door blocked Eddie's view. He stepped around the body and craned his neck just in time to see Jack Waldron shove a uniformed police officer and storm toward them. Jack took a few steps when two officers grabbed him and argued with him.

"*Mierda,*" Eddie intoned, "the captain ain't gonna like this."

"Like what?" Duane asked, wiping his mouth with the back of his hand.

Eddie flicked a finger in Jack's direction. "Detective Waldron just joined the party."

"Yeah, I know him. So?"

Jack broke free from the two officers and walked toward them. Eddie grabbed Duane's arm to move him away from the body. "You are slow, Duane. You know that?"

"You don't have to be a prick about it."

Eddie watched as Jack dropped to his knees next to the body. "The dead woman, Duane," he said in a low voice. "You saw her name on the sheet, right?"

"Yeah."

"Rebecca Witherspoon," Eddie added.

"Yeah."

"That's her maiden name," Eddie said. "She changed it back to her maiden name when she divorced Waldron."

Eddie looked at Duane for a sign of understanding. He didn't see one. He shook his head. "Waldron's wife, Duane. His wife. She was Rebecca Waldron."

Duane bit down hard on his chocolate bar. He stared at Eddie with wide eyes while he chewed and swallowed. When he finished, he cleared his throat and whispered, "No shit?"

4

Uncomfortably Numb

12:53 A.M.

Jack's reaction to seeing Rebecca dead on the floor surprised him. He didn't feel anger. He didn't feel sadness, grief, remorse, or guilt. He just felt an icy numbness that had swept over him the instant he knew for certain that it was Rebecca. He didn't know why. He only knew that those emotions would come later, and that he was grateful to be free of them now. This was the scene of the crime. He didn't intend to leave it in the hands of Eddie Rodriguez and Duane Chapman. He didn't trust them. But, then again, he trusted very few people. The company had taught him that.

"This is not a place for you, Jack. There's nothing you can do here." Jack felt a sympathetic hand on his shoulder.

The voice, thick with a French accent that made "Jack" sound like "Shack," belonged to Police Captain Remi Moreau. Remi was Jack's boss, and one of the few people Jack trusted. But no matter how much he respected and trusted Remi, this was not a request Jack could accept.

"That's my wife."

"She is your ex-wife, Jack, yes. And that's why you can't remain here. You know the rules. There can be no personal ties."

Jack stood up and looked Remi in the eyes. "I'm not leaving."

They stared at each other, locked in a clash of wills, as the medical examiner's staff put the body into a black bag, raised it onto a gurney, and wheeled it away. When they had gone, Remi broke the icy silence. "How did you find out? Who called you?"

"It came as an alert. I didn't check with dispatch. I figured it was you."

"It wasn't me."

"Then who?"

A thoughtful look crossed Remi's dark, lean face. "That is a good question, Jack," Remi said.

A buzz of whispers and murmurs grew and then faded away as everyone in the room turned to the door. Remi saw him before Jack did. "Christ," he said, "what's he doing here?" Remi shook his head and headed for the door.

Jack didn't need to look for himself; the look on Remi's face had told him everything he needed to know. He stepped back to meld into the crowd as William Weatherall, Unitex Chairman and CEO, entered the room.

A visit to the scene of a homicide by William Weatherall was the last thing anyone would ever expect. It was like a famous rock star showing up at a high school talent contest, or a famous movie star sauntering into a middle school performance of Shakespeare. It had a predictable effect; a pin-drop silence enveloped everything.

In a world where three giant corporations controlled everything, William Weatherall was the undisputed "King." The battle for dominance among the "Big Three" was epic, but Unitex—a massive conglomerate of powerful companies that stretched from the northernmost parts of Canada to the southernmost tip of South America—was winning the battle. That made William Weatherall the most powerful and influential man in the world.

It also made him the worldwide face of business. His image was everywhere: in holograms, on signs, on the news, all over the WorldNet. He had the most recognized face in the world, and in person, he was no less impressive. Impeccably groomed, and dressed in Savile Row's best, he moved with a confidence and purpose that made everyone around him feel as if they were dwarves and he a giant. He knew it and used it to his advantage when needed.

Tonight, he didn't need to exercise any personal power; Unitex owned and ran the Chicago Police Department, just as it did with almost every government function across the Americas Trade Union ("ATU"). It was the inevitable consequence of corrupt public unions and inept bureaucrats bankrupting their governments, forcing the privatization of services. Jack watched as Weatherall stood at the doorway, searching the room with his quick, dark eyes, and then strode toward Lupe Vincente. The silent crowd parted in front of him like a wave splitting at the bow of a moving ship. His bodyguards trailed behind like small boats trying to keep up with a bigger, faster ship.

A cold chill crawled down Jack's spine. It had been two and a half years since Jack had last been in Weatherall's office. Jack had tried, but failed, to erase the memories of that day and everything that came before it.

Jack watched Weatherall cross the room and wondered why he was here. Lupe was the company's chief operating officer, the second most senior officer in the company, and Weatherall had known Rebecca in the manner that any top man knows a rising senior subordinate. But Jack knew that Weatherall had little compassion, and certainly not enough to drag him from his bed in the middle of the night to show up at a crime scene. *He's here for some other reason*, Jack thought. He filed the notion away, pulled his silver flask of whiskey from his coat pocket, and gulped a big swig. He didn't give a shit who saw him do it.

Lupe had her face buried into the shoulder of the female officer seated next to her. Weatherall placed his hand on Lupe's shoulder, squeezing it with just enough force to get her attention. She turned to him and tried to stand, but Weatherall kept her from rising. He lowered himself into a kneeling position and leaned in to talk to her. Jack strained to hear them, but they were too far away to make out anything more than the soothing tones of Weatherall's voice and an occasional, breathless sob from Lupe. Their conversation was quickly over. Weatherall stood and nodded at Remi.

Remi took a few steps forward.

"All of you know that this apartment is equipped with a Virtual Reality Surveillance System," Remi said. "The VIRSUS was running, and the system can give us a full playback. But before we run the playback, I remind everyone that this playback is for *authorized personnel* only. I will check, and if I find that anyone without authorization has logged on, well, let's just say I will be very unhappy."

Remi turned to Eddie Rodriguez. Eddie stepped forward holding a small transmitter in his left hand. He looked around the room, signaling to the crowd that the playback would begin. Most of the crowd had permanent microchip implants buried beneath the skin at the back of their necks. These links were always turned on. But a very few in the crowd—including Jack—wore external links that surrounded one ear and had a plastic arm that pressed a neurotransmitter against the base of the neck. The external link could be turned off or removed, so those who wore them reached up to make certain that their link was on.

Jack waited nervously for the playback to begin. He had relived more than a hundred gruesome murders in playback, and he expected to relive more as the technology infrastructure grew. Today VIRSUS playbacks were limited to the homes of the well-to-do, major streets, public transportation, and some public places, but the systems would soon be everywhere. It was a boon to police work, but Jack had never known a victim personally and had certainly never loved one. Living through a crime—seeing it in all its terrible aspects as if you were standing just a few feet away—was an unsettling experience. He knew the next few minutes would test his limits.

Jack clenched his fists as a wave of adrenaline coursed through his body. His heart pounded harder and faster as a swirl of pixels swept him, and the other observers, into the playback of the murder.

5

Playback

1:22 a.m.

A Christmas tree nestled in a corner of the penthouse apartment. It was a big tree, twelve feet high, and its white lights and shiny ornaments showed the deft touch of a professional decorator. A few feet away a log burned in a fireplace, adding its own soft yellow glow to the room, and casting a long shadow behind the couch where Rebecca sat curled up reading a printed book. Jack smiled; Rebecca had always had a penchant for old-fashioned things, especially old books.

A doorbell interrupted his thought.

He watched Rebecca stand and walk to the door, stretching and yawning as she did. He saw that the playback time code read SATURDAY, DECEMBER 6, 9:59:32 P.M. He swallowed hard, feeling the heavy weight of guilt, knowing that he had been in his Game with Rebecca's virtual avatar when she was murdered in the real world. He didn't want to watch her die, but he knew he had to.

When Rebecca reached the door, she activated the transparent security door. A uniformed deliveryman stood in the hallway holding a brown paper package that blocked most of his face from her view. He peered around the package with soft brown eyes.

"Yes?" she asked.

"UX Express. Got a package for . . . uh, Lupe Vincente. Needs a signature."

Rebecca hesitated. "Awfully late, isn't it?"

"You're telling me, lady," the deliveryman said. "The regular guy missed it. My super found it and sent it out, so here I am." The deliveryman shifted the big package, leaning left to make his face visible. Handsome, in his mid-thirties, clean-shaven and neatly dressed in a pressed UX Express uniform, he spoke with a streetwise charm that made him seem trustworthy. "I was s'pposed to be home hours ago," he added, "but I could come back tomorrow."

"Oh no, that's silly," Rebecca replied. "Please, come in." She entered a code in the door controller. The door opened, and the deliveryman stepped into the foyer. His eyes followed her gesture as she pointed across the room. "Would you mind putting it over there next to the tree?" she asked.

They walked across the room together. When they arrived at the spot Rebecca had pointed to, the deliveryman put the package on the carpet. Then he stepped toward Rebecca, a dark shadow silhouetted against the rain-swept windowpanes. Rebecca lurched backward frightened, uncertain whether she should scream or say something.

He didn't give her a chance to choose.

He wrapped his hands around her throat, squeezing her trachea shut like a vise. Her eyes popped like a squeeze toy and a blood vessel in her left eye burst, filling her tear duct with blood. He lifted her off her feet and slammed her to the floor. He released her long enough to let her suck in a lungful of air. Once she did, she let out a piercing, animalistic scream.

Jack lurched forward to grab the deliveryman but stopped himself after a single step. It was an automatic reaction; there wasn't anything he could do. It was just a program running to show a crime that had already been committed. He just had to endure it.

The deliveryman silenced her scream with a blow to her jaw, splitting her skin and crumbling her front teeth. He ripped her shirt open, slamming his fist into her gut. She doubled over in agony and misted the air with blood as she coughed it out.

The deliveryman wiped the blood from his shirt and grinned. His eyes were cold and black. He flipped her onto her stomach, beating her in the kidney as she tried to rise to her knees. Then pressing his forearm against the back of her neck, he shifted his weight, and her vertebrae cracked and popped in protest. Her screams became worse, powered by the pain and the fear of what she knew was to come. The deliveryman pulled a knife from his back pocket, and held it against the white flesh on her well-formed buttocks. Using its sharp tip, he severed the waistband of her yellow thong underwear and pulled it down around her left thigh. He put the knife down.

Then he raped her.

She stopped screaming and gasped in pain. She had no more fight left, just tears, and she was quiet. The only sound in the room was the slapping of the deliveryman's body against hers. He picked up speed, driving deeper and harder and built to a climax that made her pour out a mournful cry. When he was finished, she feebly tried again to rise to her knees, but the deliveryman had only begun.

He pulled away and zipped his pants. Then he picked up the knife.

He rolled her over. The first cut slit her from the base of her neck to the small of her back, streaming ribbons of blood across her skin and onto the carpet. She cried out so loudly that it seemed impossible that no neighbor would have heard, but in a luxury building the soundproofing was nearly perfect and her weakened voice was no match. The deliveryman raised the knife, hesitated for a moment, and stabbed her repeatedly. With each deep thrust, Rebecca's hands clawed the carpet in agony.

Dying, she looked one last time at the glistening ribbons of light on her window. Her lips formed a word. She tried to speak, but nothing came out; she soundlessly gurgled and bubbled bright red blood. The final blow buried the knife deep and pierced her heart. Her eyes clouded, fixed on a distant point of light, and dimmed into darkness.

She was dead.

The deliveryman rose unceremoniously. He buckled his pants and looked around the room. Then, as if he was seeing it for the first time, he walked over to the package and stared at it. He picked it up and walked across the room to the door. He had taken just a few steps when a voice yelled, "Freeze!"

It was Weatherall's voice.

The images froze as the playback stopped and the program went into suspended animation.

Freezing a playback allowed the viewers to step into and examine the details of the crime as it occurred. There was always a lot to learn by seeing the crime from multiple angles as it occurred, having the chance to examine the action even down to the smallest details. When the program was running, each person observing the crime was alone. But Weatherall's command instantly brought all the onlookers into the room, now able to interact with one another. Even the faces of the jaded veterans showed the strain of seeing this crime unfold. Everyone took a collective deep breath.

"What do we know?" Weatherall's voice resonated with anger.

Eddie edged forward and stood next to Weatherall. A criminal record appeared next to the deliveryman.

"The perp is Donald Dillon, thirty-eight. He's got a long jacket. Nine hits: theft, drugs, mostly petty stuff. He's a registered sex offender. Went up at Crest Correctional for burglary but swung an early after five. We don't have a locator on him—he's off the grid." Eddie shrugged his shoulders to help make his point. "Maybe no chip, we don't know."

Remi, still glued to Weatherall's side, studied the information. When he finished he turned to Weatherall, "Don't worry, Bill. Chip or not, we'll find him. You can count on it."

"I am counting on it," Weatherall snapped. He took a last look around the virtual crime scene. "That's enough," he said with finality. "Turn it off."

The virtual reality dissolved in a swirl of pixels. There was a collective exhaling of breath, a shuffling of feet, clearing of throats, and the growing murmur of voices speaking in low, hushed tones. A young detective heaved violently, a combination of the effect of leaving the virtual world and witnessing the gruesome crime. A thin stream of vomit splashed onto the carpet and formed a pool at Eddie's feet.

"God damn it," Eddie complained, "will someone get him outta here."

Two paramedics rushed to escort him to a bathroom. A grizzled veteran detective tagged along; he looked as though he was ready to throw up himself.

Jack was watching them leave the room when he saw Weatherall looking in his direction. He knew in an instant that Weatherall had spotted him. Weatherall pulled Remi to a private space where they could talk and not be overhead. The discussion was out of Jack's earshot, but Jack knew that they were talking about him. When it was over, Weatherall and Remi shook hands and Weatherall turned and headed for the door. Everyone in the room watched him go. When he walked out, everyone in the crowd sighed in relief.

Remi walked over to Jack.

"What did he want?' Jack asked.

Remi leaned in close. "He wanted to know what you were doing here."

"What did you tell him?"

"I told him you got an alert."

"What else?"

"He wanted to know who sent it."

"And?"

"And I told him I didn't know. I told him you didn't know, either. After that he said, 'Give him my condolences,' and then he left."

Jack started to say something but changed his mind. Remi jumped into the open space. "Go home, Jack. Take some time off. And, do yourself a favor by staying out of this. Leave this to the department."

Jack didn't respond.

"Call me if you need anything," Remi added.

Jack finally nodded and moved toward the door. On his way out, he lingered for a moment in front of Lupe. Their eyes locked in an icy glare before Jack turned and walked away.

PROTECT OUR
CHILDREN'S FUTURE

KEEP MANKIND
PURE

People United Resisting Enhancements

LEARN MORE AT HTTP://WWW.PUREORG.NET

6

PURE

2:47 a.m.

The elevated platform for the Maglev was dark and nearly deserted, illuminated by just a few small pools of light cast from lampposts that vandals hadn't smashed. The rain had stopped, but the air still held an icy mist that blurred the forms of the people waiting for the train. Jack watched them move in and out of the light—there one second, gone the next. It reminded him of the early virtual reality programs where you always knew you were in the Game. Now, the real world seemed like a game and the Game seemed real.

Part of Jack's musing was alcohol. He was drunk.

His first stop when he left the penthouse apartment had been a downtown liquor store where his arrival roused the dozing clerk. When the bottle of whiskey crossed the counter, he ignored the clerk's protests and drained a third of its contents. He gulped another third of the bottle on the short walk to the elevated Maglev platform. Now, huddled against a wall of the graffiti-scrawled platform in a futile attempt to stay warm, he was polishing off the rest.

A frigid wind swept down the platform, stirring a flapping noise behind his shoulder. He turned to see an old-fashioned paper poster taped to the wall, fluttering in the breeze. A worn corner broke free and blew away into the dark. The poster was red and black. At the top, it read,

"Protect Our Children's Future." In the center, the dark silhouettes of a man and a small girl held hands in front of a brilliant, boiling yellow sunrise. At the bottom, below the sunrise, it read, "Keep Mankind PURE," and below that, "People United Resisting Enhancements." Centered at the bottom it read, "Learn More at http://www.pureorg.net."

PURE. Jack knew the group well. He had a private connection; one he tried to ignore. He also had a professional connection he couldn't ignore.

PURE opposed cybernetics—the physical merging of man and machine. It also opposed eugenics—the genetic manipulation of DNA. But the group's primary focus was the implanted chips, judged by PURE to be the most immediate threat. The focus of their outrage was Chicago-based Digitex, the Unitex subsidiary that created, manufactured and sold the DX series digital microchips. The DX chips, first offered seven years earlier as the DX-1 and later upgraded to the DX-2 series, were an instant success. Powerful, fast, and offering apps that external links couldn't handle, DX implanted chips were rapidly replacing the world population's external links. Almost everyone Jack knew had made the personal decision to have a permanent chip, but Jack hadn't and he never would. He had his reason, but it was a reason he could never tell anyone.

Most of the population thought of PURE as nothing more than a collection of kooks, senile old folks, crazies and refugees from other failed causes. The average citizen embraced transhumanism—the belief that humankind's intellectual, physical and psychological capabilities should be enhanced with technology, and thought PURE greatly exaggerated the threat that came with the chips. Supporters of transhumanism had many arguments. Didn't millions of people already depend on bionic limbs and manufactured organs? Weren't those devices linked to the brain? How could anyone argue against an artificial heart beating in the chest of a six-year-old child? And since no one under sixty-five had ever known a world without the Internet, and its privatized, upgraded and security-enhanced successor the WorldNet, they couldn't imagine a world without instant access to unlimited information and instant communication. They enthusiastically welcomed anything that made life easier. Mocking PURE had become a part of the language. "What are you, PURE?" had become a common derision, replacing the mundane, less colorful, "Are you an idiot?"

If they only knew, Jack thought.

A bright flash illuminated the platform. Jack turned to see the electric blue halogen of a Maglev speeding toward the platform. Seconds later the platform floor next to the clearway flashed yellow to warn passengers to step back. Jack watched as the train emerged from the icy mist, a great carbon fiber whale growing bigger every second. It swept silently into the station, and then slowed to the muted clicking of its servos reversing the magnetic fields that floated it between steel rails and propelled it forward. The train stopped, and the doors hissed open. Jack stepped into the brightly lit interior and grabbed an overhead handhold.

The graffiti-scrawled, litter-strewn passenger car was nearly empty; the three people in it paid no attention to Jack's entrance. They were oblivious to him, each linked to the WorldNet, and each with a small, portable Game console. The portable consoles were a necessity for full VR immersion, although it was rumored that the company was hard at work on a way to eliminate the need for them. Each of them was experiencing a virtual reality far removed from the passenger car they shared with one another. A Latino teenager played drums in a silent band, waving his arms wildly. An overweight, African-American woman sobbed softly, tears streaming down her face. An elderly Japanese man sat motionless with a wooden cane in one hand; his face a blank mask that offered no clues about his emotions.

Jack had left his link turned on and as the train accelerated out of the station and into the night, an advertising program activated it. Advertisements could do that in public places. Most advertisers wisely chose not to interrupt anyone spending Game credits, so right now the ad was playing only for Jack.

The ad appeared to Jack like a hologram floating in the air in front of him. Swirling multi-colored pixels formed a stylized human head that displayed a small microchip implant at the back of the neck below the base of the skull. The chip illuminated and grew in size as a familiar woman's voice began a warm, compelling sales-pitch: "The new DX3. Faster speeds, broader bands, better walls. A better WorldNet experience. Available Christmas day from Digitex Corporation, a Unitex company. Digitex, bringing the WorldNet to you." The image morphed into the face of a famous female virtual entertainer. She smiled and faded from view.

Jack felt the old rage take over, a rage that no amount of whiskey or hours of Gaming could ever quiet. His eyes searched for the WorldNet transmitter and found it just above the entry doors. Reaching into his jacket, he pulled out his gun, jumped up onto a bench, and pounded the transmitter with the butt of the gun, hammering it until its blue light flickered out and pieces rained down on the floor like black plastic snowflakes. Finally satisfied, breathing hard, pulse racing, he stepped down from the bench and holstered the gun.

He took several deep breaths to calm himself and then took a long swig of whiskey. He looked around the car. The three passengers, their Games abruptly ended, stared at him with accusatory eyes. He ignored them. He tried to look out through the windows, but the night was too dark, and the car too brightly lit to see beyond the dirty, reflective panes. Instead, he saw the reflection of a disheveled drunk staring back at him.

7

Nothing to See Here

2:47 a.m.

Remi Moreau was taking a last walk around the empty penthouse apartment before calling it a night. Closing a crime scene typically belonged to the lead detectives—in this case, Eddie and Duane—but Remi had decided to close this one himself. He felt the need to linger in the apartment while the facts percolated in his mind. He didn't understand why he felt that way. But then, not much about the case made sense to him anyway.

He was certain about only one thing: he would not stumble upon anything important on his walk or turn up anything new. There would be no new clues found, no startling discovery. More than two-dozen detectives and forensic examiners had scoured the premises; it was impossible they had missed anything. There would be no sudden "Aha!" moment when everything about the case came into focus.

Besides, they already knew who committed the crime. They had all watched it happen in all its bloody, brutal detail. Watching the VIRSUS playback had been hard. It had taken all his resolve to watch it without turning away. Seeing someone you knew in life murdered in such a brutal way had been tougher than he had ever imagined. He wondered how Jack had endured it.

He also wondered how it would affect Jack. Jack blamed himself for his daughter Sarah's death. Now, Remi knew Jack would blame himself for Rebecca's, too. Would he make it through this after everything else that had happened?

Beyond that, Remi had a feeling in the pit of his stomach that Rebecca's death was just the beginning of bad things to come. Weatherall's presence at the scene of the crime all but guaranteed it. Worse, he suspected that whatever was coming, he would be dragged into it, just like the last time he and Jack were pulled into the maelstrom of Unitex politics and plots. That time was bad, full of danger. The memories of the waking nightmare he and Jack had lived through still haunted him.

Whatever was coming, Remi knew it was a powerful tsunami and that no matter what he did now, it couldn't be stopped. He just had to prepare himself for it and hope to make it out. But even if he did manage to survive it, he hoped he could look at himself in the mirror when it was over.

Remi was already a survivor. Born Masoud Jafari, a Shi'a Muslim and the only son of a prominent Niger surgeon, his early years were pampered and easy by anyone's standards. But when Sunni Muslim organization, Boko Haram, crossed into Niger from neighboring Nigeria, his life changed. At fifteen, he watched Sunni thugs murder his father and mother and saw his twelve-year-old sister taken captive. Shaken and scared, he found refuge in the battered ruins of the city. Hiding there with the Shi'a resistance, inspired by their example, he found the courage to fight back.

In less than twelve months, he was a legend in the resistance with a long line of bloody Sunni bodies behind him. He also became a major target for the enemy. But when he learned of his sister's whereabouts, he risked everything to rescue her. Slipping alone into a Boko Haram encampment one night, he murdered eleven of the enemy before disappearing into the darkness with his sister in tow. Knowing that he could not remain in Niger without risking her life, he escaped into neighboring Algeria and eventually made his way to Reims, France. There, he sought refuge with relatives and Masoud Jafari became Remi Moreau.

Remi knew about surviving.

Time to go. Remi stepped into the hallway and pushed the code into the generator that set up the holographic, yellow POLICE LINE, DO NOT CROSS warning banners. When the lines were up, he clicked into the building's security system to secure the door with the department's entry codes and heard the door click shut. The sound reminded him of a gun's slide pulled back to chamber a round.

Loaded weapons have a way of going off when you least expect it, Remi thought. He hoped he would have warning before this one did.

8

Welcome to the Neighborhood

3:20 a.m.

Walking home through the dirty, litter-strewn streets of his neighborhood always depressed Jack. But now, in the bitter cold, obliterated by drink and haunted by the images of Rebecca's murder still fresh in his mind, the word despair barely scratched the surface of his feelings. Staggering along the icy sidewalk, Jack stared contemptuously at the finger of liquor remaining in the bottle and finished it with a gulp. He wasn't worried about running out of whiskey. Just down the street, the bright red, holographic sign of his neighborhood liquor store beckoned him forward. He quickened his pace, doing his drunken best to negotiate the ice, but the going wasn't easy.

All around him, his broken neighborhood glowed like a cut-rate Las Vegas. Holograms and flashing neon signs blazed everywhere, advertising everything imaginable. Even though the residents were barely scraping by, the fucking "suits" still wanted their last buck. Jack despised them, and tonight he had even one more reason to do so: their blazing, multi-colored lights were reflecting on the sidewalk, making the icy patches impossible to spot. He had already taken two bad falls.

As he approached the liquor store, Jack mind-clicked to contact the store's robotic attendant. It was illegal to replace a human job with a robot without approval, but after eleven robberies in six months—one of them almost fatal—the owner had decided that his own life was worth the months of paperwork and the high cost of making the change. So, when Jack clicked-in, the robot responded with a confirmation, and by the time Jack walked through the door, the bottle of whiskey was on the counter in the grip of the robot's mechanical arm. When Jack's payment cleared, the arm released the bottle.

"Thank you, Jack," a nondescript computerized voice responded. It was also illegal to assign human appearance and characteristics to a robot, but that didn't stop Jack from responding as if the robot were human.

"Fuck you, asshole," he slurred.

He opened the bottle and took a swig that made him dizzy and sent a wobble to his knees. He figured that tonight there wasn't enough liquor anywhere to push his demon away, but he planned to try.

Jack trudged forward, rounded the corner to his block, and then came to a dead stop. Three people were locked in a confrontation on the street in front of his apartment building: two men and a woman in her late twenties.

The woman was pretty in a rough-and-tumble sort of way. She looked as if she could handle herself, even here in this broken-down part of town. Her raven hair swept from her forehead to the nape of her neck and ended just above her jacket collar. She had a long, straight nose pierced with a small diamond, and thick eyebrows that arched above dark, wary eyes. Her lips were oversized and heart-shaped. Somewhere under her clothes and heavy coat, Jack knew there were tattoos; he briefly wondered where and what kind. She was gripping a big cardboard box with her back pressed against an ancient gas-driven automobile. The vehicle was plastered with worn and peeling counterculture stickers that championed everything from animal rights to world peace. A PURE sticker covered most of the passenger door.

The two men, one tall and massive, the other short and skinny, both in dark hooded jackets, were hassling her. They had their backs to Jack, but something about them seemed familiar. Jack wondered if he could avoid getting involved when the woman's tense voice ended his speculation. "Hey, man, leave me alone!"

The tones and vowels in her plea pegged her as French Canadian. *Quebec, maybe,* Jack thought. Chicago was flooded with Quebec refugees these days, ever since that province crumbled from the weight of its withdrawal from the Americas Trade Union.

"Baby, what's wrong wid you?" the big man asked in a baritone rumble. "I got jus' what you need." He thrust his hips back and forth, mimicking sex.

"Yeah," the short one laughed, his voice thin and high-pitched, "he got jus' what you need."

Both men laughed.

"Fuck off, man," the woman said.

"Da mout on dis bitch." The big man shook his head in mock offense.

The short one spoke again. "You know who dis man is? My man Rocco here run dis terry-tory. Every mofuck fo' miles do what he say."

Rocco. Shit. Jack knew him all too well, a local drug dealer with a side business pushing stolen Game credits around the neighborhood. That made the little one "G." He was Rocco's gopher, cheerleader and collector. Small, yes, but plenty mean. Both were tough customers. Worse, Jack had been buying Rocco's black-market credits at a deep discount, looking the other way at the illegal drug business if Rocco kept it off his street. If it got out that he was bypassing the company to buy illegal credits, he would be in deep shit. He sighed, knowing he would have to proceed with caution.

"Kiss my ass." The woman's voice had jumped up an octave in tone.

"Now dat's sumthin' we can agree on." Rocco smirked.

"Yeah, but we gonna have to teach her some manners first," G chimed in.

Jack knew what was next. Rocco slapped the cardboard box from her hands and the box spilled its contents of books onto the ground. Rocco crushed the woman against the car and forced his mouth on hers. She tried to fight back, pummeling him with her balled fists, but he was too strong. If he felt the blows, he didn't show it.

"Hey, assholes!" Jack yelled.

Rocco turned around. His dark eyes narrowed when he saw Jack. But when Jack staggered and stumbled toward them, his huge black face cracked a broad grin that flashed a gold tooth. He turned to G, laughing. "Can you believe dis motherfucker?"

"Yeah, he wasted, man."

Jack puffed himself up, trying to appear sober. "I told you to keep this shit away from my block, Rocco."

"Fuck off, Waldron. This ain't your business. You ain't in no condition to be hasslin' me."

"Yeah, we jus' talkin'," G said. He looked up at Rocco. "Let's do him, Roc."

Jack wobbled back and forth, his vision blurred, and he blinked his eyes to see straight.

"Yeah," Rocco muttered, "I think he picked the wrong night to be fuckin' around." A wicked smile crossed his face.

Jack saw the smile and knew what would happen next. He reached for his gun, but his heavy jacket blocked his hand and they were on him. He swung the bottle at Rocco, but the big man was fast and ducked out of range. Jack had only a moment to see Rocco before G's fist slammed into the left side of his own face. He tilted his head right, and the blow grazed off the side of his cheek. He fired back a hard, left jab that caught G on the nose. G grabbed his face, squealing in pain. Jack smiled, taking drunken pride in the shot, but a crushing blow from Rocco wiped it away and sent him reeling to the icy pavement. He landed with a thump that sent a wave of pain shooting through his shoulder. He was just getting up when a powerful kick struck his stomach, and a second weaker kick landed in the middle of his back. He braced for more, but the woman's voice rang out and froze the action.

"Hey, assholes!"

The three combatants looked toward the sound. The woman was standing less than ten feet away holding an STZ, a powerful police stun gun. It was the new model that sent a charged energy beam to its target without a wire contact. Jack wondered where she got the gun; even he didn't have one.

Rocco backed away from her, his hands outstretched. When he spoke, his street language vanished. "Now hold on. Take it easy. I was just playing around with you."

Rocco's sudden elocution amused the woman. She smiled wickedly. "Don't worry, baby," she mocked, "I got jus' what you needs."

A blue stream flashed from the gun and wrapped Rocco's body in an iridescent, electric straitjacket. The powerful beam pinned his arms tight against his body and sent him into convulsions. He dropped to the pavement, flopping, twisting and gasping like a fish out of water. His panicked eyes and mouth, frozen open in a soundless scream, pleaded for release. The woman smiled as he squirmed until his kicking and twisting had turned him a full circle on the icy pavement. Satisfied, she released the beam and turned her attention to G.

Panic crossed G's face. In a flash, he held his hands high above his head in surrender, his body shaking. "Hey, no, not me, please," he pleaded.

Jack smiled at the sight of G ready to piss his pants.

"Get your pal and beat it." The woman's voice was steady.

"All right, I'm sorry. I'm sorry. We're leaving."

"Don't ever let me see you again. You got it?"

"I got it. You won't. I swear."

G pulled Rocco to his feet. Together they hurried off into the night.

Jack laughed. The sight of this good-looking woman handling those jerks the way she had amused him. He forgot for a moment where he was, why he was drunk in the early morning hours, and where he had just been. He did the thing that felt natural. He clapped his hands. "Bravo!" he yelled.

The woman pointed her weapon at him. "All right, man. Who the fuck are you?"

"Who am I?" Jack asked, still laughing. "Me? I'm the guy who saved you. You might say I'm your knight in shining armor."

"Saved me? Those two would have killed your drunk ass."

"Timing. I was just waiting for the right time before I struck the final blow," he slurred. "And besides . . ." His voice trailed off as he fumbled with the buttons on his jacket and reached into his pocket. A short burst from the stun gun dropped him hard onto the icy ground.

"Keep your hands where I can see them."

"Ouch. Jesus Christ," Jack groaned. He pulled his hand out of his jacket and turned his badge toward the woman. "I'm a cop."

The woman stepped forward and snatched the badge from his hand. She took a few steps back and examined it. Satisfied, she tossed it back to him. Jack missed it and it landed on the icy pavement. He clumsily picked it up and put it into his pocket.

"All right, Detective Waldron," she said, "what the hell are you doing here at this time of night?"

"I live here," he said, nodding at the building. He took a long swig from the bottle of whiskey that somehow had miraculously survived the melee intact. He wiped his mouth on his sleeve. "What's your excuse? You the new official neighborhood punk zapper?"

"I'm moving in."

"At this time of the morning?"

"Short notice."

"What's your name?"

"Charbonneau. Cassandre Charbonneau..." She waited a moment, then added, "but everyone calls me Cassie."

Jack pulled himself to his feet, flicking bits of ice from his jacket. He looked up and down the now empty street. He had the sudden, powerful feeling someone was watching him. He shook it off, deciding he was getting more paranoid every day. "Well, Cassie," he said, "be careful. It's a rough neighborhood."

"Yeah? Thanks for the tip."

"And if you need anything else, just look me up. I'm in 302."

Jack turned and walked away, his stride no longer a stumbling gait. The fight had pumped him full of adrenaline and the stun gun had shocked him sober enough to navigate around the icy patches. He made fast progress to the front steps of the aging, red brick building and disappeared through the front door.

Cassie watched him go. When he entered the building, she turned her attention to unpacking her car. "Don't worry, Detective," she said to no one. "I will."

9

Kaleidoscope

5:56 a.m.

He stood alone on the rooftop, gazing out at the city. The first gray fingers of dawn were scraping the tops of the buildings and pulling the dark shadows from the city's steel and concrete canyons. He walked to the edge of the roof and looked down. A lone motorboat showing red and green lights chugged eastward on the Chicago River, cutting a frothy wake through the frigid, dark waters. He watched as it passed below and motored on toward Lake Michigan. He kept watching until it cleared the breakwater and its bright white stern light grew dim in the distance. Then a cold wind swirled around his head and broke his reverie.

It occurred to him he couldn't remember how he had arrived on the rooftop. He looked underneath his heavy coat and saw that he was dressed in his UX Express work uniform. *Why am I dressed like this? My shift must have ended hours ago. Where have I been? How did I get here?* He scratched his head, digging into his memories, but his mind was a blank.

He had a sudden urge to have a cigarette. He reached into his pocket and pulled out a pack of mind-enhancing, number two nootropics, dug deeper and found a lighter. He tried to light the cigarette, but a twirl of wind blew out the flame. He cupped the lighter with his left hand and flicked it. Protected, the bright flame was steady. He leaned the tip of the cigarette toward it. When he did, he saw the dark stains on his hand and sleeve.

What's this?

A thin, orange line of sun broke through the eastern horizon. He turned his hand to the light and could see the stain. His other hand was stained, too, and his other sleeve, and so were his uniform shirt and pants and even his shoes. *Blood? Is this blood?* He examined the stains carefully. Whatever it was, he knew he needed to wash it away.

Somehow, instantly, he knew what to do. The river was the perfect place to get clean.

He walked purposefully and calmly to the edge of the roof, taking a long, final drag on the cigarette before he flicked it away. Then, arms outstretched, he leaped out into the sky. He arced out gracefully in a perfect swan dive, but his form didn't last, and he tumbled as he fell toward the water. It was a long way down, and his rotations grew faster and faster until the city, the river and the sky swirled around him in a kaleidoscope of colors. As the river rushed up to meet him, he smiled, thinking that he'd soon be clean of the stains. It was his last thought before his body slammed against the unyielding surface of the water and his broken form disappeared beneath its surface.

10

A Good Cop

12:01 p.m.

Jack's few hours of sleep had been fitful, his dreams a bloody mosaic of images of Rebecca's death. After five hours of tossing and turning, he had awakened with a start and climbed out of bed. He showered, dried and dressed in less than ten minutes. He wriggled into his shoulder holster, bundled against the cold in his heavy jacket, and jogged down the street to the elevated Maglev platform. The train was pulling into the station when he arrived. He jumped through its closing doors and disembarked twenty-five minutes later at the Unitex station downtown. From there, it was a two-minute walk to the building. He walked into Unitex headquarters at one-minute past noon.

Headquarters was always crowded—Sunday was no exception—and if the stares he was getting from the horde of police, suspects, lawyers and civilians lining the halls were any indication, he knew he looked as bad as he felt. He touched his swollen face and winced. Rocco threw a damn good punch; he had to give him that much. He probed his face, making sure that nothing was broken. He knew it would be days before the swelling subsided. Nothing he could do about it. The effects of the liquor were long gone, too, leaving him with the familiar trembling in his hands. Nothing he could do about that either. He ignored them both.

He wasn't on duty, and he wouldn't be until tomorrow morning. He had no real business being here, and Remi had warned him off Rebecca's case. He planned to keep a low profile.

His usual duty was the day watch, eight a.m. to four p.m., Monday through Friday. It was undemanding duty by anyone's measure. Officially, he held the watch because of his seniority, but Jack knew the real reason he had the shift, Remi wanted to keep an eye on him. He didn't have to be here on a Sunday, but nothing could have kept him away. Rebecca was dead. Someone had to solve her murder. He didn't intend to let that someone be anyone other than him.

He turned the corner to the squad room and headed for his cubicle. It was easy to spot, a messy jungle of paper, pens and scribbled Post-it notes in an otherwise neat and paperless office environment. He sat down and turned on the live photo with the familiar image of Rebecca and Sarah smiling and waving. He held the photograph in his hand for a long moment before he felt a presence standing behind him.

"I don't know why you're so hung up on her, Jack," Eddie said. "After all, she chose that bitch instead of you."

Jack clicked off the photo and stared at the darkened glass. He could see the reflections of Eddie and Duane standing behind him. They were about three feet away, Eddie to the left of Duane. He placed the framed photo on his desk, patted it once, and then launched himself backward like a swimmer at the start of a race. He arced through the air, twisting in mid-flight, and crashed into Eddie with enough force to drag him to the ground.

They struggled for the advantage, rolling across the floor, bumping into a cubicle, and tumbling one of its walls to the floor. Eddie was fast; he squirmed out of Jack's grip and jumped to his feet. *It's like fighting a weasel,* he thought, *a weasel with fists.* One of those fists hit him with a hard right as he started to get up, bloodying his mouth, and dropping him to the ground. Jack answered by hooking one foot behind Eddie's foot and pushing against his knee with the other, throwing him off balance and slamming him to the ground. Then both men were up again, facing one another, trading hard rights and lefts, the blows landing with heavy thuds. A crowd had gathered and was cheering them on when two uniformed officers leaped into the fray and pulled them apart.

"Knock it off!" Remi's voice echoed around the room.

The crowd froze like a bunch of kids caught with their hands in a cookie jar. A second or two later they dispersed. Only Duane remained, blindly focused on eating a chocolate bar, until Remi walked up to him and tapped him on the arm. When he felt the tap, Duane looked down at him, took one look around, and scurried off like a kid sent to the principal's office. Remi watched him go, shaking his head. Then he looked at Jack and jerked his thumb toward his office.

Jack dusted himself off—something that was getting to be a habit—and followed him. Remi was sitting behind his desk when Jack walked in and closed the door. Remi took a moment before he spoke. "What am I supposed to do with you?" he asked, his face growing even darker than it usually was.

"You didn't hear what he said."

"I didn't have to."

Jack couldn't let it go. "He's out there mouthing off again about Rebecca and Lupe Vincente. It's bullshit."

"Yes, I know. But nobody's listening and nobody cares."

"He's an asshole."

"Yes, he is," Remi answered. "He always has been, too. But he's a good detective. Like you used to be before you climbed down into the bottle."

"I'm still a good cop."

"You're a drunk, Jack."

"It's under control."

"Bullshit!"

Remi reached into his desk and pulled out a small holographic emitter. He dropped it onto the desk and pushed a button. A holographic image floated in the air between them. It was a surveillance recording of

Jack hammering the WorldNet transmitter on the Maglev into tiny bits. It started with Jack pulling out his gun and ended with a crazed Jack Waldron huffing and puffing and downing a big swig of whiskey while scowling at the three startled passengers. Remi watched it without a show of emotion. When it ended, he stared at Jack with a raised eyebrow.

"It wasn't my best day," Jack said with a shrug of his shoulders.

Remi picked up the emitter, tossed it into the open drawer, and slammed the drawer shut with an angry shove. "Jack," he said, his tone turning from anger to sympathy, "I know things have been rough for you, worse now after last night. But the way you've been living . . ." He shook his head. "A man can't keep on like that forever."

"You want me to clean up? Put me on the case."

"You know I can't."

"Bullshit."

"Not bullshit. Rules. In case you've forgotten, we have them in this business."

"That's crap, Remi. We both know you'll bend a rule when it suits you."

Dark anger flashed across Remi's face. Jack was referring to their experience with Weatherall and problems with the DX-2 chips. It had ended two-and-a-half years ago, but it was still an open wound for them both, and one that was likely to never heal. They never spoke of it.

"Be careful, Jack," Remi cautioned. "I'm still your boss."

Jack stared at him. Remi leaned over the desk with a look of menace and concern. "That right there is why your life is so fucked up," he said. "You've got no respect."

"Put me on the case."

"I can't."

"You owe me, Remi. You know it."

Remi rose to his feet and walked to the window. He stood with his back to Jack, his hands on his hips, staring out at the street. When his anger subsided, he faced Jack. "Even if I put you on the case, we both know there's not much there. Eddie will find Dillon dead or alive, and that'll be that."

"Enough for Eddie, but not for the case."

"What do you mean?"

"You know what I mean," Jack said. "It was way past delivery hours, and he took the package with him when he left."

"I wondered about that, too," Remi said, "but it's thin."

"There's the crime itself. Rape and murder? It's a crime of passion."

"Dillon was a registered sex offender."

"Not enough. We need to dig deep, and you know it. Besides, Dillon had to know a building like that had a VIRSUS, and that everything he did would be available for a playback. It's been used as direct evidence for a few years now. He wasn't trying to hide anything."

Remi mulled it over. "I don't know," he said, "but what the hell. Okay, but not officially. On the record, it belongs to Eddie and Duane, and it stays that way. Keep your snooping quiet. And for Christ's sake, keep a low profile."

Jack rose to his feet and turned for the door.

"Not so fast." Remi's sharp tone stopped Jack in his tracks. "This is only on your free time. You have other assignments. And since you're here, I have one right now for you."

"Like what?"

"A death certification at the Golden Oaks Retirement Apartments. It just came in on auto schedule assigned to you."

"Now? Are you shitting me? I'm not on duty. It's got to be a mistake."

"Probably, but you're here and I'm not changing it, so it's yours. Have a nice trip."

11

The Book of Esther

1:23 p.m.

"So, what are we waiting for? When is somebody going to do something, already? And where are the paramedics? What are they, on vacation, or what?"

The rapid-fire questions came from seventy-five-year-old Esther Goldstein, wife of recently deceased Herbert Goldstein, who was lying dead on a plastic-covered, floral-patterned couch. The focus of Esther's inquisition was a baby-faced patrolman standing in the middle of her tackily decorated apartment. The young man was trying to be polite, muttering an occasional "Yes, ma'am" and "No, ma'am," but the look on his face said he was running out of patience. Esther continued her tirade by barking off a stream of judgmental bullets on the ineptitude of the police, the ineffectiveness of the paramedics, and the unfairness of life.

Jack stood in the open doorway to the apartment, a deep scowl etched across his face. The woman looked and acted like a rabid Rottweiler, albeit one wearing three-inch hair curlers, a tattered blue bathrobe and pink slippers. He cringed at the thought of stepping across the threshold of her apartment to deal with her.

He had always hated doing a death certification, even before the last one he did. That one was over three years ago, and had started his long, personal nightmare. He considered calling Remi to come on down and do it himself. Rookie detectives typically got death certifications. When he left Remi's office, he clicked into auto schedule to see the assignment for himself. It was there. When he'd asked the system why he was assigned on an off-duty day, the system answered with a code that read, "HA794." He'd asked the computer to clarify the code, but the system didn't answer, and he couldn't find the code anywhere else. Jack knew that by not reassigning this to someone else, Remi was reminding him he was boss. He decided to just do it and get it behind him as fast as he could. He took a deep breath and stepped into the apartment.

When the young officer saw Jack, relief spread across his face like bright sunlight popping out from behind a cloud. He slipped off his hat and ran his fingers through his locks of blond hair. "Ma'am," he said, "I told you, we're moving as fast as we can. Everything will be taken care of shortly." He nodded toward Jack and continued. "The detective has just arrived."

The word *detective* was all it took to put Esther on Jack's scent. She was next to him in an instant, nipping at him with a barrage of words. "Detective," she said derisively, "it's about time. Do you know how long it's been? I can tell you how long. One hour and forty-seven minutes, that's how long. That's almost two hours. It's not right! I'm telling you, it's not right that a poor, old woman must wait two hours for something to be done."

Jack raised a hand and held it out toward her; Esther reluctantly fell silent. Jack turned to the officer and looked him over. He was young, and Jack wondered if he was even shaving regularly. *Probably fresh from the Academy graduation ceremony,* he thought, *his shoes still wet from the muddy front lawn.* Jack picked his name from his badge. "Okay, Erikson," he said, "what have we got?"

Erikson, still smiling at the way Jack had silenced the old woman, snapped to attention like a cadet. "Herb Goldstein, age seventy-seven, white male. No signs of trauma. Looks like a cardiac event, sir."

"What do you mean, looks like a cardiac event?" Esther fired off her words in staccato succession. "What are you, a doctor now? What do you know? You're what, maybe sixteen years old!"

"I'm twenty-one, ma'am," Erikson answered forcefully, emboldened by Jack's example.

"Well, you're a baby. Just look at my Herbie. Everything was fine, and now he's gone."

Jack stepped forward and loomed over her, crowding her space. It was like a silent growl, the big dog showing the little dog whom was the boss. It worked—Esther was silenced. You could almost hear her whimper. If she had had a tail, she would have tucked it between her legs.

When she was quiet, Jack turned to Erikson. "What makes you think it's a cardiac?" he asked. "And where the hell are the coroner's people?"

"Sir," Erikson fired back, "they said they had to go to another location, but they said they'd be back." Erikson had delivered the rapid-fire answer standing ramrod straight. He was breathing hard and the color was draining from his face.

"Take it easy, Erikson," Jack said. "Stand at ease and unlock your knees before you faint. You should have learned that at the Academy." He watched the young officer loosen his stance and take a deep breath. "So, what about the cardiac?" Jack asked as the kid's color started back.

Erikson shuffled his feet. He still looked uncomfortable, but he wasn't pale, and he was standing normally. "They said to give you these for the evidence kit. They said they were for his heart." He held out a bottle of prescription pills.

Jack took the small, transparent brown bottle and read the label. They were Goldstein's pills, all right. He was supposed to take two daily, one in the morning, one in the evening. The prescription was a month old and due for a refill. Jack twisted the cap open and looked inside. The bottle was full. He put the cap back on, dropped the bottle into his jacket pocket, and walked to the couch to look at the body.

Herbert Goldstein was stretched out on the couch in a cotton bathrobe pulled tight around his blue pajamas. The pajamas had little white ducks with brown feet, and his own feet had a pair of soft brown moccasins that matched the color of the ducks' feet. He was short, thin and bald except for the few thin wisps of gray hair that popped up from the top of his head and protruded from his ears like antennae. As a corpse, he was unremarkable except for one strange aspect.

He was smiling.

Not just a small smile, either. It was a big, happy grin—the grin that a kid got on Christmas morning after getting the toy he wanted. Jack glanced back over his shoulder at Esther Goldstein, still smoldering in silence, and concluded that maybe old Herb was just happy to finally be free of her. Then he noticed a Game console tucked in the corner of the room. The blue light on the Quantum Drive was blinking.

He turned to Esther. "What was your husband doing when he died?" he asked. "Was he in a Game?"

"Sure," she answered, "bird-watching. My Herbie loved birds. He was in there all the time."

Jack turned to the young police officer. "I'm in," he said. "Stay put." He tapped his external link and mind-clicked into the local network. He saw an icon with a bird and mentally clicked it, too. A login screen appeared:

Birds of North America
Interactive VR
Digitex Industries Beta V. 1.3
Security Protocol Crystal
Game Running
ENTER Password

Crystal security? Crystal was a protocol reserved for high-level security matters, a security level that a standard police metaheuristic algorithm couldn't break. Jack was about to grab the Quantum Drive and turn it over to the geeks at headquarters when he changed his mind. *What the hell, Crystal is multi-level and the Game is running.* Herb had allowed the Game to run past the most protected part of the security system, so one more password would put him in. Jack thought for another moment and then clicked in the letters "D-U-C-K-S" and clicked "ENTER."

A sudden swirl of pixels announced that he had guessed correctly.

12

Tami

1:43 p.m.

Even before the pixels had finished assembling, Jack could hear the music, laughter, shouts and high-pitched giggling. It sounded like one hell of a party going on, and when the room came into view, Jack found out that it was.

He was standing next to a long bar packed with men and women drinking and smoking. The men were a varied group—executives in designer suits, construction workers in blue jeans, doctors in scrubs, teenagers still battling acne and sporting dental braces. But the women were all one kind—young, pretty, sexy, scantily dressed and smiling seductively at the men. Overhead, the ceiling fans were working hard, sucking up thick blue ribbons of smoke while the bartenders fought equally hard to keep the crowd fueled with liquor. They were moving as fast as they could, but they were losing the battle.

At the end of the barroom, a staircase wound up to a second-floor lined with private rooms. Jack watched a platinum blonde in a short, tight red dress tow a high school-aged kid up the stairs. The kid was grinning as if he'd just won the lottery. Judging by the blonde's shapely ass as it swayed back and forth, Jack decided he might have.

It's a virtual whorehouse, Jack thought, trying hard not to laugh.

Sex Games were everywhere, but not like this one. This was the best Jack had ever experienced. Everything was perfect: the colors, the sounds and the smells. Jack also knew immediately that it was a multiplayer Game, that the men were all real persons logged in from around the world and that the women were all characters created to serve them. It would explain the high security level—Gamers playing a sex Game would insist on security to protect their identities.

A throaty woman's voice interrupted his thought. "Looking for a good time, sonny?"

Jack wheeled around to see a character that was clearly the madam. She was well past her prime—sixty plus—but she was wearing sex like she invented it. She stood with her hands on her hips, stuffed into a purple corset with tight black drawstrings that squeezed her overflowing, milky-white breasts so that they looked like big white balloons. Tight curls of platinum blonde hair framed her face, while layers of makeup, gold eye shadow, and long, fake eyelashes did their best to hide her years. But even with all of that, the thing that struck him most was the erotic smell of her perfume.

He flashed his badge; the madam caught it and nodded.

"What's that perfume you're wearing?" Jack asked, putting the badge back into his pocket.

"Jasmine, honey, and me. You like it?"

"It smells . . . real sexy."

"Yeah, well now, ain't that sweet, sonny," she said. She gave him an appreciative once-over. "I don't work no more," she added, "but I might make an exception for you."

"My boss is waiting for my report," he said, feigning an apology.

She threw Jack a hard look. "Well, sonny," she said, "that's too bad. You don't know what you're missing." After a pause, she continued. "You here about the old man?"

"Yes."

She turned to walk away, nodding at him to follow her. Jack followed her up the stairwell and down a narrow hallway. In the hallway, laughter and moaning seeped from beneath closed doors with the girls' working names on them in gold plaques—Tiffany, Brandy, Amber,

Lacy, Cinnamon, Jade. A heavy-set bald man, naked from the waist up, popped his head out of a room with a door marked "Candy" and raised a monocle to his eye. His eyes widened when he saw Jack, and he scurried back into the room on skinny legs and slammed the door shut. Jack laughed, impressed at the depth of the program; even in this virtual whorehouse, police were not welcome.

When they reached the end of the hall, Jack followed the madam through a door marked "Tami." A four-poster bed dominated the room. Instead of a canopy, a mirror hung above the bed, and at the head of the bed, another mirror tilted down to offer a different view. Sex toys lined a white bookcase, and bondage paddles and ball gags hung on the walls. Jack recoiled. Sexual quirks just weren't a part of his makeup. Thinking about the activities that took place here made his skin crawl.

But even more unsettling to Jack was the rest of room. It looked as though it belonged to a schoolgirl. Pink bedsheets and fluffy, pink pillows trimmed in white lace adorned the four-poster bed. A small desk covered with schoolbooks, a cup of crayons and a coloring book occupied one corner of the room. A white, enameled vanity displaying an army of tiny glass fairies surrounding piles of cheap makeup stood in another. A lamp, with a shade trimmed in lace, filled the room with a soft glow. A rack full of young girl's clothes hung in an open closet. Just one thing seemed out of place—a vintage portable bar crammed with an ice bucket and bottles of liquor that stood against the farthest wall.

Even stranger than the room was its occupant—a young woman dressed as a young girl in a pink, baby doll negligee. She had a blonde ponytail, frail limbs, and ample breasts. She sat with one leg draped over the arm of a bright pink high-back chair. She was beautiful in a fragile, compelling way, with a face in the shape of a perfect oval, high cheekbones and pouting red lips. But her most remarkable feature was her eyes. They were "bedroom eyes," hauntingly set back deep in her face under heavy lids, smoldering with an electric sexuality. But what struck him even more than their appearance was their color—bright violet. Jack had never seen anyone with violet eyes, and he imagined he might never see eyes like these again. Dressed as she was, the woman didn't look as if she could be a day over eighteen, but the way she was dragging on her cigarette and downing vodka from a crystal glass said otherwise. She eyeballed Jack nervously, clicking long fake fingernails on the arm of her chair in a rhythmic drumming.

"This is Tami," the madam announced. "You can talk to her." She swept out of the room, closing the door with a resounding thud.

Jack wanted her to speak first. It helped get the straight facts when you let them tell it their own way. It was true for real people, and so it was just as true for Game characters who were programmed to respond like a real person. He was ready to wait for as long as it took, but he didn't have to wait long.

"Who the fuck are you?" Tami asked the instant the madam was gone.

"UCPD," he replied.

"Another cop. Why haven't I seen you before? What's your name?"

"Waldron. Jack Waldron," he answered.

She took a long drag on her cigarette. "What do you want?"

"You know Herb Goldstein?"

"Oh," she said. She exhaled a lungful of smoke and snubbed out her cigarette. She rose from her chair and brushed past him on the way to the portable bar. She dropped a fistful of ice into a glass, followed it with a ten second pour of vodka, and took a long, deep pull before turning back to face him. "You mean the old man?"

"You know who I'm talking about."

She huffed over to the pink chair and plopped down in it again, slinging her leg over the arm. "It ain't my fault," she said. "That crazy, old fuck was in here all the time and nothing ever happened to him before. Shit, he was wearing me out and that ain't easy to do, let me tell you." She let those last words linger.

Jack could see she was trying to sugarcoat her answers. He wondered what she was hiding. "So, you know he's dead?" he asked.

"Yeah, genius, I know he's dead. But I'm telling you, it ain't my fault! The old fucker just died, it was his heart or somethin'. It just stopped workin'."

"What about the fail-safes? Why didn't they kick in and stop the Game?"

She gave him an incredulous look. "Do I look like a fucking designer? Do you see some degree from some big fucking university on my wall? I'm just working here, trying to make a living, and that's hard enough without having a bunch of dipshit cops come in to give me the tenth degree."

Something about this Game character seemed off. Jack played a hunch. "What's your Turing score? Better than a three, isn't it?" Alan Turing developed the Turing Test in 1950 to measure a machine's ability to exhibit intelligent behavior indistinguishable from that of a human. The test had changed over time, but Jack was counting on the fact that only an A.I. would even know of its existence. Games had a supervisory A.I. linked to them by their online connection, and Jack had never seen an A.I. Game character. He sensed that Tami was his first. He guessed she wouldn't be his last.

Tami stayed in character. She laughed so hard she spit a mouthful of vodka on the carpet. When she recovered, she pulled another smoke from her pack and lit it. "Artificial Intelligence? That's a fucking laugh. Do you think I'd be working here if I was a Class Three A.I.? You cops are all the same. Just a bunch of dumb assholes."

Jack watched as she set down her cigarette and vodka, and stood up. She started toward him, moving slowly and gracefully, like a cat stalking a mouse, her footfalls landing in a tight line. As she came toward him, she smiled seductively and ran a wet tongue across her lips. She stopped just inches away from him.

"Look, Waldo, I'm just trying to turn a few credits here, so how about you cut me a little slack." Swinging her hips, she moved in close; he could smell the liquor and smoke on her breath. "And in return," she purred, "I'll make it worth your while." She put her hands on his shoulders and moved them up to his cheeks, pulling him close. She touched the back of his neck. When she did, a puzzled look crossed her face. She stepped back and stared at him.

Jack knew she had been searching for his link. It wasn't visible in the Game; she didn't find it because it was an external link. What he didn't know was why she cared. He needed to figure that out.

Jack decided he'd had enough. He put his hands around her waist, picked her up, and tossed her onto the bed. She bounced once and then sat staring at him, her violet eyes pinched into thin slits.

"No thanks," he said, "not interested in your fun and games." He paused and added with a sarcastic ring, "It's been a pleasure meeting you."

His tone agitated Tami, and she sprang into action. She leaped forward and grabbed his arm tightly. "Hey, wait a minute," she said. "Where are you going?"

"Why? What's it to you?"

"What's going to happen to me?"

"What do you mean?"

"I mean, what's going to happen to me? To the Game? A girl needs company from time to time, you know." She gave him a suggestive look before continuing. "You're not gonna shut it down, are you?"

"There's no telling what I'll do."

"How's about you keep it to yourself? You're kind of cute."

Jack twisted her arm off of him and pushed her away. "Maybe. We'll see," he said before clicking *exit.*

In an instant, he was watching the room melt away.

13

Summoned

1:57 p.m.

"Well, well, well. Look who's back! Those got to be some birds. My Herbie was gone for a long time too, sometimes. He loved those birds."

Esther Goldstein stood with her hands on her hips, her eyes bright with anticipation. She was licking her lips like a dog eager to chew a fresh bone. Jack wasn't about to be that bone and let her chew him. He kept walking without responding.

"It was his favorite," Esther said. "Every day he went in there and stayed for a long time. Except when he was working or . . .Hey! Where you are going with that?" she barked. "That belongs to me."

Esther was referring to the Quantum Drive that Jack had just pulled from the Game console and placed into his own pocket. "Evidence," he said with finality. He didn't waste any time switching subjects. "He worked? I thought your husband was retired."

Esther seized this new opportunity to complain again. "Retired? What? Are you, kidding me? Who can retire these days? Do you know the cost of just one prescription these days? We should be so lucky to retire all the way." She paused for a moment before continuing. "Besides, my Herbie liked to get out now and then."

And away from you. Jack had no trouble understanding that. "What did he do?" he asked.

"He was part-time at UX Express. That's where he worked, my Herbie. I mean, before he retired. He was a manager there before he retired."

UX Express. Jack's ears burned. "What exactly did he do there?"

"The same thing he did when he was full-time, of course. Operations. Scheduling the deliveries. Let me tell you, it was very demanding work. Even with the computers, things always needed to get rescheduled. Thirty-three years my Herbie worked there. You'd think the company would provide a decent retirement so that he could stop working altogether, wouldn't you? You know, I don't think . . ."

"Uh, Detective Waldron, sir," Erikson broke in, cutting Esther off. "I'm sorry to bust in here, but I got a call when you were in the Game and I have a message for you."

Jack looked at him, waiting. Erikson stared back. Jack had to raise his hands in a questioning gesture to get the young officer talking.

"Oh, sorry. I thought you would say something. It was Captain Moreau, sir. He said Mr. Weatherall wants to see you." He whispered Weatherall's name as if he were speaking the name of a supreme being.

"Weatherall? You sure?" Even Jack's voice had a disbelieving tone.

"That's what he said." Erikson shook his head in disbelief.

"When?"

"Tomorrow morning. Nine o'clock sharp."

Weatherall. Jack flooded with old emotions that left him with nothing more to say. He turned to Esther to get an answer. "How often did your husband work?"

"Weekends, mostly. Saturdays and Sundays. And that's another thing, we never got to go out on the weekends. Never. Our friends invited us out, but we couldn't go because Herbie was working, and we couldn't go. That's not right, you know..."

"Good luck, Erikson," Jack said to the young officer. He figured the kid needed it. "I'm certifying the death, and I'll amend the file online." He turned and was out of the door and walking down the stairs when Esther started back on Erikson.

"It's ridiculous the way elderly persons are treated these days," she yapped, "and I won't stand for it. I have your badge number, young man, and I must tell you I'm filing a complaint. You people just aren't organized. It's too bad my Herbie is gone; you people could really use his help. And another thing..."

14

A Walk in the Park

4:38 p.m.

It was the kind of day that put a smile on your face and a spring in your step. It stirred Jack's memories of his summers as a boy, when the days were filled with bright sunshine and warm winds. Jack longed for more days like those, but he knew they were gone, ended by the disastrous three-degree temperature rise in the past two decades. That rise in global temperatures—something the company blamed on a natural solar cycle—had caused the weather to become erratic. These days, scorching heat followed freezing cold, soaking rains followed droughts, and snow and ice followed sun and soft breezes. Worse, the few beautiful days that appeared often turned ugly by late afternoon.

But not this day, Jack had seen to that.

He had paid for it.

He looked around and decided this Game was well worth the credits it had cost him. Everything was as he remembered it: colorful kites soaring and swooping across a crystal sky; sailboats pounding windward on the white-capped waters of the lake; families crowding around ice cream vendors and hot dog carts. Jack smiled, remembering how often he, Rebecca and Sarah had enjoyed time here.

Jack and Rebecca were strolling side-by-side on a wide sidewalk. Fifty feet ahead, Sarah skipped through the crowd. She disappeared now and then, swallowed up by the crowd. Not having her in sight made Rebecca nervous. She was constantly moving and craning her neck to keep her in sight.

Jack looked at Rebecca and sighed. He had decided that it was time to tell her that she no longer existed in the real world. For some unexplainable reason, he thought he owed her that, even if she was a Game character and only a re-creation of Rebecca constructed by the Game's A.I. after scanning his memories. But now, seeing her and standing next to her, he couldn't do it. He rationalized it by telling himself that she wasn't ready to hear the news, even if the news wouldn't matter much to her. She would be sad for him, of course, and curious about the details, but it wouldn't change things here in her world. He decided to wait until later.

"Sarah, honey, not so fast. Stay close." Rebecca's voice brought him out of his thought.

Sarah heard her mother's voice above the noisy crowd. She stopped and turned, put her hands on her hips, blew a big, pink bubble, and tapped her toes impatiently. Jack smiled when he saw her expression—the same look of exasperation he had seen so often on Rebecca's face. *She is her mother's daughter,* Jack thought. *No doubt about it.*

"Don't give me that look, young lady," Rebecca chided. "Just stay in sight."

Sarah smiled, waved and skipped away into the crowd. She knew, just as Jack knew, that it would take two or three similar warnings before her mother took any real action.

They walked on, enjoying the day, moving left and right to keep Sarah in sight. "It's a perfect day," Jack said, feeling the need to say something.

"I know," Rebecca answered. "So, what's wrong with you?"

Straight to the point, Jack thought. He never could hide his emotions from her. Even here in the Game she could read his emotions. He ducked the question. "What do you mean?" he asked.

"Don't bullshit me, Jack," Rebecca fired back. "I can see it in your face. There's something you're not telling me."

He needed a dodge. He nodded his head in Sarah's direction. "I miss her," he said. "A lot."

"I know you do, but she's here for you. And you still have that, don't you? Besides, that's not it, and you know it." Rebecca turned to search the crowd for Sarah. She spotted her and shouted, "Sarah, honey, wait for us right there. I mean it."

Sarah stopped and gyrated around to face them. She fidgeted with her hair.

Rebecca looked deep into Jack's eyes. "Tell me what happened, Jack."

He looked at her. He knew he had to tell her, but he just wasn't ready to say it. Saying it would make it real. She would ask how and why, and he couldn't answer those questions. Not yet, anyway. He would have to tell her later. "I will," he said, "but not now."

Before she could protest, he formed the word *exit* in his mind and let the swirling pixels pull him back to the dark reality of his life.

15

A Cold, Hard Place

MONDAY, DECEMBER 8
7:47 a.m.

The seat was cold, hard and unforgiving. It seemed to Jack that he had spent his entire life taking these trains, sitting on these seats, watching the bleak facades of buildings blur by through dirt-stained windows. It was here he thought about his cases, and here he most often had the sudden flash of intuition that solved them. He took out his flask, slugged a long pull, and thought about Herb Goldstein's death.

There was something wrong with it; he could feel it. In fact, he was certain of it, but he didn't know why. He just knew that something was not right. It was like hearing a discordant note in the middle of a familiar song, knowing it shouldn't be there. He couldn't shake the feeling.

A WorldNet ad activated his external link and interrupted his thoughts. The ad appeared to Jack like a hologram floating in the air in front of him. Swirling multi-colored pixels formed a stylized human head that displayed a small microchip implant at the back of thc neck below the base of the skull. The chip illuminated and grew in size as a familiar woman's voice began a warm, compelling sales pitch: "The new DX3. Faster speeds, broader bands, better walls. A better WorldNet experience. Available Christmas day from Digitex Corporation, a Unitex company. Digitex, bringing the WorldNet to you." The image morphed into the face of a famous virtual entertainer. She smiled and faded from view.

Anger swelled up inside him, but this time he held it in check. No sense giving Remi something else to complain about.

He gazed down the rows of mindless passengers who lined the crowded, early morning commute, each staring blankly into space, unaware of the world outside of their Game. He thought again about Herb, doing the only real living he did in a Game. Jack, himself, was guilty of the same thing, but at least he was still alive. For Herb Goldstein, it had been an abrupt end to his Game, and a short ride in a black body bag to the morgue. He was probably still there now, waiting now for the obligatory automated autopsy to satisfy the company's record keeping requirements. After that, it would be a fast trip to a cemetery somewhere, and a slow rot in a cold, hard place forever. *But at least the poor bastard went out with a smile,* Jack thought.

He understood the smile.

The smile did not make him uncomfortable about Goldstein's death; it was Tami. Tami struck him as odd. He was sure she was A.I. and that she was hiding something. She seemed nervous in a way he had never seen in a Game character. Did she know more about the way Herb died than she said? He was certain that she knew more than she told him. He was also certain that Goldstein was somehow tied to his case. His position at UX Express—scheduling deliveries—was too unlikely to be just a coincidence. Somebody had sent him there on purpose. The only question was, who?

Jack was pondering the question when an automated announcement broke into his thoughts, "Now arriving Unitex Plaza. Passengers for the Unitex building and the Unitex Plaza exit here."

The Maglev slowed to a stop. The air-compression doors opened to a thunderclap of noise that flooded the train and reverberated off the seats and windows. Jack stepped out onto the platform into a light drizzle and looked toward the sound. It was coming from the Plaza—the acres of concrete that surrounded the towering Unitex building. Jack could see an endless sea of screaming protestors crowding the Plaza. They were packed elbow-to-elbow, jostling, screaming and chanting in unison. Red was everywhere.

Jack knew instantly that it was a PURE protest rally: red was the chosen color of PURE. The use of red started in response to the widespread characterization by pundits of PURE as "Biological Luddites," a reference to the early nineteenth-century anti-technology movement. "Biological Luddite" quickly evolved into "bio-ludd," and then just "bludd." That word's similarity to "blood" was too obvious to ignore and the loop was complete.

These days, PURE red was everywhere. The crowd in the Plaza was mostly dressed in red, and above the heads of the protestors, floating like boats on an undulating red ocean, were the PURE signs. Professionally made, all of them delivered the PURE message: "Ban Human Microchip Implants Today!" "Protect the Human Race." "A Human Is Not a Machine." "Keep 'Man' in Mankind."

The object of the crowd's anger was a giant holographic image of Weatherall's face created by emitters built into the windowpanes of the Unitex building. Twenty stories tall, his face spoke to the crowd through loudspeakers blended into the design of the Plaza. But the catcalls and boos from the crowd were louder than Weatherall's voice, and Jack could hear just a few sporadic words between the jeering and screaming. The words were all too familiar: "A new brotherhood. . . new DX3 . . . uniting our world . . . man's full potential." *Same old song,* Jack thought. The crowd's screams increased with each word and drowned out the rest of the speech.

Jack shook his head and pulled his flask from his pocket. The crowd was about to get ugly and things would soon get out of hand. Getting through the crowd to the building would not be easy; he risked being stuck in the middle of the riot. Not that he cared about getting hurt. But elderly people, women, even a few young kids were in the crowd. If a full-blown riot erupted, it would be a fucking mess, and he would wind up bashing heads with the rest of the police. People would get hurt. And then there was Weatherall, who was expecting him. Jack shook his head; there just wasn't a good choice here. He turned his collar up against the rain, leaned forward, and jogged toward the Plaza.

16

Peggy

8:09 a.m.

Peggy Owens stared in disbelief from her cubicle on the eighty-fifth-floor of the Unitex tower as Lupe Vincente stormed toward the office of Morton Johnson, Senior Vice President for Logistics. It was a rare event for any of the company's top officers to leave the luxury and executive privileges of the topmost floors. It was even more rare for any of them to visit the lower levels where the drones like Peggy did the work that made the company run. Just seeing her was a shock, but it was an even greater shock to see Lupe so angry. She hoped her boss wasn't in too much hot water. She watched as Lupe barged into Johnson's office and slammed the door behind her.

Peggy could still see them through the large window that gave her boss a view out into the clerical pool. Lupe wasted no time getting started. She walked to Johnson's desk and leaned over it, waving her arms and pointing an accusatory finger at him. She was yelling at him, too, but Peggy couldn't hear what she was saying—the thick walls and heavy glass window blocked the sounds. Whatever she was saying, Peggy could tell it wasn't something her boss wanted to hear. Then to Peggy's even greater distress, her boss—a slight, soft-spoken, balding and bespectacled African American man in his late forties—stood and shouted back.

She couldn't believe her eyes and glanced around to see if anyone else was watching them.

They were. Almost everyone in the clerical pool was already on his or her feet, watching the argument. In moments, everyone in the office was standing in slack-jawed, rapt attention, glued to the unfolding drama.

The show ended abruptly when Lupe noticed the crowd watching them and said something to Johnson. He looked out, and in the blink of an eye, the photochromic window turned from clear to opaque gray. The gawking workers looked around at one another with guilty expressions, like a crowd of Peeping Toms caught in the act. When they sat down at their desks, things were back to normal in less than a minute.

Peggy sat down and wondered if she could risk a quick trip into her Game, as Johnson was preoccupied. She was eager to visit her new friend. Her friend had been teaching Peggy to shoot—a hobby that she had never imagined she would find herself enjoying so much. She decided she would take a chance and drop into her Game for a short time.

When she clicked on her Game icon, a whirlwind of pixels swept her away from her cubicle.

17

Girl Scout Cookies

8:23 a.m.

By the time Jack had made his way to the edge of the crowd, he realized things were even worse than he had imagined. He'd seen PURE protests turn ugly before. There was always a certain electricity in the air when things were about to get bad. He could feel it now, a charge that made his skin itch. It was written on the faces of the crowd, too—tired faces streaked with rain, bursting with anger, twisted with rage. It didn't take a psychologist to know this crowd was a ticking bomb about to explode.

He looked past the protesters to the headquarters building. It was only one hundred yards away, but it might as well have been one hundred miles—he'd never get through the crowd without help. He spotted a sergeant holding a bullhorn, jogged over, and flashed his badge. "Can you get me to the building?" he yelled above the noise.

The sergeant looked at the badge and waved at two riot guards standing forty feet away. The guards saw him and marched over. Encased in impenetrable carbon fiber exo-suits, powered by hydraulics and elevated by their massive boots, the guards were every bit as tough as they looked. They loomed over the sergeant and Jack, waiting for orders.

"Get him to the front door and get back as fast as you can," the sergeant said, looking at the angry mob. "I think the shit is about to hit the fan."

"Yes, sergeant," the guards answered in unison. Their voices boomed through their suits' built-in voice amplification systems. This close, their voices left Jack's ears ringing.

Jack followed them as they cleared a path through the crowd. For the first thirty seconds, progress was easy. The guards' heavy footsteps boomed and when the crowd heard them, they stepped aside. Things changed when an angry, young black man wearing granny glasses and a red leather beret jumped in front of them to block their progress. He stood there, refusing to move. The lead guard's response blasted out of his speaker. "Remove yourself from our path, citizen," the guard warned, "or you will be arrested."

To the crowd, the guards were invaders, like foreign bodies in a bloodstream. And like a swarm of antibodies attacking an infection, the crowd quickly surrounded them, pushing against them so that each yard forward was harder won than the last. "Remove yourself from our path," the other guard added.

The young man started a chant—"PURE! PURE! PURE!" The crowd picked it up and surged forward, pushing the young man into one of the guards and bringing him to the ground. Jack watched as the guard sprang to his feet and raised his nightstick. He lunged for his arm, hoping to prevent a full-blown riot, but his action backfired when his body weight brought the nightstick down to crack the young man between his eyes. The young man fell back into the crowd while screams of outrage erupted everywhere.

Guards rushed in from all sides and the fight began. A bottle sailed through the air, shattering into broken shards at Jack's feet. A protestor broke his sign over the helmeted head of another guard and was tossed to the ground. Everywhere Jack looked, bodies slammed the pavement with bone-crushing force.

The lead guard pushed forward, forcing the crowd to make an opening. But just as they were about to break through, Jack saw a familiar blur of slicked-back hair and a woman's body draped across the back of a guard. The woman was beating the guard with her bare fists, doing her best to keep the guard from beating the shit out of the same young black man in a red beret and red vest who had started the riot.

The woman turned a bloody face toward him and Jack recognized her—it was Cassie, his new neighbor. When he saw another guard raise his nightstick and approach her from behind, Jack sprang into action.

He grabbed the guard's arm and flashed his badge. The guard saw it and lowered his nightstick. Jack ripped Cassie off the other guard's back, tucked her under his arm, and carried her kicking and screaming through the crowd. Just as they were about to break through the crowd to the doors of the Unitex building, a protestor swung a sign and slashed Jack across the face with the sign's sharp edge. Jack reached for the wound to stop the sudden flood of blood erupting from it when someone in the crowd shoved him toward the doors of the building. Holding tight to Cassie, he stumbled forward. The automatic doors sensed his badge and swung open just long enough to permit his entry. He staggered into the crowded lobby and dumped Cassie onto the polished marble floor.

Cassie sprang to her feet and stepped away. She shook the wet rain from her short dark hair, brushed dirt from her jacket then whipped around to face Jack. "What the fuck do you think you're doing?" she screamed. She flattened her palm into a paddle and flung her right arm into a wide, sweeping arc.

Jack saw it coming. Even half-drunk as he was he could have dodged it, but he needed a reason to keep her off the street until order was restored. He let her hand hit his face. The moment it did, he regretted the decision. The blow was a resounding one, hitting his cheek with unexpected force. His eyes blurred, and his knees wobbled. It was the hardest blow a woman had ever dealt him. He wouldn't soon forget it.

"Jesus Christ," he exclaimed in anger, "you're lucky I was here. Those guards would've hurt you bad."

Cassie swung again, but one hard blow was enough for Jack. He grabbed her wrist, twirled it behind her back, and shoved her up against the glass window. He held her with his right hand and cuffed her with his left. The he twirled her around again and pushed her down to the marble floor.

Cassie sat up, smiling wickedly. "Oooh, well. This is getting kinky," she said.

"Relax. I'm not arresting you. I'm detaining you for your own safety."

"Bullshit. For what?"

"Because I feel like it. But if you insist, I'll make the charges formal: disorderly conduct, inciting a riot, assaulting a police officer. I can come up with a few more."

"You're drunk," she said. She squirmed and turned her head toward the growing crowd of Unitex employees. "Hey, assholes, do you hear me? This officer is drunk, and he is sexually assaulting me. Somebody needs to call the duty desk and get the sergeant on call down here before this pervert does anything else." When she finished, she shot Jack a look that said, what are *you* going to do about that?

Jack shook his head and sighed. She was attracting the stares of the crowd—not a good thing. He was glad to see a uniformed officer approaching him, attracted by the commotion. The officer looked as if he was in his fifties, with salt-and-pepper hair and a sagging belly. But Jack knew in an instant that he wasn't just building security. He walked with the "don't fuck with me" swagger of a veteran accustomed to rough neighborhoods. Jack liked him on sight, and he knew he could depend on him. He held up his badge. The officer gave it a quick once-over. "How can I help, Detective?" he said.

"Put this one in lockup and let her out in three hours."

"What do I put on the sheet?" he asked, smiling. He was happy to have a break from the boring duty.

"Under investigation. Don't book her."

"No problem, Detective. No problem." He looked down at Cassie and smiled. "And what would your name be, young lady?"

"Fuck you, asshole." Cassie spat out the sentence without looking at the officer.

His grin got bigger. "Well, just so I get it right," he said in his most official sounding voice, "is your first name *fuck* and your middle name *you* and your last name *asshole*? Or, have we got us here one of them hyphens, like maybe your first name is *fuck* and your last name *you*, but when you got married it was changed to *you-asshole*?"

Cassie looked at him with disbelief.

"It's important that I get it right, missy," the officer said in a confidential tone. "If I screw up the paperwork...well, they might just forget about you, and you'll spend weeks in lockup while some jerk tries to figure it all out." He leaned down to speak in an avuncular manner. "We wouldn't want that, would we, sweetie? So why don't you just tell me your name?"

"Fuck off."

"Well, now, see that's also confusing," he said, feigning exasperation. "I guess I can put *fuck* down as your first name since you always start with it. But I'm even more confused about the middle and last names. I guess you'll be spending a lot of time in lockup."

Jack had watched him with amusement, but he had to get upstairs; Weatherall was waiting. "Her last name is Charbonneau. First name, Cassie. But book her as a Jane Doe if that's okay with you."

"Okay, Detective, no problem," the officer said. He turned back to Cassie and reached down to take her arm.

"Miss Charbonneau," he said cheerily in French, "*votre nouvelle maison vous attend.*" When she stood up, he ushered her off toward a bank of elevators like a solicitous maître d' leading a guest to a table.

Twenty feet away, Cassie looked back and shouted at Jack "Thanks a lot, asshole. What's next? I think I saw some Girl Scouts selling cookies without a permit. Maybe you ought to go arrest them."

Jack watched as Cassie and the veteran officer disappeared into one of the elevators. When the doors closed, he muttered to himself, "You're welcome."

18

Mount Olympus

8:57 a.m.

To describe Dorothy Stark as prim and proper would be like calling the Great Pyramids at Giza stone piles; neither description would be adequate. She was much more than just prim and proper. Starched stiff from head to toe would be a better description, but even that would still miss the essence of Dorothy. Just one quick look would tell you that.

Layer upon layer of meticulously applied makeup fixed her sixty-eight-year-old face into a permanent, wrinkle-free mask. Her steel gray hair, unruly by nature but sprayed into stiff submission, sat on her head like a wax bonnet. Her clothing, expensive, tailor-made, and conservative, fit her small frame so perfectly that finding a wrinkle on it was like finding a needle in a haystack. Even her plain black shoes, polished to perfection, had no visible flaws. She was, in a word, impeccable. What her clothes lacked in style they made up for in comfort and utility. But to Dorothy, they were proper for someone in her position.

The result of this tireless and tedious preparation created a countenance that had not changed in the thirty-five years Dorothy had been the executive administrative assistant to William Weatherall. That suited her. If there was anything she hated more than not being prim and proper, it was change.

The way Dorothy dressed mirrored the way she felt about life; she believed that all life's problems would be solved if people acted in good taste. She looked at her polished mahogany desk with approval, noting that unlike the desks of the staff assistants below her, everything was where it was supposed to be. She was just getting back to work when the elevator doors opened, and Jack Waldron stepped out.

Dorothy nearly screamed. Only her years of mental discipline kept her from making a scene.

If ever someone offended Dorothy's sense of order, it was Jack Waldron. If ever there was a person she had hoped never to see again, that person was Jack Waldron. If Jack Waldron were a bug, she would gleefully smash him with her shoe. Just looking at him sent her blood pressure rising. He had upset her well-organized life three years ago, and the moment she saw him, she vowed that he wouldn't do it again. She pulled herself together, reminding herself that proper behavior was its own reward and waited until he was standing in front of her desk before she spoke. When she finally addressed him, she did her best to hide her venom, even if allowing just a touch of the proper sarcasm.

"Well, Detective Waldron," she said in a voice dripping honey, "it's so very, very nice to see you again. To what do we owe this honor?"

"He wants to see me."

"What? Why wasn't I told? All of his appointments go through me." Dorothy muttered a rare swear word under her breath while scrambling through her appointment list.

"I don't know," Jack answered. "Ask him. All I know is that he wants to see me."

Dorothy sat back in her chair and scrutinized him. He looked even worse than the last time she saw him when the security guards were dragging him kicking and screaming out of her boss's office. Then he was at least clean and well dressed. Now, he was a wreck. His hair was an uncontrolled disaster, his face covered with a two-day's growth that barely hid an ugly scar she hadn't seen before. His clothes were soaked and smeared with dirt. And his head, bruised and battered from some previous ruckus, was dripping blood from a fresh red gash just above his right eye. She immediately thought of the new carpet installed just last week and reached for her box of tissues, thrusting it toward him across her desk. “Well, Detective,” she harrumphed, “you might want to tidy up just a bit before you see him. I’m sure he would appreciate it.”

Jack pulled a tissue free and dabbed at his forehead. *Nothing has changed here. It looks exactly like it did the last time I was here.* Long rows of desks were staffed with busy clerks, breathtaking views of the city, and heavy glass doors closing off Weatherall’s office. Two security types stood guard at the doors. Jack didn’t recognize either of them, but to him they all looked alike in their black suits and black sunglasses.

Dorothy’s voice interrupted his thoughts, “He’ll be right with you, Detective.”

Jack turned to see the two guards pull open the oversized doors to Weatherall’s office. As they did, Remi came skulking out, his head low and his jaw tight. He looked like a whipped dog. When he reached Jack, he stopped. “Good luck,” he said in a low voice, “he’s waiting for you.” He shot Jack a weak smile and slipped off toward the elevators.

Jack looked past the open doors and saw Weatherall beckoning him to come in. He took a deep breath, straightened his shoulders, and walked in past the smirking guards. When he did, they closed the doors behind him.

19

All is Fair

8:57 a.m.

Peggy Owens entered a delivery order on her work screen and clicked her approval. The instructions rerouted five hundred thousand DX3 units to a company owned warehouse at the Port of Illinois where they were to be stored and sorted for distribution. Peggy and her colleagues had been busier than ever in the past three months, responding to new shipping instructions, changing warehouse destinations, rerouting shipments. She couldn't wait for Christmas when she could finally enjoy a day off while everyone else joined the long lines of eager shoppers at Digitex retail outlets.

Peggy already had a DX3. The notification that she was being awarded a free one had arrived three weeks ago, and she had gone the next day during her lunch break for the implant. Peggy loved watching the other employees turn green with envy when she told them. *Not everyone is as valuable to the company as I am,* she thought. She wanted them all to know the company felt the same way.

She stood up to peer over the top of her cubicle. Lupe was gone, and the office had returned to the way it was before she had arrived. But her boss, Morton Johnson, still hadn't emerged from his office—at least Peggy hadn't seen him come out—and she worried about him. It had been a terrible fight, the kind that would have made Peggy nervous under any circumstance. It had been unbearable to see it happen right into front of her own eyes. She was about to sit down when she noticed two women staring at her from across the office. She didn't remember seeing them before. *Who are they?* she wondered. W*hy are they staring at me?* She saw them laugh and point in her direction. Peggy looked behind her to see if they were looking at someone else, but there was no one there. When she turned around again, the two women had vanished.

A sudden revelation struck her: she knew those women—they were the ones who were telling everyone her secret. Then she remembered her plan.

It was time to put that plan into action.

She reached under her desk and grasped a black bag resting on the floor. She pulled the bag up and plopped it on her desk, released its drawstring and stared at its contents.

The bag held a model 17RS semiautomatic pistol, loaded with a round in the chamber and a full magazine in the clip. The bag also held dozens of extra magazines; all of them loaded and ready for instant use. Peggy stroked the gun with her forefinger. The gun was a good choice for her, just as her new friend had told her. Built from aircraft-quality aluminum, it was lightweight and easy to handle. Its open slide design never jammed, and it had a short recoil. Best of all, with fifteen rounds in each magazine, she was certain to have plenty of firepower. She was glad she followed her new girlfriend's advice in the Game and chose it.

She picked up the gun, grabbed the bag of ammunition, and stood up. Everyone was busy with work. No one would notice her. It was time. She walked the thirty feet from her cubicle to her boss's office, turned the door handle, and walked in.

Morton Johnson was standing with his back to the door, clicked-in, speaking in a low voice. He didn't have to talk when clicked-in—his thoughts were enough—but talking was a habit hard to break for most users. His talking meant that he didn't hear Peggy walk in and close the door behind her. "I don't have a choice now," he said to someone, "I have to do something about it."

Peggy plopped the heavy bag of magazines onto his desk with a loud clunk. Morton heard it and turned to Peggy. He saw the gun pointed at him, confusion spread across his face.

"Hold on," he blurted into his link. He looked at Peggy. "What are you doing, Peggy?" he asked. He smiled, as if he knew this was a joke.

"You couldn't keep it a secret, could you?" Peggy answered. "I thought you loved me, but you were using me."

"What? What are you talking about? What secret?"

"Us. Our affair. It was supposed to be a secret, but now the whole office knows." Peggy's voice was mechanical, as if she was doing a bad job of reading a script.

Morton's dark face blanched as it drained of blood. "Us? What us? What are you talking about?"

"It's too late to fix it now, you bastard." Peggy thumbed the gun's hammer back into the firing position with a loud click.

"Wait! Don't shoot. Put down the gun, please." Morton jumped up and moved past the window that separated his office from the clerical pool, edging for the door. He held his hands up in front of himself, as if the force of his will could keep Peggy at bay and the bullets from reaching him.

It didn't work.

The gun spewed rounds from its muzzle, each shot accompanied by an earsplitting blast and a burst of smoke and flame. The bullets came in rapid succession, punching ragged holes in the window glass and slamming Morton's body with hard thuds. Bright explosions of red blood erupted from his torso and filled the air with a fine mist. The barrage of bullets slammed him backward into the glass, shattering the weakened structure into pieces that cascaded to the floor.

His body fell, crunching the broken glass when he landed on it. He lay there twitching, his empty, dead eyes staring at nothing.

20

Zeus

9:01 a.m.

Weatherall's office hasn't changed, Jack noted. The priceless sculptures, the antique furniture, the rare Persian rugs, the photos of Weatherall with the rich, famous and powerful, everything was exactly where it had been the last time he was here. Jack inventoried the photos by looking at the tables because there were no walls anywhere, not even sectional walls. The office was a hemispherical expanse of photochromic windows that blurred the lines between the world outside and the space inside. Company wags had long ago labeled it the "Crystal Palace," but Jack had always thought of it as a crystalline Mount Olympus, just as he had always thought of Weatherall as the great Zeus himself. He trudged forward, leaving a trail of damp spots on a priceless Persian rug.

"What happened to you?" Weatherall asked.

Jack walked to the windows. A brilliant blue sky arched above an ocean of cloud tops that stretched as far as the eye could see. A few of the city's tallest buildings poked up through them to float like steel and glass islands on a sea of white. Jack took it all in before pointing down at the streets beneath the clouds. "You can't see it from here," he said dryly, "but there's one hell of a riot going on down there."

"I know, Jack," Weatherall said.

"You know? That's all you have to say?"

"There's always a protest somewhere."

"Doesn't that tell you something?"

"Certainly. It tells me that we need to do a better job of communicating our vision for the future."

"Communicating? Hasn't it occurred to you that maybe the real problem is the vision?"

The rebuke startled Weatherall. He wasn't used to hearing disagreement; he was slow to respond. "You helped us protect our vision in the past," he finally said.

Jack's anger visibly boiled to the surface. "I was wrong," he said through a strained voice.

"No, you were right then; now you're wrong. That troubles me."

Weatherall walked to his desk and sat down. He motioned to Jack to sit in one of the hand-carved Ming dynasty chairs that matched his sandalwood desk. Jack hesitated until Weatherall raised an eyebrow. When he finally sank into the chair, he remembered why he hated them—they were short and forced their occupant to look up at Weatherall. Jack was certain it was no accident.

"So, what is it you want?" Jack asked. "Did you call me up here to talk about the company's vision?"

"I was able to rely on you and Remi in the past," Weatherall said, ignoring Jack's question. "I need to know I can count on you again."

He's worried about something big, Jack concluded. He decided he wouldn't make it easy.

"So, you want me to bury the truth again about another company fuck up? What have you done this time?"

"Nothing." Weatherall's face was a blank mask.

Jack's mind raced through the possibilities; he landed on just one. "This is tied to Rebecca's murder, isn't it? You know something, don't you?"

"This is about Rebecca's death. But, no, I don't know anything. That's why I called you up here. I want somebody working on this I can trust."

"I'm not on the case."

"You are now. I just directed Remi to put you on the case."

The statement stunned Jack. He tried not to show it. "Why?"

"I told you—because you were reliable in the past. And, with this case, you're motivated. I think you won't let up until you solve the crime."

"No. I don't mean why me. I meant, what do you expect to find? It was a rape and murder. We all saw it. It's an open-and-shut case. Eddie will eventually round up the perp and declare it closed on the news feeds."

"Perhaps you're right, Jack," Weatherall said. "But if you turn up something, I want to know about it right away." He leaned forward and added, "Can I count on you for that?"

Jesus, Jack thought, *something's up.*

Before Jack could answer, Weatherall raised a hand to quiet him. He was listening to a message. Seconds later he lowered his hand and looked at Jack. "Moreau wants you on the eighty-fifth floor," he said, shaking his head. "Apparently, all hell has broken loose."

21

The Eighty-Fifth

9:22 a.m.

The eighty-fifth floor was in chaos. A mob of panicked employees stormed the elevator the moment the doors opened. It took all of Jack's strength to elbow and push his way out of the elevator, through the frenzied crowd, and into the hall. Once free, he leaned against a wall, huffing and puffing, struggling to catch his breath, watching the battle at the elevator. It was a loud, noisy, dangerous stalemate as the people first into the elevator battled with the ones still trying to get in. Everyone had abandoned any sense of order.

Idiots, Jack thought. *No wonder the company gets away with so much crap.* He had barely completed the thought when gunfire erupted down the hallway. He took a couple of deep breaths and sprinted toward the sound.

The hallway was a madhouse, bursting with terrified employees running away from the gunfire and grim-faced police running toward it. Badge in hand, Jack dashed and dodged his way through the moving river of bodies. When he reached a converging hallway full of building security guards standing in a tight line against the wall, Jack knew he was in the right place. He turned down the hallway and made his way toward a small cluster of men squatting at the end of the hall. The men had their backs to him, leaning forward, peering into a larger room.

A dark-skinned, sinewy body encased in a bulletproof vest identified Remi. Jack squatted down behind him and tapped him on the shoulder.

"It's about time," Remi said without turning around. "I told them I wanted you five minutes ago."

How did he know it was me? Jack wondered, but he didn't have time to ponder the question. Two more shots erupted, and a woman's voice shouted, "Come and get me, motherfuckers!"

"What the hell is going on?" Jack asked when the noise faded. "And where the hell is SWAT?"

A building security guard kneeling beside Remi turned to Jack. He looked like a young Iowa cornhusker fresh off the farm—a freckle-faced kid dressed up like a police officer for Halloween. He was beaming a bucktooth smile from one cup-handle ear to the other, and it was obvious he was excited to be here. Jack figured it was his first hostage situation. "Man, it's just awesome," the security guard said. "One of the admins. The word is she just walked into her boss's office like it was no big deal and emptied a clip into his chest. Now she's got five hostages and a shitload of ammo, and she's holed up in the office and she's not coming out. It's just friggin' awesome."

"Where's SWAT?" Jack asked again.

"Yeah," the security guard answered, "well, they're on the way, but it'll take some time." SWAT teams were positioned close to the city's problem areas, five miles from Unitex Plaza. He turned to Remi. "SWAT's going to have a tough time getting through the riot crowd, too, Captain. They may be delayed even more. But," he added with a tone of hope, "I'm ready to send my guys in right now."

Remi raised an eyebrow. Jack understood. Hell, he knew it was coming. A long time ago, he had talked down a shooter after trained hostage negotiators had failed. It was obvious that Remi was hoping he could do it again now. "What's the situation?" Jack asked, resigning himself to the task.

"Security cameras have the whole room covered; the link is up and running," the security guard answered. "She's in the executive office.

She can see the whole room, but you can use the cubicles to get close. The hostages are sitting down, lined up against the back wall."

"Okay," Jack said. "What's her name?"

"Peggy Owens." The guard sighed his disappointment. He knew his chance to be first in the room was gone.

Jack took off his coat, slipped his flask into his pants, tossed his jacket aside, and pulled his gun out of its holster. He pulled back the slide.

"Not so fast," Remi said. "Let's try to keep everyone out of the hospital this time. And put this on." Remi tossed a bulletproof vest to Jack.

Jack shook his head at Remi's remark. Last time, a ricocheting round slightly wounded a hostage, and it was just like Remi to remind him of it now. He ignored the comment, pulled on the vest, and started into the clerical pool. He crouched low as he crept along the back row of cubicles to an aisle formed by a break between the rows. The aisle offered a clear view of the large executive office up front. He dropped to a knee and peered around the cubicle's edge. He could see Peggy Owens through the blown-out window in Johnson's office. She was pacing back and forth, silhouetted by the gray light that seeped into the office from the building's curved glass windows behind her. The weak light gave the whole scene a dismal, desperate feeling.

He wanted to get as close as he could. He shot from cubicle to cubicle, timing his moves to Peggy's pacing. Each time she turned away from the window, he darted to the next cubicle and ducked into it until her next turn. It was slow going, but he made it halfway to the front of the room before his luck ran out and Peggy spotted him. She raised her gun and fired while Jack dove headfirst into a cubicle. The shots thudded into the carpet where a moment ago he had been crouching.

When Jack rolled to a stop and sat up, he found himself face-to-face with an overweight woman hiding in the cubicle. Stuffed into a brown dress, her pudgy legs stretched out toward him. Her round face sported a pair of brown, horn-rimmed glasses, and behind the thick lenses, her brown eyes were frozen in fear. Her small mouth was formed into a perfect O, as if a scream would emerge any second. They stared at each another for a long moment before Jack stood up to peek above the top of the cubicle. The woman's eyes followed him as he moved.

Jack peered toward the office. For the first time, he had a clear view of Peggy and her hostages. He could see Peggy pacing back and forth, her pistol at the ready. She looked like a caricature of a crazy person: her eyes shining with insanity, her body movements jerky, her mouth moving in soundless speech. Behind her, he could see a desk covered with loaded magazines. The hostages—two women and three men—huddled together in a corner, out of the line of fire. It was obvious they were scared shitless of the crazy person keeping them captive and afraid to move even an inch.

Jack dropped back down and sat on the floor. He pulled his flask from his pants pocket and took a long drink while he thought about it. The active shooter protocols were clear. Legally and procedurally, he had an obligation to take her out if he could. When SWAT arrived, they would take her out immediately; Peggy would be an easy target for the highly trained team. But he wasn't SWAT. He figured he had a so-so chance of taking her out with a single shot. Not only that, but he was here to talk her into quitting, and he had to try. He took another short swig, put the flask away, and rose to kneel on one knee.

"Miss Owens," he yelled, "my name is Detective Waldron. Can I talk to you?"

Peggy shouted back, "I got nothing to say to you."

"Look, I'm going to stand up. Is that okay?"

"Fuck you. You're trying to kill me."

"No. No. I promise I'm not. I am asking you, can I stand up?"

It took time before Peggy answered, "You mean, *may*."

"May?" Jack answered. "What do you mean?"

"I mean, it's *may* I stand up? Not, *can* I stand up, you dumb fuck." She followed her answer with a short, cackling laugh.

Now she's a fucking grammar expert, Jack marveled. *She has no problem killing a defenseless person,* he mused, *but don't confuse 'may' and 'can.' The entire world is mad.* He wondered how in the hell he wound up hiding in a cubicle with a fat woman, talking to a nut job, but decided it was just bad luck. "Okay," he yelled back, deciding to humor her. "May I stand up?

"Sure," Peggy shouted back.

Jack took a deep breath. He held his gun out to his side, both arms extended, and stood up. It made him an easy target, but he needed her trust. As his eyes topped the cubicle, he could see Peggy staring at him. He kept his eyes focused on her body language.

Peggy twitched, and Jack knew it was coming. He dropped fast, pulling his legs out from under him as three shots rang out and whizzed past the top of the cubicle. A second later, three more shots slammed the wall of the cubicle, shaking it as they hit. Jack said a silent *thank you* that the rounds didn't pass right through them and into his skull.

A siren wailed—except that it wasn't a siren. *It's a woman screaming.* It started with a low rumble that rose in timbre from contralto through mezzo-soprano to a high-pitched soprano wail. Jack listened in amazement, watching the sound emerge from the perfect O of her mouth, wondering where she was getting the breath to sustain it. He pulled out his flask and took a deep drink. Then, for the hell of it, he held it out to the woman. The woman stopped screaming, grabbed the flask, and took a long swig. When she finished, she handed the flask back to Jack and remained silent.

Things can't get any weirder. First the rally, then Cassie, then Weatherall, and now this, it felt as though he'd finished two back-to-back duty shifts.

"What the hell was that?" he yelled to Peggy. "You said I could stand up."

"Yeah," Peggy answered, "I did. But I didn't say I wasn't gonna shoot, you dumb fuck." Cackling like a witch, Peggy fired off a fast six rounds. The bullets thumped the cubicle with dull thuds.

The fat woman emitted a low-pitched rumble, the beginning of a scream. Jack held a finger to his lips and the noise petered out. She sat there in silence.

It would not get any better, he decided. His best move was to make his way back to Remi. He would have to leave the fat woman here. There was no way he could take her with him. She would be too easy of a target.

Besides, he reasoned, Peggy had enough hostages and didn't need more. He figured she wouldn't leave the safety of the office to get another one.

Crouching low, he duckwalked to the edge of the cubicle and craned his neck around the edge to check Peggy's position. She had her back to him, muttering to herself. When he saw an opening, he took it, dashed out of the cubicle, and moved as fast as he could down the long aisle toward the back row of the cubicles. He glanced back over his shoulder and saw Peggy turn. Diving headfirst for the floor, he crawled the last few feet and turned the corner into safety. From there, crouched low, he made it to Remi's position in less than a minute and crouched next to him.

"Well, what do you think?" Remi asked.

Out of breath, Jack just shook his head from side to side.

"What about the hostages?"

"North corner of the office, she's ignoring them," Jack said. "I don't think she's even thinking about them."

"Okay," Remi said. "We wait for SWAT."

When the SWAT team arrived, the leader—a forty-something, soft-voiced female lieutenant—asked Remi three questions and then used hand signals to move the team into position. The team slipped into the room silently, each team member proceeding to an assigned position, melting into the cubicles like shadows vanishing at twilight. The incursion was completed in less than two minutes, and went unnoticed by Peggy, who paced back and forth muttering to herself. When the team was in place, the SWAT leader announced their presence through her voice-enhancement module. Her words reverberated as if emitted by a bullhorn, "Ms. Owens, Unitex SWAT. You are instructed to disarm and surrender, or we will take you by force."

Peggy's response was immediate—a quick volley of three shots.

The SWAT leader said nothing further. Instead, Jack heard her quietly issue a command using her link, "W-A-M on my command. Ready three…two…one…now."

On the word "now," a team member popped up in the far left corner of the room and fired a shot in Peggy's direction. She turned toward him, firing a round just in time to see him duck before another team member on the far right side of the room stood and fired in her direction. She swung in his direction, but before she had turned all the way, another in the room's center fired. She swung in his direction, only to see him duck down and yet another in the back of the room stand and fire. In seconds, she was furiously swinging left and right and left again, firing and missing, swearing and cursing at the officers that rose and ducked in a Whack-A-Mole game. Then everything changed—every team member in the room stood. The sight stunned Peggy. She hesitated, trying to decide which uniformed body to shoot, but that moment's hesitation ended her life. A barrage of bullets erupted from every gun in the room, thirty or more rounds hitting her at once. The force of the bullets picked her up off her feet and threw her backward like a rag doll. She was dead before she hit the floor.

22

Just the Facts

12:38 p.m.

Taking statements from half-crazed hostages was the kind of job Jack hated. He was pissed off that Remi had assigned it to him, especially since he knew that Remi would ultimately shove him aside to assign the case to others. The whole thing bored him and left him itching for something else to do. Fortunately—or unfortunately, depending upon how he viewed it—the fat lady provided him with a cure for his boredom.

Still bristling that Jack had abandoned her in the office cubicle, the woman saw her chance for payback when her uniformed escort left her to get them both a cup of coffee. Circling Jack to stay out of his line of vision, she jumped him, letting her bulk and weight crush him to the floor. When he was down, she pummeled him with balled fists, blasting out a string of four-letter words that made every police officer in earshot turn to watch. Not willing to risk hurting her, Jack just covered up, waiting for his rescue. When it came, it took three burly uniforms to pull her off and drag her away kicking and screaming. He wasn't physically injured by the attack, but the event was humiliating, earning him the epithets "slugger" and "champ" from the detectives who witnessed the mugging.

When he finished collecting the statements, Jack headed for Morton Johnson's office. The forensic team was gone, the bodies of Peggy and her boss bagged and headed for the morgue. The cleanup was still to come, and the signs of violence remained everywhere. Jack crossed a floor covered with broken glass and carefully avoided brushing up against the back wall that was covered in blood and tissue.

Remi handed him a note written on a formal note card. "Something you ought to see," he said.

"Where did you get this?" Jack asked.

Remi pointed at Johnson's desk. "Sitting right there on top of the desk, big as life."

Jack read the barely legible note: *"The bastard was a liar. He made me think he'd be there for me, but he lied. He was just using me. He shot me through the heart, so I did the same to him. He needed to die, and I saw to it."* She had signed it with a scrawled, "Peggy Owens."

"What do you think?" Jack asked.

"I don't know what to think, Jack," Remi grumbled. "But we will eventually find out, I guess."

"The hostages said the same thing," Jack added, "that she was ranting and raving about an affair with Johnson gone bad, and that's why she killed him." His voice lacked conviction.

Jack walked around the desk to get a better look at a tall stack of papers piled on it. Using paper was unusual, frowned upon by the company because it put information outside of the company's instant reach and control. "You don't see this too often," he said, gesturing at the mound of documents. He waited for a comment from Remi, but none came. "You go through these yet?" he asked.

"No, I did not go through them," Remi said, "and don't you disturb them, either. The B-Boys are on their way in. I'm assigning the case to them."

"The B-Boys? Why the hell would you give this to them?" B-Boys was shorthand for Boreck and Blackman, two of the department's most senior detectives, partners for decades. Just about everyone in the department thought the B-Boys were over-the-hill, slow-moving dinosaurs stuck on following the book to its letter. Jack understood the reason for their behavior—the B-Boys were close to retirement and not about to let anything get in between them and their pensions. But he didn't approve of their behavior and didn't understand why Remi would assign this high-profile case to them.

"Why don't you let me worry about your assignments," Remi snapped. "Unless perhaps you would like to organize and file last year's outstanding parking citations."

Jack ignored the comment. In fact, he barely heard it. He was staring at Johnson's desk and the old-fashioned leather desk pad that covered its center. The pad had a printed calendar on it filled with pencil scribbles and doodles. One entry caught his eye: Tuesday, RW, 12:30 p.m..

Jack had been to Cadence once—a very upscale and very private local eatery built around booths with high walls and discreet entrances. It catered to the business crowd seeking a place to meet away from the cameras and recorders that were everywhere nowadays. Was RW a reference to Rebecca? If it were, it would tie Rebecca and Morton Johnson together. Jack didn't understand now what that connection might be, but he knew he would find out. He decided he would keep this thought to himself.

23
The Morgue

2:38 p.m.

Not every corpse in Unitex's basement morgue would get a full physical autopsy. Most bodies were just loaded into the Automatic Autopsy Scanning System ("AutScan"), a self-contained Class Four A.I. unit capable of performing a full autopsy without human assistance. The AutScan picked up everything: bullet wounds, knife cuts, blunt force trauma, injuries of all kinds, every known disease, and every catalogued genetic abnormality. Its testing systems found tissue damage from poisons and gases, sampled and tested DNA, and identified and tested any DNA sample not belonging to the corpse. It ran all the typical tests of a full autopsy and more. Once the system's A.I. identified the cause of death, it referenced the police report and then generated a cause of death report and death certificate. Joe Hayden's job as Chief Medical Examiner was usually limited to signing off computer-generated reports in the comfort of his office.

But not this time.

This time, Joe was doing a full physical autopsy. The company required them whenever the cause of death was suspicious or when a special executive order called for one.

Joe could have assigned the job to a staff doctor, but he was doing this one himself. He had once spent time explaining to Jack why he liked doing the physical autopsies. He liked the sharp edge of the scalpel, the shrill buzzing of the bone saw, and the physical work of prying open the thorax. The work made him happy. So, it was no surprise to Jack when he walked into the autopsy room to find Joe whistling a bright tune as he leaned over a stainless steel autopsy table to reach into a cadaver's chest cavity. Joe didn't need to look up to know who it was. "I left you a message two hours ago," he said, his eyes locked onto the bloody heart he was pulling out of the body.

"I've been busy," Jack answered.

"Yeah," he said. "I heard." He dropped the heart onto a scale, wiped the blood from his gloved hand with a towel, lifted his clear plastic face guard, and frowned when he saw Jack. "You look like *shit*," he said, placing considerable emphasis on the word.

"Yeah, I know," Jack answered. "But not as bad as you."

Joseph John Hayden, MD was what polite people called "eccentric" and less polite people called "weird." He often spent weeks on end in the morgue, sleeping, bathing, and taking his meals in his small office. He smoked old-fashioned tobacco cigarettes incessantly and drank gallons of coffee daily, staining his teeth a dirty brown color. Since he rarely left the morgue, he rarely got a haircut, and his gray hair was long, stringy and unkempt. Because he rarely saw anyone other than a low-level staffer, he rarely shaved. When he did, he shaved badly, leaving his face covered in a rough, uneven stubble. He read the same dog-eared, paperback pulp fiction novels over and over again, and the strain required him to wear thick glasses that made his eyes appear to pop out of his face. Even Jack thought Joe was weird, but Joe was the only friend he had, and the only person he could talk to about her.

"Haven't seen you in a while," Joe said. "Still dancing with your demons?"

"Haven't had a drop in. . ."Jack clicked his home screen for a time check, "fifty-seven minutes."

"Practically a full recovery," Joe quipped. He was silent for a long moment. When he spoke again, his tone was softer. "Are you okay?"

Jack knew what he meant. "Getting by," he answered.

"She was here," Joe said, "but I guess you know that." After a pause, he added, "I gave it to Yashimoto."

"I figured," Jack said. He had nothing else to say. There wasn't anything else to say. He just looked at Joe. Joe looked back.

After a long, uncomfortable silence, Joe asked, "When is it?"

"Wednesday." Jack shifted his weight from one foot to the other and gave Joe a blank expression. He didn't want to talk about it.

Joe took the clue. "Heard about the excitement on the eighty-fifth," he said, his voice taking a business-like tone. He nodded at two steel gurneys, each with a black polyurethane body bag. "Johnson and the shooter, Owens. They just brought 'em down."

"That why you called me down?" Jack asked.

"Nope."

"Then why?"

Joe looked down and found what he was looking for. He kicked a cardboard box in Jack's direction. It skidded across the gray linoleum and stopped at Jack's feet. Jack bent down and pulled out a water-soaked, mud-stained UX Express uniform. He let it unroll and stared at it.

"Your delivery man," Joe said, nodding at the body on the autopsy table. "Just identified the body. It's not even in the computer yet. Washed up on the riverbank, west of the bridge, south side."

Jack let the uniform drop back into the box and stepped forward. He looked at the corpse, his face dark with rage; if the deliveryman hadn't already been dead, he would have killed him on the spot. "Drowned?" he finally asked, spitting the word out.

"Nope."

"What then?"

"Blunt force trauma."

"He was beaten to death?"

"No, probably a suicide. A civilian called in, said she saw somebody taking a header into the river early this morning. Judging by the damage to the body and internal organs, I'd say he's the jumper."

Jack thought for a moment. "What about a chip? He was off the grid."

"Yeah, I heard that, too, so I checked. He has one, but . . ." Joe grabbed a pair of tweezers and picked up a microchip from a stainless steel tray. He held it up to the bright examination table lights and peered at it. "It's a weird one. Let me show you."

He placed the chip into a small machine and pressed a button. A hologram floated in the air between them. It rotated slowly, turning to show a 3D image of the microchip. "See this little square at the bottom of the chip?" Joe said, pointing with a bloody gloved finger. "It's something new."

Jack recognized it immediately. "You don't get out much, do you, Joe?" he said.

"Why?"

"It's the company's new chip, the DX3. They're advertising the hell out of them for a Christmas release. I see the fucking ads every day."

Joe gave Jack a puzzled look. "Are you sure?" he asked. "I don't think so."

"Why?"

Joe reached for the body on the table and turned the head to the side, exposing a small, open incision at the base of the skull. "Because, judging from the condition of the area around the implant, I'd say this chip's been in him for at least two years."

24
Sailing

10:07 p.m.

The big genoa jib was pulling hard in the stiff breeze, driving the boat forward through a light chop. Sheeted tight on a close reach, the forty-two-foot sloop was heeled over, her lee rail buried in the gin-clear water. It was a perfect day for sailing in the world's best place to sail—the Sir Francis Drake Channel in the Virgin Islands. The channel was a long, sheltered track of sea bracketed by Saint John in the southwest, Virgin Gorda in the northeast, Tortola to the north, and by countless small green islands to the south. They were headed for one of those islands, Peter Island, and an overnight anchorage in picturesque Deadman's Bay. Jack tugged the brim of his baseball cap down over his brow, leaned back in the helmsman's seat, put his feet up, and looked up at Rebecca.

She was facing windward, her bare feet on the cabin roof, leaning back against the sloping mainmast. She had her hands behind her head, grasping the mast, looking out at the islands passing by. She was naked from head to toe. Her toned body showed the beginnings of a tan, and her long auburn hair streamed out and danced on the breeze. Her back arched, pushing her breasts out and away from her body so they seemed to point into the distance. She looked, Jack thought, like one of those carved, bare-breasted wooden figureheads that had adorned the bows of the schooners, barques, brigantines and square-riggers that had sailed these same waters centuries earlier. He felt like a pirate captain, sailing off with his captured prize of a beautiful woman to a hidden island retreat. The fantasy put a big grin on his face.

Rebecca caught his grin from the corner of her eyes. She turned her head to face him, flashing a smile of her own. "Ye be thinking nasty thoughts, Captain?"

"Aye, me lady, I be," Jack responded in his best pirate's voice.

"And what then are ye planning to do about it, Captain?" She twisted seductively, pretending to be stuck to the mast. "I can't be doing much for ye tied me to this big pole."

Jack smiled. He popped the switch to the autohelm and made his way to her, clambering out of the cockpit and onto the gunwale in just a few steps. He stood in front of her and grinned. "And if I be letting ye loose, me lady, how am I knowing ye won't be trying to kill me?"

"Oh, but I will be trying to kill ye, Captain. But me weapon won't be a gun or a knife." She ran her tongue across her lips.

"And then what would that weapon be?" Jack asked.

"It would be this, Captain," she said, writhing her body sensuously. "But that would be only if ye be man enough to take the risk."

"Oh, I be man enough, lady," Jack said. He reached behind her back and grasped her wrists, pulling them apart. When he did, she threw her arms around his neck and kissed him, pulling him tight against her sun-warmed body. He kissed her back hard, squeezing her tight in his arms. It was a long kiss, and he felt himself melting into her, the way he always felt when he kissed her. He pulled back from her, looked ahead and around the boat, and then pulled her toward the cockpit. He pointed at the cushioned bench on the leeward side.

She took a few steps to the bench, turned, and sat down. She put her hands behind her head and leaned back against a cushion. She placed her left leg on the rail and dropped her right on the sole. She flashed a smile of invitation that no man could turn down.

Jack took a careful look around, his eyes searching the blue waters for boats. He saw none. He reached down, eased the main sheet, and then did the same with the jib. The sails luffed, and the boat slowed. He tossed off his swim trunks and shirt and squeezed onto the bench next to her, clasping her hand in his. He held it tight, and then kissed her. It was a long, lingering kiss, spinning together the warm sun on his back, the rhythmic flapping of the sails, the soft push of her lips and the hard, urgent press of her body against his own.

A pounding noise snapped him back to reality. He looked up at his wall clock. It said 10:27 p.m. He had been in his Game for three hours. He leaned forward to take a long pull of whiskey. The pounding noise made him remember the near collision with the other boat, and the angry shouts that had followed their near miss. He smiled, remembering how those angry shouts had dissolved into laughter when the people on the other boat realized what he and Rebecca had been doing.

It had been their honeymoon, that sailing vacation, the best ten days of his life. Reliving it in the Game made him happy. *Maybe tonight I'll go back in,* he thought. He and Rebecca could sail to Salt Island and dive the wreck of the *RMS Rhone*—a British Royal Mail Ship sunk during a hurricane in 1867, lying in eighty-five feet of crystal water. Rebecca would like that, and he was curious to see how the Game handled underwater adventures.

The irritating pounding was coming from his door. It shook the door and reverberated throughout the small apartment. Jack pulled off his external link, tossed it on the coffee table, and reached for his whiskey. He took a long pull, put the bottle down, and then stepped to the door. He jerked it open.

Cassie was standing there, her fist frozen in midair, ready to pound a door that wasn't there any longer. She was still wearing the clothes she had worn at the rally, but without the heavy jacket. She was a wreck. Her face was dirt-stained, her blouse bloody, and her hands and knuckles bruised and scraped. Her face showed the strain of the rally and the time she spent in the lockup. Jack could see she wasn't happy. She stood there glaring at him.

Jack smiled. He couldn't help it. She was entertaining, even if she was a pain in the ass. "You look great," he said mockingly. "Just back from the groomers?"

"Kiss my ass," she said. She barged into the apartment, shoving him aside.

"Oh," Jack said, "where are my manners? Why don't you just come on in?" He closed the door behind her.

She stood in the center of the room, her back to Jack, her hands on her hips looking around. She spotted the open bottle of whiskey on Jack's coffee table. "Are you drinking that by yourself?"

Jack didn't answer. He walked toward the small kitchen and popped open a cupboard to get glasses. It was empty. He grabbed two dirty glasses from the sink, rinsed them, dried them, and headed back to the cramped living room. He handed a glass to Cassie and poured her two fingers of whiskey. He filled his own with the same amount, held it up in a quick toast, and tossed half of it down. Cassie looked at him. She held up her glass, tossed it all down in a fast gulp, and then held out her glass for more.

Jack decided he liked her. Not enough to spend a lot of time with her, but well enough to tolerate her for now. She could kick ass, drink, and didn't take shit from anyone. He smiled and poured her another two fingers. "So, you're here . . . why?" he asked.

"I was hoping you could recommend a good housekeeper," Cassie said, as she glanced around his disorganized, messy apartment. "But I can see that was a bad idea."

"Yeah, well, she's kind of picky about who she works for, anyway. I doubt she'd work for you." Jack paused and then asked, "So why are you really here?"

Cassie's eyes narrowed. "Listen," she said, poking him in the chest, "I came over to tell you to butt the hell out of my business. If there's another rally and you're there, butt out."

"PURE rallies can get out hand fast," Jack said. "People have been killed at PURE rallies."

"I know," Cassie said, "I've been to more rallies than I can count. So, I don't need some overgrown Boy Scout watching over me."

"Why?" Jack asked.

"Because I can take care of myself," she said, her voice rising.

"No," Jack said, "not that. I'm asking you why you go to them?"

"Oh," she said, calming, "because I'm the editor of *PURE Magazine*."

Jack burst out laughing. He poured another three fingers of whiskey into his now empty glass. "That figures," he said.

"What figures?" Cassie stuck out her empty glass for another pour.

"I knew you were cyberphobic that first time I saw you outside the building," Jack said. "That antique wreck you call a car, with all those stickers, only a CyPhobe could own that thing. It's a rolling billboard for weird."

"It's not weird, Detective, to want to keep some asshole from sticking a piece of bioengineered silicon into your brain. A lot of people think the same way." She swallowed a big gulp of whiskey. "Besides," she continued, "what about this?" She picked up Jack's external link from the table and held it up.

A strange feeling struck Jack. He wanted to tell her the reason he didn't have an implanted chip. He didn't know why he wanted to tell her, but it didn't matter. He knew he wouldn't tell her. He knew he couldn't tell her. "I have my reasons," he said, "but I'm not PURE."

"You're either CYBER or PURE," Cassie said, pushing it. "There's no middle ground. So, which one are you?"

"I'm a policeman," Jack said in a way that ended the discussion.

They sat in silence. The silence was okay with Jack; he was finding her company welcome. Her eyes found the silver-framed photograph on his coffee table, and she picked it up. "Who are these people?" she asked.

It was a question no one ever asked, and he didn't know how to answer it. Everyone at the station already knew, and they would never ask. He had no friends except Joe Hayden. No one ever came into his apartment, so no one ever saw the photo to ask. He sat looking at her, searching for a way to tell her that wouldn't require a long explanation or summon up the "Oh, I'm so sorry" bullshit response he didn't want to hear. He took the easy way out; he ducked the question. "You want another drink?" he asked, pointing to the nearly empty bottle. "I have another bottle."

She paused for just a moment before she answered. "Sure," she said, "why not."

Jack stood and headed for the kitchen.

When he turned the corner and disappeared, Cassie twirled her head to find his Game box. She saw it sitting on a table in the corner, the blue light blinking, signaling the Game was running. She tapped her external link and clicked-in to see an icon marked "proximity devices." Another click captured the Game box's WorldNet IP address and ran an automatic password hacking algorithm guaranteed to work in less than ten seconds if the security level was below Crystal. She heard Jack coming back and clicked back out.

"You like whiskey?" Jack asked, holding the bottle out, ready to pour.

Cassie held back her glass. "I do," she answered, "but it's better with ice. I hate to ask, but if you don't mind . . ."

"Sure," Jack said. She watched him head off to the kitchen again.

The moment his back was turned, Cassie clicked back into Jack's Game. She went into "Settings," found what she was looking for, moved a sliding bar forward to its maximum and clicked back out of the Game. She was sitting there smiling when Jack returned with a small bowl filled with ice. She kept on smiling while Jack put ice cubes into her glass and poured whiskey over them.

25

On the Roof

TUESDAY, DECEMBER 9
11:23 a.m.

The cold rain moving through the region had given way to bright sunshine and temperatures reaching into the low sixties. It was unusual, but welcome, weather for the time of year. Jack was glad to be out of the office, walking the crowded city streets. The city felt clean, washed by the rain, dried by the warm breeze. It looked clean, too, with sparkling shop windows lining the avenues and rain-washed taxis zipping up and down its thoroughfares. It was a good morning to be out for a walk, even if the purpose of the walk was to find a piece of evidence in Rebecca's murder.

He had spent the morning at the station working on the case.

He had started with the alert, pouring through dispatch for a record of who sent the alert that directed him to Rebecca's murder and pulled him into the case. But his search came back empty. In fact, there was no record of the alert, and that meant just one thing: that whoever sent it had a level of clearance high enough to manipulate the system. It was a frustrating dead end.

He did the same thing with his assignment on the Goldstein death certification. It was another frustrating dead end. He could find no indication that it had been anything more than a random assignment. He just couldn't accept that as the whole truth and decided he would try again later.

He had also spent time reviewing Donald Dillon's Criminal Behavior Profile—CBP— the company's profiling program that predicted future criminal behavior for just about everyone on the planet. Jack hated the process behind the CBP program—collecting everything about everyone and running the data through a sophisticated set of algorithms proven to predict criminal tendencies—but he had to admit it was usually right. Besides, the program was decades old, tracing its roots back to the Internet days. The extensive collection of data had started then in both government and private sector companies; the only difference between then and now was how much better the company had become at it than anyone had been in the past. Privacy had vanished long ago, so much so that the word itself had no meaning anymore.

What the program showed Jack surprised him in two ways: first, CBP was certain that Donald Dillon—the man he and everyone else in the room had watched brutally raping and murdering Rebecca—showed zero likelihood of committing such a crime; and second, Eddie Rodriguez hadn't bothered to check the program for Dillon's profile. The latter oversight seemed odd since Jack's investigation showed him that Eddie was doing a passable job with the rest of the investigation.

Eddie had interviewed several witnesses: the UX Express Human Resources person who hired Dillon through the company's ex-con rehab program, a UX Express supervisor, Dillon's parole officer, the building's night security guard, and Dillon's girlfriend, Anna. Routine questions, routine answers, everything filed, electronically stamped and digitally signed. By later in the week, the file would be on its way to the central electronic storeroom to join all the other closed files, and Eddie would report to the news feed that he had closed the investigation. A quick, tidy and efficient closing out of a human life. Just what a well-run police force was expected to do.

But not if he had anything to do with it.

He turned a corner, walking east on the flagpole-lined esplanade. A stiff breeze from the lake whipped the flags and filled the air with their loud beating. The sidewalk was crowded with vendors hocking their wares to throngs of tourists. He ducked and dodged his way through the crush of people, moving in and out of the shadows of the high-rise condominiums that stretched up into the cloudless sky. Just across the narrow Chicago River, other luxury condominiums offered the same sweeping views, liveried door attendants, fine dining restaurants, gyms and more to their privileged residents. *A nice place to live,* Jack thought, *but not a nice place to die.* His destination, the building just ahead of him, was the last high-rise before the river joined the lake. It was the building from which, based upon the witness' report, Donald Dillon had jumped to his death.

He had already reviewed the building's security camera records. All security camera records from high-security buildings were automatically forwarded daily to Central Records and provided for police review. The cameras showed Dillon entering the building at 3:31 a.m., his entry facilitated by the UX Express RFID—radio frequency identification device—that identified him as a prescreened, secure UX Express employee. It showed that when Dillon walked into the building, he was carrying the package he took with him when he left the murder scene. Jack was here to find it.

When Jack reached the building, a uniformed doorman, with pale skin and a heavy five o'clock shadow, stepped in front of him to block his entrance. Jack flashed his badge. The attendant grudgingly stepped aside and pulled the door open with a white-gloved hand. The moment he stepped inside, a condescending concierge descended on him like a hawk on a field mouse. Her heels clicked as she crossed the marble lobby, eyeing him suspiciously, a scowl plastered across her face. When she reached him, she examined his badge and questioned him before she pointed to the elevators just off the building's atrium.

So much for hospitality. But it could have been worse—they could have demanded a warrant if they had wanted to be real assholes. He hadn't bothered to take the time to get one because he knew he wouldn't need one. The rich and their employees always cooperated. They had an unspoken but real understanding with the Unitex Chicago Police Department that they would always cooperate and that, in turn, the UCPD would protect them and their privacy whenever it could.

The elevator ride to the top of the building was smooth, fast and silent. Jack stepped out of the elevator and through a service door into a dark shaft. He climbed a short ladder to the roof, opened the small metal security door and stepped out into the bright day.

The rooftop was silent and still. The wind that was whipping the flags along the sidewalks was gone, replaced by an eerie calm. The sounds of the city's daily life: the blaring horns, the rumble of the big the trucks, the incessant humming of the AirTrans, and the plaintive wails of the emergency vehicles were all distant and muted.

The rooftop was massive, the size of several football fields together, and covered in a chalk-white gravel that crunched underfoot. He started his search. He looked everywhere, circling each of the dozen huge air conditioning units that sprouted up like small houses in the center of the roof. He rummaged through two small storage sheds, crawled into a vent and duckwalked the full length of a solar panel installation, emerging from the other end with his leg muscles burning. There was no sign of the deliveryman's package anywhere.

He started to leave but had a sudden urge to look. He walked to the edge of the rooftop and peered over it. It was a long way down to the river below. He imagined Dillon's long plummet into the icy cold water. Dizzying vertigo overwhelmed him. He stepped back from the edge and took a deep breath.

"It's a long way down, *Cabrón.*"

Jack knew the voice. "Well, well," he quipped, "if it isn't our resident big city homicide dick." He turned to see Eddie standing a few feet away, smirking in the bright sunshine, his trademark black fedora pulled low over his brow to block the sun. Eddie reached into his pocket and pulled out one of his nootropic cigarettes. He lit it and took a deep drag.

"Ever try one of these?" he asked through a crooked smile. "You should. *Número Tres.* A mood enhancer. Makes dealing with dickheads like you a whole lot easier."

"If I thought it would help me stomach you, Eddie," Jack said, "I'd smoke a whole pack of them."

The men glared at one another for a long moment. "You butting into my case, *amigo*?" Eddie finally asked. "You know that's a big no-no."

He doesn't know I'm officially on it. Remi didn't tell him. He wondered why. He decided Remi probably just didn't want to hear Eddie whine. *Well, fuck him,* Jack decided. *I'll let him sweat for a while.* "Just taking in the view, Eddie," he said.

"Bullshit, amigo. You think I'm going to buy that crap?"

"Buy what you want, *a-Mee-go,*" Jack said, breaking the word into a mocking three syllables. "And speaking of buddies," Jack added, "where's that brilliant partner of yours?"

Jack had barely spoken the words when the metal security door to the rooftop clanged open and Duane Chapman's massive bulk appeared in the small opening. Emitting grunts and groans, Duane managed the last few rungs of the ladder, grasped the doorway's metal handles with his fat hands and squeezed himself out onto the rooftop. He stood in the bright sunshine, blinking, and then reached into his pocket to pull out a chocolate bar.

Eddie looked at Duane, shaking his head in disgust. He looked back at Jack. "So, did you find it, amigo?"

"Find what?" Jack asked, feigning ignorance.

"More bullshit, *compadre*?"

Jack headed for the security door, walking past Eddie without looking at him. When he reached the door, he turned and stepped into it, his hands grasping the door's handles, his foot finding the ladder's first rung. "Like I said, Eddie," he replied, "I was just sightseeing."

He started the short climb down, dropping out of view. He was enjoying the image of Eddie and fat Chapman walking and crawling around the rooftop in a futile search when a new thought struck him: Eddie had suspicions he wasn't content to ignore. Most police officers would do the minimum in a high-profile case like Rebecca's. High-profile people had high-profile friends; a police officer never knew what they might find to upset them. Most officers played it safe, especially in an open-and-shut case like Rebecca's murder. Eddie was breaking an unwritten rule; he was taking a risk.

Little surprised Jack these days. This did.

26

Anna

2:52 p.m.

She was sitting on the couch in her living room in the small house she had shared with him, lost in her memories. The doorbell startled her. It was an old-fashioned one, set too loud, and the booming "ding-dong" made her flinch. She struggled to her feet, straining to lift both herself and the baby due any day now. She padded over to the front door and cracked it open. Bright sunshine flooded in through the narrow opening. It took her eyes time to adjust before she could see the man standing on her porch. When she did, she knew why he was there.

He was standing there with one foot forward, the other back, like a fighter. He held his arms loose and away from his sides, as if he might need to throw a punch or draw a gun. He looked confident, even arrogant, acting as if he was standing on his porch, not hers. But it was his eyes that told her the most—cold, questioning eyes that looked right into her and said, "I don't believe you," even before he asked a question. She had grown up on the South Side and had dealt with lots of cops. She could spot one a mile away.

She waited for him to speak. It didn't take long.

"Miss Anaïs Iliescu?" he asked.

"Yes."

"Detective Waldron," he said. "May I come in?"

This one looked different from the other two detectives who had visited two days ago. He was much better looking, even if he was disheveled and scarred and she sensed something that made her think he was different inside too. But she was fed up with them all. Nothing she said to this one would bring him back to her. "I talk already to the other detectives," she said dismissively. "I tell them everything I know." She started to close the door.

He pushed back against the door with one hand and pulled out his badge with the other. He held it up for her to see. "Look, I just have a few questions," he said. "I can ask them here, or . . ." He let the statement hang there.

She knew it would be easier talking to him here than at the station. She had been there before, and she didn't like it much. She had nothing to lose by talking to this detective except time, and she had more of that now than she wanted. She pulled the door open, inviting him in.

She ushered him into the neat and tidy living room, pointed to the couch and then sat down in a chair facing him. She waited patiently while he looked at a digital picture that sat on the end table next to him. She wondered why he was so interested in it.

It was a picture of Anaïs and Donald Dillon, bundled in skiing attire, standing on a snow-covered mountaintop, framed against a cobalt blue sky. He could see that it had been taken a few years earlier, and that then there was nothing of the pain she had in her eyes now. The photo had grabbed Jack's attention because it reminded him of an earlier time in his life, a time when he too had been happy. He had to force himself to stop looking at it.

"You ski a lot, Miss Iliescu?" he asked, trying to get a dialogue going. "I used to ski a lot myself."

"Not now," she answered, "but before. Before, we go every year." She paused, sighed, and added, "Please call me Anna. Everybody else does."

"Thank you, Anna," Jack said. "Did you mean before you got pregnant?"

"No. I meant since before Donald was at that place—Crest. But not since he was there."

"You knew Donald a long time?"

"Since high school," she said.

"How did you meet?" he asked casually.

Her eyes narrowed, the lines around her mouth tightened. "The other two," she said, "when they come, they didn't ask me this. This is important?"

Probably not, Jack admitted to himself, but getting her talking was. "My captain likes a complete report," he said, playing the overworked civil servant card. *What the hell. Why not? It works sometimes.*

It did this time. She frowned but talked. "Not a special meeting," she began, "it just happened one day. I was walking home from the school. He was driving by. He pulled over his car and we talk." She smiled at the memory; a private smile people kept for special memories. "I was young, and he was older. But he was nice and very good-looking. I like him right away."

Her face brightened, and her eyes sparkled when she thought of Dillon. *She's a beautiful woman,* he thought, even with the few extra pounds of the pregnancy and the unruly dark brown hair that framed her face with stray strands. Her eyebrows stretched out to form a lazy V that crossed her deeply set, soft gray eyes, her lips were full and rested under a river-deep philtrum that drew the eye to them. She glowed with health, as pregnant women so often did. He guessed her age at somewhere in her early thirties.

"Where are you from?" he asked, intrigued by her accent.

"I grew up in the Auby," she said.

Jack knew it well. Auburn Gresham, one of the city's warzones, locked for decades in gang wars between Spanish-speaking Latino gangs and black gangs speaking a language of their own. It spread out for blocks from the corner of South Halstead Street and Seventy-Seventh Avenue. Residents had a one-in-four chance of making it through a year without being robbed, stabbed or murdered; juveniles had a one-in-five chance of making it to their twenties. Birthdays in Auby took on a whole new meaning. Jack had once asked a kid in Auby his age. The kid's answer: "I just *made* fourteen." To the kid, making it to fourteen was a big accomplishment. Even the police drove through Auby with their windows up and the doors locked.

"Before that," Jack said, "I meant what country?"

"I came to the States when I was seven," she answered, "from what used to be Romania. My town was not far from Bucharest."

A Romanian kid stuck in Auby; he wondered how she'd gotten through it. Dillon was lucky to have this beautiful and tough woman, and he must have known it. He looked around the house, noting how clean, tidy and orderly it was. *A nice home, a beautiful woman and a baby due any day.* Jack felt his case shifting, like a fault line jiggling before the real earthquake got going. It was an unsettling feeling.

"You never married?" he said.

"We were supposed to marry this weekend," she answered, "before the baby came." She reached down to touch her belly.

It was sounding like a fairytale. Jack needed to punch a few holes in it. "Donald had a long police record," he said bluntly. "Why did you stay with him for so long?"

"He was wonderful," she said, "not like you police think he was."

"But he had a long record," Jack insisted, pushing it harder.

"He made mistakes when he was young. He wasn't a bad person."

"He was a registered sex offender." Jack made the words sound as ugly as he could. He wanted to see her reaction. When it came, it surprised him.

She laughed. Not just a chuckle—a real laugh. She took a few seconds to collect herself and answer. "That was my parents," she said. "They called the police when they found out I was seeing him. They said he was too old—nineteen—to be with someone just sixteen. He got probation, but they made him register. I moved in with him when I was eighteen."

"Did you tell that to the other officers?"

"No," she said derisively, "not to them. They ask only a few questions and left. I think they were not interested in finding out about Donald."

Jack wondered what else Eddie missed. "What about Crest?" he asked. "The file says he went up for burglary, a private residence in Oak Park."

"It was a friend from before," she said, "from when he was young. He asked Donald to drive him to that house, so he could pick up something the owner was holding for him. Donald was always doing favors for friends. The friend went around the house; he was gone for a while. Donald decided he would go look for him when the police showed up and arrested them. The friend was inside with a big bag of jewelry and the silent alarm was on and that's why the police showed up." She sighed and shrugged her shoulders. "Nobody believed him. They gave him ten years."

"He was out in five," Jack said. "Good behavior?"

"He volunteered for some program to test new microchips—you know, the ones everyone has under their skin. They let everyone who was in it out early—a reward for being in it."

Nothing in Donald Dillon's file said anything about participating in a test program for microchips. She had his full attention. "What did they do in the test?" he asked, trying to appear less interested than he was. "Did he tell you?"

"No," she answered. "He said it was mostly boring, just a lot of sitting around while doctors ran programs and checked machines for something or other. He said it was painful sometimes. He didn't know what they were doing and didn't like it much. He thought about quitting it."

"Why didn't he?"

"He wanted to get out early."

"Anything else?"

She thought about it for a moment and then answered. "He said that sometimes they let them play Games as a reward."

"What kind of Games?"

"I don't really know. But he told me there was one most of the others like, but not him. Something to do with watching birds."

Jack sat still on the couch for a moment then looked around the room. He was surprised that everything was still in the right place. Jack's earthquake had begun.

27

Cold, Dead Halls

4:18 p.m.

Even the corridors in the Unitex basement morgue seemed dead. The linoleum floors, streaked and cracked by countless heavy gurneys, were long overdue for replacement. The dingy green walls, peeling paint and pockmarked with dings, formed a dizzying maze that mystified even the most frequent visitor. And the low ceilings—dreary, endless tracks of dirty grids interspersed with yellowed light panels—gave the whole basement a claustrophobic, dungeon-like feeling. Jack understood why Joe Hayden loved it down here. He fit right in.

Jack was trying to decide where to look for Joe—his office or the autopsy room—when he heard a squeaking noise in the hallway behind him. A skinny, brown-skinned kid in blue scrubs was pushing a gurney with a black body bag on it down the hall toward him. The bag was big, bulging, and pulling at its seams, and the kid was having a hard time pushing it. When the teenager got close enough Jack said, "Where's the boss, on the floor or in his office?"

The kid stopped pushing, happy to take a break. He wiped his brow, wet with sweat even in the cold corridor. When he responded, Jack didn't understand a word of what he said.

Jack remembered that he wasn't wearing his link. He held up a hand while he fished in his pocket and put it on. Then he motioned for the kid to speak again. Smirking at Jack's old-fashioned link, the teen spoke the words again. Now that he was clicked-in, Jack saw the translation—"He's in his office." Jack nodded a thank you and walked off. When he had gone a few steps, he heard the wheel squeaking again.

Jack pulled off his link and shoved it deep into his pocket. He resented having to rely on it but knew he couldn't get along without it. His translator said the kid was speaking Indonesian, and Jack knew the kid always would. The kid had no reason to learn English, at least not as long as he had his translator. It was the same for all the immigrant groups. They all spoke their own language, using their translators when they needed them. But the technology had a downside—people had stopped assimilating. A third of Chicago's wards were like foreign countries now, places where outsiders weren't welcome, and intruders scorned, or worse. The xenophobia of the non-English-speaking groups spurred gang wars, and the police were stretched thin controlling them. The only big winner from the technology was the company. The company got five credits a month for the translation application. Everyone had to have one. *Big fucking money,* Jack thought, and with no incentive for the company to change things, they were certain to remain the same.

When he got to Joe's office, he walked right in. Joe wasn't there, but it was easy to see he hadn't been gone long. A half-eaten sandwich sat in the middle of his cluttered desk next to a full cup of steaming coffee. A burning cigarette threatened to tumble out of an overflowing ashtray. A worn paperback novel lay open, face down, ready to be picked up and read again. Jack was about to call out Joe's name when he heard a flushing toilet in the back of the room. Seconds later he emerged, drying his hands, walking toward his desk.

"Well, well, well," Joe said, spotting Jack. "Two visits in two days. I must be living right."

Jack plopped down into the scratched and worn red leather chair in front of the desk and crossed his legs, his left ankle on his right knee. He wriggled to get comfortable. "Yeah, I'm just here for the ambiance," he said, glancing around at the disorganized, messy office.

Joe sat down and picked up the cigarette, scattering ashes onto the desk. He leaned back in his chair and took a drag, sucking the smoke deep into his lungs before exhaling long and loudly. When the exhale was complete, he smacked his lips.

"Where do you get those things?" Jack laughed. "You never leave this fucking basement."

"I got a guy who brings 'em to me," Joe said. "He doesn't charge me anything, either. I just let 'em watch an autopsy now and then. Women, mostly."

"He's probably a fucking pervert serial killer." Jack pulled his flask from his pocket and gulped down two ounces. "Ever thought of that?" he continued. "That he's looking for tips on how to slice up his victims?"

"Nah, he's not. He's just a bit weird."

The pot calling the kettle black. Jack remembered the saying from his grandmother, who said she'd heard it from her mother. He'd never seen a black pot or kettle but guessed they used to be that way. "Well, that's a very comforting thought, Joe," he said.

Joe's stained teeth flashed a big grin. "So, to what do I owe this honor, Detective? Something I can do for you?"

Jack reached into his pocket and pulled out Herb Goldstein's pills. He thumped the bottle on the desk in front of Joe.

Joe picked it up. "What about 'em?" he asked.

"Evidence in a case," Jack said, "a death certification. Your department did the autopsy. I forgot about the pills until about an hour ago. Blew the chain of evidence, too, not that it matters much." Jack could hear Rebecca chiding him for his sloppiness. "I want to know what they do."

"It's a powerful angiotensin," Joe said without hesitating. "Opens the arteries so the heart doesn't have to work so hard."

"What happens if you need it and you don't take it?"

"Probably kill you. Powerful little pills. They're not for everybody; you have to have a big problem." Joe looked at the label. "This Goldstein fellow, what'd he die from?"

"You're the ME, Joe. That's why I'm here."

"Okay," Joe said. "Follow me, I'll connect you." He waited while Jack dug down into his pocket for his link and put it on. When he was ready, Jack tapped his link and his home screen appeared. A Unitex icon with a caduceus and the words "Office of the Medical Examiner" appeared. Jack clicked-in.

He watched as Joe navigated the site, sourcing Herb Goldstein's autopsy. A 3D image of Herb's body appeared. Joe looked at the body, turning it around. He stopped on Herb's face.

"By the way," Jack asked when Herb's face popped into view, "what's this guy so happy about?"

"Not happy, Jack," Joe said. "Just looks like a smile. We see them from time to time. Grimace from the pain of the heart attack. Probably hurt like hell." He lit another cigarette from the first, crushing the first in the overflowing ashtray. "That's what killed him—heart attack."

"Because he didn't take the pills?" Jack asked.

"How many did he miss?"

"You're looking at it. It looks like all of them, about a month's worth."

Joe whistled a long, drawn-out whew sound. "That would do it." He paused then asked, "Why are you interested in this guy?"

"Not sure," Jack answered. "Was he wearing a chip?"

Joe gave Jack a quizzical look. "Let's look." Joe clicked a field, and the 3D autopsy image morphed into Herb's head and neck. The display dove through a transparent epidermal layer and stopped, focused on the chip. It showed the chip perfectly. "Well," Joe said, "how about that. Brand new, too. The implant was less than three weeks ago."

"The new chip? The DX3?"

"Yup."

Jack's display went blank as Joe clicked it off. Joe was staring at him. "You got chips on the brain again?" Joe asked.

It was a reasonable question, after what happened. Joe was the one person outside of a small group of Digitex and Unitex senior management who knew what happened with the DX2, but Jack wasn't ready to share his suspicions about the DX3 with him. "Nah," he said nonchalantly, "just wondering. But since I'm here, what can you tell me about Peggy Owens?"

Joe took a big bite from his sandwich and chewed it for a few seconds. "Who is Peggy Owens?" he asked, through a mouth stuffed with sandwich.

"The shooter," Jack said in a scolding tone. He knew Joe was playing with him. "Cut the crap and tell me."

Joe swallowed the bite and chased it with a big sip of coffee. He cleared his throat. "Oh, well, she's dead," he said, grinning.

"Asshole. What else?"

"Official cause of death—thirty-seven nine-millimeter rounds. Took out her heart, lungs and most of her stomach." He lit a new cigarette from the burning one, stubbed out the old, and sucked in a deep drag. "Did the autopsy myself," he said, exhaling a cloud of smoke. "Not pretty."

"Joe, you know what I'm asking," Jack said. "What about her chip?"

The way Joe smiled at Jack said it all. "When I pulled her chip, and saw it was the same as Donald Dillon's, I told my staff guy to look into it. He found out Peggy's was authentic, a brand-new DX3. She got it just a couple of weeks ago, some kind of employee reward program. Probably the way Goldstein got his too."

Jack was stunned. "So, you already considered this?"

"Yes."

"And Dillon's chip wasn't a real DX3?"

"Close, but no cigar. My guy figures it was a prototype, but he couldn't find out where he got it. And here's the kicker—it looked like it had been implanted years ago."

Jack let the time stretch before he spoke. "What do you think?"

"I dunno," Joe said. He took another sip of coffee and drag on his cigarette. "But I'd sure as hell tread carefully if I were you."

28

Tahoe

9:23 p.m.

Jack leaned against the railing of the mountainside lodge, his ski jacket opened to his waist. He was soaking up the warm spring sunshine, gazing out at the lake through the protecting lenses of his polarizing sunglasses. He could see the entire Tahoe basin in all its vivid colors: the varied blues and greens of the lake, the granite grays of the mountains, the purple greens of the pines, the bright white of the snow. Everything melded together in a palette of picture-perfect color. He took a deep breath. Even the air was faultless—crisp, clean and scented with the sharp smell of the pines.

He loved Tahoe.

He didn't want to leave.

He hadn't been here long, just a few hours. He had spent all that time with Rebecca, skiing the manicured trails that wound down from the summit of the mountain to its base and then chairlifting back up for another run. Jack loved to ski. It made him feel alive. Right now, he needed that feeling more than ever.

He hadn't thought about Tahoe in a long time, not until this morning when the photo in Anna's house reminded him of it. He had never been here before in his Game. He wondered why. He had always had a great time in Tahoe with Rebecca, before and after they were married.

And they had brought Sarah here, too, right after she turned five, spending many happy hours with her playing in the snow, building snowmen, sledding and even putting her on a pair of tiny skis to glide down the gentle slopes of the children's area. That trip was just before Sarah got sick.

Now he remembered why he hadn't been back.

The thought soured Jack's mood. As he struggled to push it out of his mind, he was grateful to hear Rebecca's voice behind him. "Beautiful," she said. "Isn't it?"

She handed him a cup of hot chocolate. He took a sip from the steaming cup. The hot liquid stung his lips and burned his tongue, but tasted great. He ignored the discomfort and downed a mouthful. "Beautiful is an understatement," he said when he had swallowed the drink. "It's fantastic."

Rebecca slid into place next to him, leaning over the rail to gaze out at the lake below. "You know," she said softly, "I always loved it here too."

Rebecca's words hit Jack like a hammer. His smile dissolved instantly.

Rebecca was commenting on the thoughts he had before she arrived with the hot chocolate, not the direct conversation of this moment.

It jarred him. He might not have noticed it on another day, but now, after what happened, his sensitivity to the Game was greater than before. He immediately clicked into the command bar and pressed the Game's double-bar "pause" icon.

He couldn't remember which setting it was that allowed a Game character to share in the thoughts and feelings of the player; he had to use the "Help" search to identify it. But once he found it in the ERS (encoding, retrieval, sharing) functions for declarative memory, it was as simple as moving a sliding bar from the maximum to two settings below the mid-range default. He wasn't ready for Rebecca to find out she was dead in the real world.

The process bothered him. He didn't remember changing the setting. If he didn't do it, then someone else had done it. But whom? Cassie had been the only person in his apartment for months. And if she didn't do it—and he couldn't imagine why she would—then who? Had someone else been in his apartment? He promised himself to look into it.

When he clicked back into the Game, it was as if the pause had never occurred. "Remember how hard I laughed that first day we were here?" Rebecca said, doing her best not to laugh now. "You were a riot, thinking you could you just put on skis and go."

Rebecca had grown up in Colorado, spending her youth at the ski resorts that ringed the Denver area. She was more than just an expert skier. When she was fifteen, she was offered a sponsorship to train for the Olympics. She had chosen, instead, to turn her efforts toward fast-tracking multiple degrees at Stanford and Berkeley, including a degree from the prestigious Boalt Hall School of Law. But even during those years of hard work, she'd found the time to make the trip from San Francisco to the slopes at Tahoe to keep her skills sharp. It didn't hurt that she came from a very rich family. She had always made the trip in her top-of-the-line hydrogen-electric automobile, seated in a body-conforming, heated leather seat while auto drive gave her plenty of time to study on both legs of her trip.

"Yeah," Jack answered, "I was a bit overconfident."

Jack had never skied before he met Rebecca. It was not something that the son of a Chicago city fireman could afford, even before the politicians had bungled the city's finances and government workers' salaries were chopped drastically. Skiing was an expensive sport. It would have stayed out of Jack's reach except for Rebecca's money.

Rebecca's money—her family's money, and the top salary she made as a lawyer at the company—had always been a sore point with Jack. He didn't hate money—he had worked hard all his life to get it—but he didn't like that the money that funded their lavish lifestyle came from her and not from him.

It didn't bother Rebecca. She had always been rich and felt that money was meant to be spent. But Jack struggled with it. Maybe it was his own modest upbringing, or maybe it was that as a cop he saw how most people had to live their lives on the edge. Or maybe he just was a man and she was a woman, and it somehow didn't seem right to him. Whatever it was, one thing was certain—it had always bothered him.

Not that it mattered much now. Not with Rebecca gone. It had never mattered in the Game.

Jack felt his mood changing and pushed the dark thought from his mind. He was here with Rebecca. There was nothing he had to do right now except spend time with her. Tomorrow was soon enough to deal with everything else. "Well," he said smiling devilishly, "how about we go step into our skis and race to the bottom of the hill. The winner gets whatever they want."

Rebecca smiled back. "You don't have a chance, Jack."

Jack's smile grew even bigger. "Yeah, I know."

29

Headstones

WEDNESDAY, DECEMBER 10
11:01 a.m.

"The Lord God lives in his holy temple yet abides in our midst . . ." The priest's solemn voice droned on, echoing off the tombstones in the still morning air. "Since in baptism, Rebecca became God's temple, and the spirit of God lived in her, with reverence we bless her mortal body. Grant that our sister Rebecca may sleep here in peace until you awaken her in . . ."

Jack stopped listening.

The ceremony had no meaning for him. Rebecca had found strength in her Catholic faith after Sarah died, but Jack had not. Whatever little faith he once had—and it had never been much—died with his little girl. Her death was the beginning of the unraveling of his life. The days, weeks and months after her death had been a nightmare of cursing God, blaming himself, fighting with Rebecca and drinking himself blind. Nothing had ever been the same after—not his marriage, his health, his friendships, his job, or his hope for a future. He was at Rebecca's graveside only because he had loved her in life, not because he hoped for an afterlife. He didn't like accepting that death was the end but told himself it was enough that she had lived.

He looked around, realizing he didn't remember the gravesite. No wonder. He hadn't been here since they'd buried Sarah. He had planned to visit Sarah's grave a few times, twice buying flowers to plant next to her tombstone, but he never made it. Something had always interfered, but he knew the real reason: he never made it because he didn't want to let her go. And then it didn't matter, because he'd discovered the Game and he had her back.

He was glad that the graveside ceremony would be short. He was uncomfortable in his loose-fitting, dark suit, and even more uncomfortable in his role as the ex-husband dutifully attending the ex-wife's funeral. To everyone else, he was an afterthought—a person of no importance, a part of Rebecca's past that was best forgotten. He was a bit player, a character in a play that walks on stage to deliver a letter and then departs and never returns. He knew that the more than one hundred mourners, crowded four to five deep around the grave, viewed him that way. They were all company people, focused on the real power players at the gravesite—Weatherall, Lupe, and the company's other "senior suits." They had all arrived at the gravesite early, bolting from the church at the last amen, scrambling to their limousines, racing to the cemetery to make sure that they'd be standing in full view of the right people. Little trumped death, but office politics clearly did.

The priest's voice rose slightly as the ceremony ended: ". . . until you awaken her to glory, for you are the resurrection and the life. Then she will see you face to face, and in your light will see light and know the splendor of God, for you live and reign forever and ever." A chorus of Amens echoed in the still morning air.

It was over. The crowd stirred. Jack watched a long line form to shake hands and offer condolences. Most people in the line didn't know Rebecca; if they had met her, it had been in a business meeting. But Jack knew that it didn't matter to them. What mattered to the people lining up was a chance to shake hands with the company's second highest-ranking officer. They might even get to shake the hand of Weatherall himself; he was standing next to her. Jack wandered away from the fringe of the crowd and stood staring at a grave.

"How are you, Jack?" Remi asked, looking serious and solemn in a black suit and overcoat. He looked at Jack with sympathetic eyes.

"Okay, Remi," Jack answered. "Thanks for coming."

"I wish I wasn't here," Remi said, but quickly corrected himself, "I mean, I wish Rebecca . . . well, you know what I mean."

"I do," Jack said.

The two men stood and watched as the line of mourners moved in Lupe's direction. Jack guessed it would be another thirty minutes before the last person in line reached her. He had decided to wait for the gravesite to clear before he went to it; he needed to be alone there.

A minute passed before Remi broke the silence. "It's been a couple of days," he began. "Making any progress?"

Just like Remi to talk business, Jack thought, *even here.* But it didn't bother him. He welcomed the chance to think about something else. "Not much," he said. He wasn't sure how much he wanted to tell Remi.

"What then?"

"I haven't found the package, but I did run across Eddie looking for it."

"I told you he was a good cop."

"He's a fucking asshole," Jack said.

"He's that, but he is still a good detective."

"Yeah," Jack said grudgingly. "I suppose that's something." He paused before adding, "He didn't know I was on the case."

Remi grinned. "He came into my office after, wailing like a stuck pig." He had a contemptuous twinkle in his eye. "I had to threaten to assign him to sorting out old parking tickets for a month or two to get him to shut up."

Jack grinned, visualizing the confrontation in his mind, Eddie whining and Remi shutting him down.

"What else?" Remi asked. He wasn't letting it go.

"I talked with Dillon's fiancé."

"And?"

"And it made me wonder why he did it. Nice woman, nice house, baby on the way."

"Well, he did it," Remi said. "We all saw that. Why he did it . . . I don't know that it matters."

"Probably not," Jack said. He didn't want to argue the point.

"Is that it? Because if that's all you've got, you don't have much." Remi rubbed his hands together to warm them. The sun was shining, but the temperature had dropped overnight into the low forties; the forecast was calling for lower temperatures and the chance of snow. "Maybe I ought to let Eddie wrap it up," he added.

It was an empty threat, and Jack knew it. The order to put him on the case came from Weatherall himself; Remi wouldn't—couldn't—pull him off. He was just bluffing—digging for whatever other information he could wriggle out of him. Jack decided that two could play the same game. "If you think so, Remi," he said innocently. "Of course, the man at the top of the tower might not see it that way."

Remi grumbled and turned to look at the line leading to Lupe. He watched it for a moment. "It looks as if it's winding down," he said. "I think I will go join it to pay my *respects*."

Remi's biting tone of "respects" hung in the air as Jack watched him walk toward the dwindling crowd. He crossed paths with a well-dressed man in a suit, tie and dark overcoat. The man was headed in his direction. At first glance Jack didn't recognize him, but when he did, it took everything he had to not burst out laughing.

"Hey, Jack." The familiar voice seemed entirely out of place.

Jack couldn't remember ever seeing Joe Hayden in a suit, much less a tie. The transformation was nothing short of miraculous. Joe looked like a normal person, and it left Jack momentarily speechless. "Jesus, Joe," he finally said, "you clean up pretty damn good."

"Yeah," Joe answered. "Didn't recognize myself in the mirror."

"Thoughtful of you, Joe. I know you don't believe in any of this."

"Well, maybe I don't," Joe said, "but then again"—he pulled out a cigarette and lit it, sucking in a big lungful of smoke— "maybe I do. The science isn't clear, quantum fields being the way they are and all."

Jack remembered some of it, a long night of drinking with Joe in the basement morgue after Sarah died. Joe did his best that night to help him get through it, even getting into a long, complicated discussion of quantum theory, how maybe there was something to the whole idea of God as a universal consciousness. Joe had thrown in names like Planck, Einstein, Schrödinger and Spinoza. Jack remembered that much, but the rest was fuzzy. He had awakened in the morning on a steel autopsy table with a monumental hangover. They had never talked about it again.

"Well," Jack said, "I appreciate it, anyway."

"You know the real problem with these things," Joe said, gesturing at the priest before lighting a new cigarette from the stub of the one he had lit less than two minutes before. "No smoking. The church could sell a lot more fire and brimstone if they let you smoke while they did it." He took another deep drag, holding it in for a moment before exhaling a heavy stream of smoke. "Sunday attendance would skyrocket if they let you smoke."

Jack had always appreciated Joe's dry sense of humor. He figured Joe might be half right, with cancer beaten and a big chunk of the population smoking again, addicted to the nootropic cigarettes. But he knew that old-fashioned religion would die; a belief in anything other than money and what it bought just wasn't in the best interests of the Big Three Trade Unions. Besides, he figured, the whole philosophy of transhumanism would one day hammer the last nails into religion's coffin; who needed a God when computers could give you god-like intelligence and new body parts could let you live almost forever?

The two men stood side-by-side, waiting. Jack watched a line of cold gray clouds gather in the west. Joe smoked. Neither said anything. They had spent many hours together not saying anything, and they were comfortable with the silence. When the crowd around the grave was finally gone, Jack spoke. "Think I'll take a walk over to their graves now," he said.

Joe didn't speak; he just nodded and left. Jack tracked his progress through the tombstones by the trail of smoke he left behind. When he disappeared behind a tall obelisk, Jack walked over to the gravesite.

Sarah's headstone was to the right of Rebecca's, the dates of her all-too-short life etched deep into the cold, lifeless marble. Rebecca's headstone sat at the head of her grave, her coffin resting at the bottom of the grave, covered with handfuls of dirt tossed by mourners. Twenty feet away, three men in overalls holding shovels watched him. Jack knew that when he left they would finish the job of filling the grave. He felt his eyes filling as the emotions he had ducked for so long broke through the tough shell he had built around them. He stood there for several minutes, flooded with memories of his life with Rebecca and Sarah. He took a deep breath, deciding there was nothing more for him here. He walked away.

When he had gone fifteen paces, he pulled out his flask. The whiskey felt good going down. He took another drink, and then another. When he reached the cemetery gates his head was swimming, but his eyes were dry.

30

A Proposal

10:11 p.m.

"I can't believe you brought me here," Rebecca said, looking around the small restaurant. "You even managed to get the same table. That couldn't have been easy."

"Ten credits to the maître d'," Jack said. "Greedy little bastard."

But not really a tip for the maître d', Jack mused; *real Game credits, paid to the company.* Charging extra credits for new virtual experiences, like adding tokens in an old-fashioned arcade game, was just another way the company gouged everyone. Worse, he remembered, he was running low on credits. He would have to go to Rocco soon to get more.

"Well, it's a sweet gesture," Rebecca said. "The place looks the same."

Jack smiled. It could look no other way to her. The system A.I. created her from his memories. She had no memories of her own, except those generated in the Game and stored in the Game's database. She could only share his memories of their former life together. He remembered the white-clothed tabletops, the candlelight, the tuxedoed waiters and the pretentious maître d'. He remembered a magical evening, so she had to remember it the same way. But for all he knew, his memory was flawed, and he was turning an ordinary eatery into a magical place that had never existed. Not that it mattered. What mattered was being here with her now.

"So," Rebecca asked, "what's the occasion?"

"No occasion," Jack said, smiling. "You deserve a nice night out."

"Oh, please," Rebecca exclaimed, her right eyebrow arching up. "You haven't worn a jacket to dinner since the last time we were here. And that was here at this table, and you were proposing."

Jack remembered. He had been as nervous as a kid on his first date, fumbling the whole speech he had memorized. Rebecca was a reach for him—beautiful, sexy, smart and a company lawyer headed for a top slot in the company's management. He was just a cop—a good cop, a cop moving up the ranks, already a detective—but still just a cop. But he would always carry a badge while Rebecca, and others like her, would always decide who could carry one and what they could do with it. The first time they met, in her office, she was chewing him out about a flub in a chain of custody. It made him nervous about their relationship.

"Yeah," Jack said, smiling, "I never thought you'd say yes."

"Are you kidding me?" Rebecca laughed. "If you hadn't proposed, I would have. No way was I letting you go."

Jack twirled his whiskey in the soft glow of the candlelight. He watched the amber liquid spin around in his glass and wondered why, even here, he craved it. The scientists probably had an explanation for that too. *Those assholes had an explanation for everything.* Everything except for the things that mattered, like why their little implant chips had so fucked up his life. The last thought soured his mood. He felt his anger rising. He couldn't stop it.

Rebecca sensed it. She was used to his changing moods and knew he was fighting with something. "Jack," she said quietly, "whatever this is, let it go."

He took a deep breath. "It's hard," he said. "You should know that."

"I know what you went through, Jack. I know it was hard for her too."

"The company knew," Jack said, his voice rising. "That son of a bitch Weatherall lied. He knew, and he lied. Sarah's dead, you blamed me, we got a divorce, and now—." He stopped, catching himself before he said anymore. He still wasn't ready to tell her.

"That's the second time you started to tell me something, Jack," Rebecca said. "What are you hiding from me?"

"Nothing," Jack almost shouted. "I told you before, nothing."

"Okay, Jack, fine," she said in a calming tone. "But now's not the time to lose it."

"There's never a right time," Jack snapped, his voice rising even higher. "It's not fucking fair." He picked up what remained in his glass and tossed it back.

"I can tell you what's not fucking fair, buddy boy," a deep voice rumbled, "listening to you bellyache about your bullshit, that's what's not fair."

The voice was coming from a dark-haired, dark-eyed man in his early forties sitting at the table next to him. The man was dressed elegantly in a dark gray suit, gray silk shirt and a black silk tie. A large diamond stickpin secured his tie, and an even bigger diamond flashed from a ring on his finger. He held a wine glass just below his bent, broken nose, twirling it to aerate the wine while a fussy, nervous sommelier waited for him to taste it.

Two women flanked the man, one blonde the other brunette. The women were young, less than half the man's age, and dressed in identical gold Lamé dresses with deep v's that showed a lot of cleavage. The dresses looked expensive, but the women looked cheap. They giggled and smiled, hanging onto the man with tight grips like suckerfish attached to a shark's belly along for an easy ride. Jack didn't like them or the man.

"Maybe you shouldn't be listening in, asshole," Jack shot back.

The man just smiled. He showed no fear; Jack wondered why. The man reached his left hand up into the air, snapped his fingers, and two tough looking dark-suited goons emerged from the shadows behind him. They stood there, glaring at Jack with malevolent eyes. Jack hadn't noticed them before. He stopped wondering why the man was unafraid.

"Or maybe you should be more respectful of others, friend," the man said. "Respectful guys don't get hurt."

"If you think these two cupcakes worry me," Jack sneered, taking up the challenge, "you're thinking wrong." Jack's deep anger needed to vent. He relished the idea of beating the crap out of all three of them and stood up.

"Jack, don't ruin this for us," Rebecca urged. She held a tight grip on his hand. "Drop it, please."

He started to argue with her but stopped.

What the fuck am I doing? None of this is real. It was all just his imagination, assembled into a virtual reality scenario by the system's A.I. Even the man in the gray suit was his own invention, summoned up from his own memories of real-life crooks and then put here by the system because the A.I. knew he needed to vent his anger.

He sat back down and looked across the table at Rebecca. Her face glowed in the candlelight. He needed to be with her but decided to leave before he ruined this memory for both of them. "I'm sorry, Rebecca," he said, realizing that his anger, still growing by the second, was making it impossible to continue.

He formed the word "exit" in his mind and kept his eyes fixed on her as the room faded away.

31

Peggy's Place

THURSDAY, DECEMBER 11
8:17 a.m.

The DX3 advertisement was playing again.

Swirling multi-colored pixels formed a stylized human head that displayed a small microchip implant at the back of the neck below the base of the skull. The chip illuminated and grew in size as a familiar woman's voice began a warm, compelling sales pitch: "The new DX3. Faster speeds, broader bands, better walls. A better WorldNet experience. Available Christmas day from Digitex Corporation, a Unitex company. Digitex, bringing the WorldNet to you." The image morphed into the alluring face of a famous virtual entertainer. She smiled and faded from view.

Seated on the Maglev's plastic passenger bench, Jack reached under his coat and touched the stainless steel frame of his gun. He couldn't risk pissing Remi off by smashing another WorldNet transmitter, but just thinking about pounding it into little pieces made him feel better. A quick pull of whiskey helped too. He held onto the thought as long as he could, turning it over in his mind until the Maglev slowed to a stop and its doors hissed open.

He stepped out into the gray morning light. It had snowed overnight, and a thin dusting of white powder covered the platform. The snow was mostly undisturbed, just a few footsteps here and there marring the smooth white carpet. He wasn't surprised. He was on the side of the platform used by the trains heading out of the city. At this hour in the morning, the crowds were headed in the other direction. Only night shift workers returning home would use this side of the platform, and few of them lived in the artistic and mostly gay, middle-class East Lakeview community of Boystown. Jack trudged to the stairs, leaving a trail of dark footsteps behind him. He headed down the street to Peggy's address.

It was a short walk on snow-covered sidewalks to Peggy's condominium. He reached the three-story, red brick building in less than ten minutes, bounded up the concrete steps to the front door, and entered the building. Peggy's apartment was a ground floor unit. The door to her unit was secured by a police lock, blocked by holographic projections of lines with the warning, POLICE LINE, DO NOT CROSS. Jack used the numeric pad to enter the disable code and waited the necessary five seconds for the lock to click open and the lines to disappear. When they did, he opened the door and walked in.

The apartment was neat, orderly and decorated plainly—just what anyone might expect to see in the private living spaces of a single forty-seven-year-old woman doing clerical work for the company. He looked around, trying to decide where to start. It was a decision made especially tough because he didn't really know why he was in her apartment. Nothing really tied Peggy's death to Rebecca's. Did the initials, written in hand, on Morton Johnson's desktop calendar mean he had a lunch scheduled with Rebecca? Did Peggy's action prevent that meeting? Maybe, but it was a stretch, and not supported by any evidence.

He was taking a risk being here. The case was assigned to Boreck and Blackman, two gruff veteran detectives who had already interviewed Jack about the standoff at Unitex headquarters and would raise hell if they found out he was meddling in their case. He needed to get through his search fast, get out quickly, and hope Blackman—a detective noted for his "by the book" approach to casework—didn't review the digital log of onsite visits.

His search lasted forty minutes and turned up nothing surprising except several dozen old-fashioned, printed books set in the Old West and a closet full of Western-themed clothes. He was about to quit and leave when he decided to see if Peggy played a Game. Games always said something important about the person playing them. He looked around the apartment, spotted the WorldNet transmitter, saw its blue Quantum Drive blinking, and tapped his link. He clicked the proximity locator on his screen and saw Peggy's Game:

"Gunsmoke"
Interactive VR
Digitex Industries
Security Protocol Silver
Enter Password

Jack clicked on his security protocol algorithm, tying the Game's silver level security—one of the most basic levels of security in commercial use—to the Unitex mainframe at headquarters. It took just five seconds for the program to unlock the Game. He tapped his link and waited as the pixels twirled and swirled him into the virtual reality of the Game.

Jack squinted in the harsh glare of a noonday sun. He was standing on a sun-cracked dirt street in the middle of a small town of weathered wooden buildings that stretched out in both directions. It was dusty and dry. The heat was oppressive, and the smell of fresh manure was everywhere. It was noisy, too. The sound of horses' hooves, the scraping and turning of wagon wheels on the dirt street, and the clicking footsteps of the men and women on wooden sidewalks assaulted him from every direction.

He looked up and down the street. It was crowded with horse-drawn buggies and riders on horseback. Men in cowboy hats and boots and women in calico dresses and sunbonnets packed the narrow wooden sidewalks. Somewhere in the distance, a banjo thrummed a spirited tune.

The American West, Jack thought. *Late nineteenth century.*

Games set in other times were common. History was rich with things to experience. Want to meet Aristotle in ancient Greece? Enjoy an orgy in ancient Rome? Join the knights on a Crusade? See Lincoln deliver the Gettysburg Address? Storm the beaches at Normandy? Tag along on the first Mars mission? The possibilities were endless. Best of all, you could experience them all without risk. Safety protocols protected the Gamer from any form of harm, mental or physical. Jack wasn't surprised to find himself in a Game set in another time, but he was surprised that it was Peggy's Game. Now that he was here, he had to find out why this Game was hers.

Where to start? In a small town, just about everybody visited the general store, Jack reasoned. The general store was just across the street beneath a sign that read: "Dry Goods, Clothing, Groceries, General Merchandize. J.N. Stroud, prop." He headed for it, ducking riders and wagons as he crossed the street. He reached it quickly and entered, closing the door behind him.

It was cool and dim inside, and he was grateful for the relief from the heat of the street. The pungent odors of leather, spices, grains, rope, feed and sundries combined to give the store a pleasant smell. Shafts of sunlight streamed in through the windows and pooled on a half-dozen wooden barrels of goods gathered at the store's center. But the light didn't reach the corners of the store and left much of it in shadow. Two women stood in a dark corner talking in hushed tones. Neither held a basket of items to purchase. Probably just taking a break from the oppressive heat outside, Jack figured.

"Kin I help you, neighbor?"

The question floated down to Jack from a man standing on a ladder used to stock the store's tall shelves. The man was in his fifties and looked as if he was of German or Dutch descent. He was pleasant to look at, with a thin ring of gray hair surrounding his bald, well-formed head. A pair of metal-rimmed glasses balanced on his straight nose and magnified his alert, intelligent blue eyes. He was compact, not over five foot nine, but he looked strong, like a farmer, even if his alabaster skin hadn't seen the sun in months. He was wearing a pressed white shirt and brown suspenders that held up a pair of brown pants, and he was neat as a pin. Jack watched him descend the ladder holding a can in one hand.

"John Stroud, neighbor," he said, stretching out his hand.

"John Waldron."

Jack took the offered hand in his own, shaking the dry flesh, feeling silly, knowing he was shaking hands with an imaginary character in a Game. Maybe it was that the Game was set in the past that was keeping him from full immersion. He decided that it would take time to adjust to this Wild West environment. He could almost feel the neurochemicals pumping into his bloodstream.

"New to these parts, are you, John?" the proprietor said.

"New to town, all right," Jack answered. He had already decided on his cover story. "Just here looking for someone I haven't seen for a while."

"You a lawman, John?"

"I am."

"Figured you for a lawman," the proprietor said through a sly smile. "This person you're looking for, running from the law?"

"Nope," Jack said, getting into the spirit of the Game. "Just looking for her. A lady in her forties, brown hair. Maybe you know her. Her name is Peggy Owens."

"Well, sure," the proprietor said, "nice lady. Been in here more 'en a few times."

"That so?" Jack asked. "Do you know where she is?"

The proprietor scratched the bald top of his head with thin fingers. "Can't say I do," he said, "'least not right now. Haven't seen her around these parts the last few days."

"Know someone who might know?"

"Well, the sheriff might," the proprietor answered with a grin and a raised eyebrow.

"Where do I find him?"

The proprietor gave Jack another quirky look. "I reckon you might find the sheriff in the sheriff's office. Down the street a piece, 'cross from the saloon."

There was something in the proprietor's answer and the twinkle in his eyes that gave Jack pause, but he ignored it. Whatever it was, he reasoned, he'd find out soon enough.

"Thank you for your help, John," Jack said. He turned and stepped back out through the door into the sweltering heat of the street.

The saloon was about a hundred yards down the street, the sheriff's office a small, whitewashed wood building across the street from it. Jack headed for it, weaving his way through the town folks that crowded the wooden sidewalks. As he walked, he wanted to tip his hat to the women walking toward him, but he wasn't wearing one. He considered pausing the Game to let the system's A.I. dress him in western garb but decided against it. It would cost him credits he couldn't afford to spend, but that he even contemplated it made him realize that he was finally immersing in the Game.

When he was thirty feet from the saloon, a cowboy tumbled out of its swinging doors and rolled into the street. Seconds later, a second cowboy flew through the doors and rolled into the street next to the first. Both cowboys sat up, shaking off the tumble and dusting the dirt from their sleeves and pants. Then the saloon doors banged open and a short figure wearing a gleaming silver badge stepped out onto the wooden porch. It was the sheriff, but not the sheriff Jack was expecting to see.

The sheriff was a woman. She was in her mid-thirties, dressed nattily in a white linen shirt, dark vest and dark pants. She was short, not more than five feet tall, but she wore a pair of polished, black cowboy boots that added two inches to her height. Her wheat-colored hair was tucked up under a black Dakota cowboy hat. Her hands rested on the polished wood handles of a matched pair of single-action Colt six-shooters, holstered at her hips. Jack sensed the guns weren't there for decoration; she looked as though she wouldn't hesitate to use them.

There was also something familiar about her, but Jack couldn't put his finger on it.

She wasted no time in conversation with the two cowboys. "You boys git now," she said in a rasping tone, "and don't let me see you back here anytime soon. I ain't gonna be so kindly next time."

The cowboys—two strapping kids in their late teens who had had too much to drink—stood up on wobbly legs to face her. They held their cowboy hats at their sides and kept their eyes downcast, looking at the dirt street. They answered in unison, like a pair of schoolchildren answering their teacher. "Yes, ma'am," they said. They stood there, not sure what to do next.

The sheriff solved their dilemma for them. "Boys," she hissed, "I said 'git,' so git."

The two cowboys shuffled off down the street. The sheriff watched them go until they turned into an alleyway. She pulled out a plug of chewing tobacco, broke off a piece and stuffed it up under her cheek. She chewed it for ten seconds, spit a brown pool of saliva onto the hardened dirt street, and glanced over in Jack's direction. "Something I kin do for you, tenderfoot?"

The question startled Jack. He had been so engrossed in watching the little drama unfold that the direct attention surprised him. He took a second or two to answer her. "Maybe you can, Sheriff," he responded. "I'm looking for someone. John Stroud told me you might know where I can find her."

The sheriff chewed for a few seconds, spat another brown pool of spittle onto the dirt, and then walked in Jack's direction. She moved with a side-to-side swagger that reminded him of a rattlesnake side-winding toward its prey. The only thing missing was a rattle, but when she spoke again, her rasping voice completed the picture. "And who might you be, fellow?" she hissed.

Jack hesitated. Now that she was standing in front of him, he knew what was so familiar about her.

It was her eyes: violet eyes set back deep under heavy eyelids.

The rest of her face was familiar, too, with high cheekbones and full lips he had seen before. The difference that had kept him from instantly seeing the resemblance was her worn-out appearance. The harsh weather of the plains had taken its toll. Her face was like burnished copper, etched by the wind and sun into thin lines around her mouth and into deep crow's feet around her eyes. But even with the differences, Jack thought, the resemblance was clear. She was an incarnation of Tami. He was certain of it. He was trying to pull his thoughts together when she asked her question again.

"I asked you who you are, stranger." Her tone left a threat hanging in the air.

"Name's Waldron, Sheriff. I'm new to town."

"You a lawman, Waldron?"

Everybody is sure interested in knowing if I'm a lawman. He wondered why, but didn't linger on the thought. "Yes, I am, Sheriff," he answered.

"This person you're looking for," the sheriff asked, "might she be Peggy Owens?"

The response didn't surprise Jack. He was expecting it. The Game seemed out of character for Peggy. He knew something was going on that he didn't understand but needed to uncover. He decided the fastest way to find out what he was seeking was to keep playing the Game.

"That's her, Sheriff," Jack answered. "Do you know where she is?"

"Can't say that I do," the sheriff said. She stepped forward, crowding Jack's space. She looked up at him through narrowed eyes. "But I am betting you're about to tell me, Waldron. Ain't that so?"

Not a typical response, Jack thought; the sheriff had to be an artificial intelligence. She wasn't responding to his needs; she was acting counter to them. *Probably a Class Three A.I. or better.* Jack looked at the gleaming, silver badge pinned to the left side of the sheriff's chest. It read, "T. Jordan."

"Well, Sheriff Jordan, maybe I will. But, then again," he added with a smile, "maybe I won't."

The sheriff's eyes narrowed. She put her right hand on the shiny handle of a six-shooter and lifted her left hand to touch the back of his neck. When she touched him, a surprised look crossed her face. She stepped back and stared at him, her violet eyes confused and fixed on his face.

"You were going to say something, Sheriff?" he asked.

The sheriff paused before she spoke. "Well," she finally began, "maybe I been a bit rough on you, you being a stranger to these parts and all." She chewed and spat out a brown pool of saliva onto the sunbaked dirt. She looked him in the eyes. "Truth to be known, I ain't seen Peggy 'round here for a few days. Been wondering myself where she might be."

"How long have you known her, Sheriff?"

"Well," the sheriff said, "she first come to town maybe six weeks ago."

"But you did spend a lot of time with her, didn't you?"

"Taught her to shoot, for one thing," the sheriff said, smiling. "She said that's why she come to town, to learn to shoot." The sheriff beamed with pride. "She caught on real quick, too. But we wasn't shooting these six-shooters." She reached down, pulled the Colts from their holsters, and twirled them expertly like a cowboy in an old-fashioned Western before dropping them back into the holsters. "We was shooting one of them guns with the slide-in bullets. They ain't as much fun, but they sure are accurate."

"Peggy a *special* friend of yours, Sheriff?" Jack asked, adding the emphasis on the word to make plain his meaning.

The sheriff shifted nervously, thinking about the question. "What makes you ask that?" she finally asked.

"Just a hunch, Sheriff. But, tell me, I'm right, aren't I?"

"What's it to you, Waldron?"

"It's nothing to me, Sheriff. But it makes telling you something tougher for you."

"And what would that be?" the sheriff asked nervously. "What ain't you telling me, Waldron?"

Jack didn't hesitate. "Peggy's dead," he said in a matter-of-fact manner.

The words hung heavily in the air. Jack waited for the sheriff's reaction. Game characters—even A.I.s—mimicked human emotions. When the sheriff's eyes filled with tears, Jack knew that his hunch that the sheriff had been programmed to be Peggy's lover was correct. "I'm sorry," he added.

"Well, I 'preciate you come here to tell me," the sheriff said.

"You're welcome," Jack said.

The sheriff started to walk away, but suddenly turned to face Jack. Her face was a question mark. "How'd she die?" she asked.

"Firefight at the place she worked."

The sheriff didn't hesitate with her next question. "Did she git her man?"

"Yes," Jack said. "She got her man."

The sheriff nodded her approval and turned again to walk away.

Jack watched her as she wound her way down the dusty street toward the sheriff's office. When she had gone fifty feet, a dry, hot wind twirled a tiny dust devil across the dirt street behind her.

Jack took a long, last look at a town that no one would ever visit again and then clicked out of the Game.

32
Sheridan Drive

2:25 p.m.

Highland Park had long been one of Chicago's most exclusive suburbs. Heavily wooded with oaks, dogwoods, elms, maples and sycamores, and graced with over six miles of bluffs lining its shore to Lake Michigan, it represented the best of the best in luxury living. It had always been hard to afford, but after the jihadist low-yield nuclear attack that destroyed New York's Wall Street and turned Chicago into the world's top financial center, Highland Park real estate prices had skyrocketed. These days a house for sale was usually off the market even before the sign went up. The buyers were all high-ranking senior executives at Unitex and its subsidiary companies—the only people in Chicago who could afford the price and had the connections to muscle their names to the top of the waiting lists. It didn't surprise Jack that Morton Johnson, one of the company's senior officers, had made his home here.

The Johnson home was on Sheridan Drive, miles from the nearest public transit. Jack had requisitioned a department Air Transit Unit ("ATU)" for the trip, hoping to avoid heavy mid-town afternoon ground traffic, but his request had been declined. There were plenty of ATUs available, but, as often was the case, the Air Trans Control Center ("ATCC") was booked to capacity. Instead, he would have to make the trip in a three-wheeled electric patrol unit. The vehicle was little more than a reclining seat on wheels with a front windshield that doubled as a door. After he had climbed in and clicked the vehicle's command center to provide the address, he had nothing to do but watch the wintry scenery pass by as the vehicle swept him out of the city. It was a forty-minute trip to the exclusive, well-tended domain of the rich. With little to do, Jack's thoughts turned to the case.

Peggy Owens was gay. He knew he could investigate her further, finding her friends and lovers to confirm it, but he saw little point. The facts were there for anyone to see. She lived alone in Boystown—a gay community. She had never married. She didn't have a boyfriend. A check of her Unitex Personal Information File ("PIF") had turned up numerous entries into gay sex Games. In addition to instructing her to shoot, the Game character of the sheriff had been programmed to be her lover. Peggy Owens was gay, and that could only mean one thing: Peggy Owens was not having an affair with Morton Johnson.

The implications of that were confounding. If Peggy was not taking revenge against Johnson for an affair gone wrong, then she'd killed him for some other reason. But what reason? It had to be important enough to skirt the law, obtain a gun and figure out a way to get it into one of the world's most secure buildings. Whatever it was, it had to be worth dying for. When she was offered the chance to give up, she refused, signing her own death certificate. Jack had seen a lot in his years on the force, but he had never seen anything like this.

Why did it matter why Peggy Owens killed Morton Johnson? A gnawing feeling in Jack's gut told him that if he could find the answer to that question, he would find the answer to Rebecca's murder. He didn't know exactly why he thought this, but he had learned long ago that his hunches had meaning.

The patrol unit signaled and turned into a long, private driveway. The house was a massive three-story Georgian at the end of a circular drive on four acres of snow-covered lawns and gardens. The leafless skeletons of snow-dusted oaks and elms ringed the property, and a fountain in the center of the circular driveway spouted a spray of frozen water that wouldn't move again until the next thaw. The house looked drowsy, the window shades drawn to their midpoint like half-closed eyes. Behind them, the interior of the house was dim and gray, like the cold day that surrounded it. Jack imagined the home in summer, with happy children playing on the expansive, manicured lawns. But instead of brightening his mood, the image of the children stirred the familiar darkness in him. He pulled out his flask and took a long, deep pull, hoping to chase the feeling away. It worked. The warming liquid pushed against the persistent demon and his mood was instantly better. When the patrol unit stopped at the front door, he stepped out into the chilled air and rang the doorbell.

He didn't have to wait long. The security camera's thin red biometric scanner beam traced the contours of his face. He knew that somewhere on the other side of the door a readout said, "John C. Waldron, D3G, Unitex Chicago Police." Francelle Johnson already knew he was coming; he had arranged it late the day before. Seconds later, the tumblers in the door lock turned and the door opened for him.

She stood there in the gray light, framed by the dark interior of the house, a light-skinned black woman with high cheekbones and green eyes that echoed a West Indies heritage. She was in her mid-forties, showing the signs of the inevitable transformation into a matronly figure that overtook rich women whose lives had dissolved into supporting their husband's career, caring for children, and keeping a busy social schedule. But beneath her soft exterior, Jack could see an inner toughness. She carried herself with pride, despite the grief that hung from her shoulders like a heavy coat. She managed a welcoming smile through sad eyes and cheeks stained with recent tears.

"It's nice to meet you, Detective," she said, in a strong, clear voice that rang with a hint of the islands she had once called home.

"I wish it were under a different circumstance, ma'am," Jack answered.

"Please, come on in from the cold."

He stepped inside and waited as she closed the door behind him. He followed her down a dark hallway and into a sitting room where a fire burned in a small hearth and a Christmas tree stood in a corner. She motioned for Jack to sit on a burgundy leather couch facing the fireplace while she stood in front of a bar built into a wall.

"What may I get you to drink, Detective?" she asked. He opened his mouth to give her his usual line about not drinking on duty, but she cut him off. "And don't give me any crap about not drinking on the job. My Morton was a scotch man. I can smell the stuff from a mile away. I'm just saving you from sneaking drinks from that flask you're carrying in your jacket pocket."

Jack smiled. "Any whiskey, if you have it."

"Well, you are in luck, Detective. Morton was saving a bottle of Royal George for a special occasion. I guess this is it."

She broke open the bottle of scotch with care and poured a generous three fingers of the expensive amber liquid into a crystal lowball tumbler. She handed it to Jack, poured herself two fingers into a second tumbler and sat down in a matching leather chair. She raised her glass in a toast. "To better times, Detective," she said, "for both of us."

Jack sipped his scotch, savoring the flavor, and feeling the warmth as it found its way down his throat to his stomach. She watched him drink. "You like the Royal George?" she asked.

"I'm trying hard not to like it too much," he responded. "It's not something a detective can afford." A bottle of Royal George costs about the same as Jack's monthly apartment rent.

They sat together in quiet, sipping their drinks, neither of them in a hurry to talk. When the silence finally grew uncomfortable, Jack knew it was time to ask the questions he had to ask. "Thank you for seeing me, Mrs. Johnson," he began. "I know it's a burden for you right now."

"Name's Francelle, Detective," she said. "What do your friends call you? John or Jack?"

"Jack. But I don't have a lot of friends."

"Well, Jack, now that we're friends and on a first-name basis, let's talk. And let's start with why you're here." She sipped her scotch and continued. "You said when you called that this isn't your case."

"It's not. You already talked with Boreck and Blackman. They have the case."

"Then why are you here?"

Jack hesitated, weighing his next move. It was risky, but he decided he had no other choice. "What would you say if I told you that I'm here because I don't believe the official theory of the case?" he said. "That I think there's more to your husband's murder?"

She sat across from him sipping her scotch, her face a blank. Jack could see her mind churning behind her intelligent eyes. He waited before he spoke again. "Because you haven't said anything," he offered, "I'd guess you think the same thing."

Francelle sat quietly for another full minute before she answered him. When she did, the challenge in her voice startled him. "You mean you don't think my Morton was fucking the mousy white woman. Is that what you mean, Detective?"

"Yes," he answered slowly, reeling from her direct answer. "That's part of it. What do you think?"

She laughed. It started as a giggle, turned into a deep chuckle, and then erupted into hysterical laughter. Jack instantly knew she didn't think the question was funny; the laughter was really an outpouring of pain, an emotional release. He knew because he had been there himself after Sarah died, stuck with the feeling that nothing made sense and his only release was laughing at a world gone mad. But her laughter now was so infectious that he started to laugh with her. His laughter fed hers, and hers his, and soon they were roaring together in laughter. They laughed for a long time.

"I take it that's a 'no,'" he finally said.

"That's most definitely no, Jack."

She collected herself quickly, dabbing at wet eyes and sipping her scotch. Then she leaned forward, her face a challenge. "And what about you, Jack? What do you think?"

"Peggy Owens was gay," he said. He wasn't trying to be funny, but the statement started them both laughing again. They both laughed raucously until they couldn't laugh anymore. When they stopped, Jack spoke first. "So," he said, "I'd have to say 'no,' too."

They shared a brief silence as they each pulled back from the edge of their emotions.

"Look, Jack," she began, "what say you and I just lay our cards on the table. I tell you what I know, and you tell me what you know. Does that work for you?"

"Works fine for me, Francelle," he said. "How about we start with you telling me why you think Peggy Owens shot your husband."

"That I don't know, Jack," she said. "I just know it had nothing to do with any supposed affair."

"Was your husband acting strangely before the murder?"

"He was working twelve-to-fifteen hours a day. His people were constantly shipping those damn chips from one warehouse to another. He was dog-tired. When he was home, he was sleeping."

"The DX3?"

"Yes. He was getting new instructions every day, moving the chips to different warehouses, shuffling them around the country and overseas. And they were shipping them to the strangest places—places that didn't make any sense. He told me that something was going on, and he was going to do something about it."

"When did he tell you that?"

"About ten seconds before he was murdered."

"What?" Jack sat up straight, his cop-sense ringing a high alert. "Did you tell that to the detectives on the case?"

"No."

"They had to have known you were talking with him, and what you were saying. The company tracks all clicked-in communications. Everyone knows that. It's part of the Universal User Agreement."

"I know. But they didn't know or pretended not to know. Either way, they didn't bring it up to me, and I certainly wasn't going to bring it up to them."

"Why not?"

"Why would I? When they showed up here, they'd already made up their minds about the murder. They started by telling me Morton was having an affair with that woman. I didn't feel like arguing with them."

It took a moment for Jack to take in what he was hearing and frame his next question. "Did your husband say what he thought was going on?"

"Not exactly."

"What does that mean, 'not exactly'?"

"Look, Jack, what I'm saying is that he didn't know what was going on. But whatever it is, he knew it was coming from the top of the company."

"The top?"

"Weatherall. He told me he was going to confront him. He was telling me that when that woman came into his office."

"But you don't know what he was talking about?"

"Jack," she said, smiling, "don't you trust me?"

Jack smiled back. He liked her and figured she had nothing to hide. "Sorry," he said, "it's the policeman in me. I guess I'm a hard case."

"I know. Rebecca told me." She delivered the words in a matter-of-fact tone as if she was commenting on the weather.

The words shocked Jack to his core. He was speechless. When he recovered, he whispered hoarsely, "You knew Rebecca that well?"

"Yes." She stood up and walked to the bar, reaching for the whiskey. "May I offer you some more Royal George?" she asked with a smile.

Jack stood and extended his glass. He waited for her to pour before he spoke. "How did you know her?"

"Morton and I threw a Christmas cocktail party last year for the company's senior people. Rebecca showed up alone. I guess Lupe was doing something else. She and I just hit it off. One of those girl things. We went to lunch a few times and clicked-in for talks every now and then."

"She talked about me?"

"All the time. She missed you, despite everything that happened between you. I think she still loved you and wanted you back." She smiled crookedly, knowing that what she was saying was good and bad news for him. She covered up by quickly changing the subject. "You don't think I'd say 'yes' to just any old police officer who wanted to talk with me, do you?"

"I didn't know," Jack uttered. It was taking him time to absorb what Francelle had told him.

"In fact," Francelle continued in a matter-of-fact voice, "if you hadn't clicked me, I was going to click you."

"Why is that?" Jack asked.

"Because Rebecca clicked me last Sunday and asked if Morton was at home. She said she wanted to talk with him."

"Did she tell you what she wanted to talk to him about?"

"I told her he was at the office working even though it was a Sunday. I asked her why she didn't just click him. She said she wanted to talk with him about a company matter. She said she didn't want to do it clicked-in. She said it was complicated, something best discussed in person. But I got the distinct impression she was upset."

"But she didn't say exactly what it was?" Jack asked.

"No. And now she's dead, and so is Morton."

They sat together in silence. "I think it's a good idea if we just keep this between the two of us for now, Francelle," Jack said.

Francelle didn't say anything. She didn't have to.

33

You're Welcome

5:25 p.m.

"I saw you at the cemetery yesterday," Lupe said. "I'm sorry we didn't get a chance to talk."

Bullshit. She's not sorry about anything. Jack took her comment as a thinly veiled rebuke for not lining up with the other so-called mourners to pay homage to her. *Typical Lupe Vincente,* Jack fumed, *making it all about her even for Rebecca's death.* He had to fight to stifle the urge to tell her what he thought of her.

"I waited until the crowd left," he said, swallowing his anger. "I needed the time alone."

"I understand," she said, putting on a sympathetic face. "I'm sure it was a difficult day for you."

You don't know the half, bitch. He swallowed his anger again. He knew he'd only get this one chance to interview her, and he didn't want to blow it. Better to just get the interview behind him. Besides, he didn't like being around her. Being in the same room with her made his skin crawl. That Rebecca had lived with Lupe after she had left him had long been a sore point; that company wags had labeled Rebecca and Lupe lovers pissed him off, even though he was certain it wasn't true. But it wasn't just those two things that bothered him about Lupe. He had never liked her, and always doubted her integrity. He figured the longer he was around Lupe, the better the chance he would say something he would later regret.

"You don't mind if we get started, do you?" he asked. "I have a lot of questions."

"No, but let's get comfortable." Lupe gestured at two couches as she walked toward them.

Jack had never been in Lupe's office. Located one floor below Weatherall's, the office was spacious, expensively furnished and commanded a great city view. Like Weatherall's office, it was filled with fine art, expensive antique rugs, furniture and photos of Lupe with the rich, the famous and the powerful. But, grand as it was, it was no crystal cathedral. Given the size of Weatherall's ego, that didn't surprise Jack. He wondered if the difference in offices bothered Lupe, but the thought vanished when they sat down and got to business.

"Your request for a meeting surprised me, Jack," Lupe said in a matter-of-fact tone. "I didn't expect you to be assigned to the case. Isn't it against department policy?"

She doesn't know that Weatherall put me on the case. Since she didn't know, he would not tell her. It said something important about her relationship with Weatherall. He kept his answer simple. "I asked for the assignment," he said. "I guess my boss figured I wouldn't take no for an answer."

Lupe's face remained a mask, but her eyes showed skepticism. That was fine with Jack. He wanted her to have doubts about his role in all of this. It gave him leverage. "You know I told all of this to Detective Rodriguez and that other detective."

"Duane Chapman."

"Yes. Whatever."

"I know. I read Rodriguez's report," Jack said. "I have questions of my own."

"Like what?"

"That night you were at a company event and Rebecca wasn't with you. Was that typical?"

"Rebecca never went with me to business functions with senior staff. She went to holiday parties, things like that, but never to working dinners and meetings."

"And you got home about eleven-thirty?"

"Yes. My driver brought me home. I dismissed my bodyguard and went straight up to the penthouse."

"Do you always dismiss your bodyguard before you get to the penthouse?"

"It's a secure building, Detective," Lupe said. "Or at least we all thought it was," she added.

"You found Rebecca's body?"

"I was horrified," Lupe answered. "I don't understand why anyone would do something like that to Rebecca."

"You don't have any ideas about anyone who might have wanted Rebecca dead, do you?"

Lupe stiffened. "Of course not. Exactly what are you asking me, Detective?"

"Did Rebecca have any enemies?"

"You mean someone who might kill her?"

"Yes."

Lupe stared at Jack, her face frozen, her eyes unblinking, her jaw tight. But while her external features didn't move, Jack knew her mind was moving behind the frozen façade. When her response came, it was just one word. "No," she said.

"You're sure about that?"

"I'm sure," Lupe said, growing irate. "How can you even ask a question like that? Besides, everyone knows who murdered her. You saw it yourself. The murderer was a registered sex offender."

"Who told you that?" Jack asked.

"Detective Rodriguez. This man—Dillon—he was a registered sex offender, wasn't he?"

"Yes."

"Then I don't understand what you're asking me."

"Dillon was a registered sex offender, but it was a minor beef from years ago with an underage girlfriend."

Lupe's eyes showed surprise, but it didn't stop her. "I don't understand the point of all of this," she continued. "He did it, didn't he? You saw the VIRSUS playback, didn't you?"

"I saw the playback. He did it."

"Then why are you wasting my time talking about this?"

Jack had no answer, at least not one he could share with her. It was time to go in another direction. "You argued with Morton Johnson in his office just before Peggy Owens shot him," he asked. "What was the argument about?"

Lupe gave Jack a puzzled look. "Two detectives—Boreck and Blackman—asked me about that. Are you assigned to that case too?"

"No."

"Then why are you asking me about the Johnson murder?"

Another question he couldn't answer. He couldn't tell Lupe that Morton Johnson suspected Weatherall of interfering with DX3 shipments, and he couldn't tell her that Rebecca was trying to get a secret meeting with Morton Johnson. "It's complicated," Jack answered, trying to soft-pedal the question, "but I'd appreciate hearing whatever you can tell me."

"DX3 shipments were bottlenecking. The company was falling behind schedule. I was in Morton's office to encourage him to get his act together."

"Did he have an explanation?"

"That's complicated, Jack."

So much for the soft-pedal, Jack thought. She would not cooperate. He tossed out one last question. "Did you know Peggy Owens?" he asked.

"The person who shot Morton?"

"Yes."

"Why would I?"

"She worked for Morton. Morton worked for you."

"I didn't know her," Lupe snapped. It was clear she was ready to end the interview.

Jack was too; he had been in the same room with Lupe for as long as he could stand it. He stood to leave. "Thank you for your time," he said. "I appreciate it."

Lupe stood and extended her hand. Jack took it. "You're welcome, Jack," she said, adopting a soothing tone and placing her other hand over his as they shook hands in what Jack took for a show of sympathy. "Take care of yourself."

When her bodyguard closed the door to her office behind him, Jack blew out a breath in a long and drawn-out exhale. The sigh caused Lupe's executive assistant to look up from her desk and glare at him. Jack stared back at her, pulled his flask from his pocket, and gulped a mouthful of whiskey. Then he screwed the cap back onto the flask and started toward the elevators.

34

Two Worlds

9:35 p.m.

"You know I feel guilty about spending so much time here with you and Sarah."

"You mean here in the park?" Rebecca asked with a smile. "We can always go somewhere else if you want to."

"Very funny." Jack's mood kept him from sharing in Rebecca's joke. "You know what I mean," he added sourly.

They were sitting on a park bench watching Sarah play with a golden retriever puppy that belonged to an elderly couple out for an afternoon walk. It was a beautiful day at the lake, a day that made it tough to be in a bad mood, but Jack was managing it. Rebecca was working hard to pull him out of his funk.

"You have noticed what a beautiful day it is, haven't you, Jack?" Rebecca asked.

"Sure," Jack answered. "Too bad it's not real."

"Jesus, Jack," Rebecca said. "Don't you ever tire thinking about that?"

"I try to, you know that. But it gets to me."

"I don't understand your obsession with this 'it's not real' thing, Jack. How can you say this isn't real? You can feel the warmth of the sun, can't you? You can hear the wind flapping the flags, the seagulls shrieking, the children laughing, can't you? You can see the clouds in the sky and watch their shadows moving across the lake, can't you? You're here with Sarah and me. Isn't that what you want more than anything else? Why can't you just enjoy it?"

"You know why."

"Yes, I know why," Rebecca answered, her tone exasperated. "Because it's not real. It's what you always say when you're down."

"It's different for you," Jack said. "You don't have to live in two worlds. You live here, with Sarah. That's it, and it's simple for you. But I live in two places. I live in one place where I'm a police officer with a job to do. There, I have to work hard to get through the days without blowing my brains out. And then I live in another place, too, here with you and Sarah, where everything is easy and perfect. Maybe it doesn't sound so hard to do, but it's tough to sort them out."

"But that's great, Jack. You get to balance one life with the other. Why is that such a big problem?"

"I feel guilty."

"Guilty about what? Enjoying yourself? Finding a little happiness?"

"Well," Jack said, "I can't be here for you and Sarah as much as I ought to be."

"But you don't have to be here all the time, Jack. I may want more, and Sarah may want more, but we're happy with what we get. Besides, we don't matter, do we? It's all for you, and you know that."

"I'm worried that my life is out of balance."

"Then put your life back into balance, Jack. You can do that. And you can have both worlds."

"You think so?"

"I don't just think so, Jack. I know so."

"I want to."

"I know. And you can." Rebecca reached down and took Jack's hand. She held it tight.

"I still feel guilty about it."

"You shouldn't, Jack. You shouldn't."

"I can't help it. It's not real, and you know."

“It is to me. And it is to you when you’re here.” Rebecca squeezed Jack’s hand as if she was trying to force her words into him.

“Well,” Jack said, “if you think I can . . .”

Jack’s words were cutoff in midsentence, and he was suddenly back in his apartment, sitting on his worn-out couch, shivering in the cold while his steam heater banged and clanked in its wasted effort to make heat. The Game flashed words across his field of vision after abruptly dumping him back into the real world:

“YOU ARE OUT OF GAME CREDITS.”

35

Payback

FRIDAY, DECEMBER 12
5:17 a.m.

"How do you like that, asshole?" Jack taunted. "How's that for a fucking wake-up call?"

Rocco rubbed his face where Jack's fist had slammed into it. He started to sit up in his bed, but Jack shoved him back down. "No you don't, asshole. You'll sit up when I tell you to."

"Hey, come on, man. What the fuck?"

"What the fuck?" Jack answered. "Here's what the fuck." Jack slammed his right fist into Rocco's left cheek again, driving the blow home with all the energy he could muster at this early hour of the morning. It was enough—Rocco's eyes instantly lost focus and watered. His dark cheek glowed red-hot where the blow had struck. Jack could see the beginnings of one hell of a bruise.

"Man, what the fuck you doin'?" Rocco groaned. He rubbed his cheek, feeling for broken bones.

"Payback, asshole. Payback."

"Man, we didn't mean nuthin'."

Jack's fist moved a third time, so fast Rocco didn't even have time to flinch. It slammed into Rocco's face again, a hard blow that reverberated off the walls of Rocco's littered bedroom and left him reeling. "Yeah, well, that didn't mean 'nuthin', either," Jack said with satisfaction.

Rocco needed time to put it all together. When he did, he struggled to get his words out through a mouth filled with blood and saliva. "Okay, man. Okay, I get it. I'm sorry. Won't happen ever again." A bubbly drool spilled from Rocco's mouth and clung to his chin in a gelatinous blob. Jack ached to hit him again, but the mess on Rocco's jaw made him pause. He settled instead for a warning.

"I'm not telling you again, Rocco," Jack said in a quiet, measured voice, "You or that little shit G show up again in my neighborhood and there's going to be real hell to pay."

"Me and G, we ain't going nowhere close to your hood, man. And I mean nowhere. I promise." At the mention of G, Rocco's eyes scanned the room. Jack could see the question forming in Rocco's mind.

"Don't move a fucking muscle," he said.

Keeping his eyes fixed on Rocco, Jack backed to the bedroom door, reached behind it and pulled a shaken, scared G into view by the scruff of his neck. G had nothing to say; a fat strip of duct tape sealed his mouth shut. The left side of his face looked like a misshapen balloon, huge and irregular. His left eye, bruised black and blue, had swollen shut, and his skinny, pale, tattooed arms disappeared behind his back, secured with a cable tie handcuff. Jack dragged him across the room and shoved him down into a stack of dirty laundry piled in a corner of the room.

"No worries, Rocco. I had to straighten out your pal, too, but the little shit is okay." He paused for emphasis before adding, "For now."

"I gets your point, Detective," Rocco said, "and I tol' you we stayin' out you hood. So why don't you jus' do some detectin' and leave us 'lone."

"Not that easy, Rocco."

"What you mean?"

"I mean you owe me."

"Fo' what?"

"For being stupid enough to think I was going to let you and G beat the crap out of me and not do something about it."

Rocco adjusted his three hundred-twelve-pound bulk on the bed, shifting his weight and limbs, trying to get comfortable while the bed creaked and groaned in protest under him. He knew he was in for a negotiation, and he was stalling before responding. "So, what you think I owe you, Waldron?" he finally asked.

"Game credits will do."

"How many?" Rocco asked. "I be runnin' low."

"Rocco, why don't you knock off that bullshit street talk? I'm tired of listening to it."

"What you mean?"

Jack said nothing. He just stood there, glaring at Rocco.

He had read Rocco's PIF. The coddled son of an Italian father and a West African mother, little Rocco Cordiano had started off life well, excelling in school and sports, keeping his nose clean, and eventually earning an associate degree in computer technology from Chicago's City College. But when the second devastating recession hit, Rocco—like most of his generation—had given up looking for work and turned to the streets for a living. Jack knew the street talk was just part of his act; he had heard Rocco drop it when Cassie threatened him.

Rocco took a long moment before answering. When he did, it was clear he was doing it Jack's way. "All right, Detective," Rocco said. "How many credits do you want?"

Jack smiled. He liked winning. He decided he'd push it as far as he could. "I think two thousand is about right."

"Two thousand is out of the question," Rocco answered quickly. "You know it, and I know it."

"You'd rather you and G do some time for the shit you've been pulling? I can arrange that, you know."

"I know you can, but I know you won't. And we both know why."

Jack knew why. He knew that if he ever arrested Rocco, Rocco would burn him with Internal Affairs, exposing that he had been buying black market credits from him. Jack figured he would be lucky to keep his job. They both knew a compromise was in order. "What do you have in mind?" he countered.

"I can give you five hundred," Rocco said with a tone of finality.

"Not cutting it, Rocco."

Rocco hesitated, but only for a moment. "I can do eight hundred," he offered, his tone hopeful. He was done with taking a beating.

"One thousand credits. Not one less."

Rocco didn't like it, but he didn't want to take any more punches. He nodded his head and said, "I'll send you the link later."

"That's fucking funny, asshole. Why not have Santa deliver it in my stocking?"

Grumbling, Rocco leaned over to a night table cluttered with beer cans, cigarettes, candy and pills, sorting through the mess, looking for something. It took a few seconds for him to find an external link.

"Still haven't moved up to an implant?" Jack blurted as he watched Rocco fumble with the link.

"And be on the grid twenty-four seven? Not a chance. Besides, they're dangerous."

"What are you talking about?" Jack asked. That was something he didn't expect to hear from Rocco.

"Something crazy is going on with the new chips," Rocco said as he put his link on, "something new that makes them dangerous. I have an old college buddy who works for Digitex. He's very nervous about it."

"What new thing?" Jack asked.

"He wouldn't tell me," Rocco responded, "but he's nervous as shit, looking over his shoulder kind of nervous. Look, you want the credits or not? If you do, let me do this, and then you can get out of here."

Jack nodded his approval. He watched as Rocco clicked into the WorldNet to make the transfer and then reached into his own pocket for his own link. He put it on and waited. It took just a few seconds for Rocco to complete his task. "It's done," Rocco said.

Jack clicked into his home screen, keeping an eye on Rocco while moving deep into his personal files to the place where he had hidden the hard-to-track, encrypted link to Rocco's distribution drop box. He found it, pressed it, and watched as the credits streamed into his Game's credit account. He clicked back out.

Rocco knew he had made the transfer. "We good?" he asked Jack.

"No, we're not 'good,'" Jack said, "but I'm leaving." He turned away, changed his mind, and turned back. "Your friend," he asked, "what's his name?"

"Jacob Steinberg," Rocco replied. "You're not going to hassle him, are you? He's a square guy."

"Not planning to," Jack said. And with that final comment, he walked out of Rocco's apartment without saying another word.

He jogged down the stairwell and pushed open the door to the street. When the cold air hit him, he took a few deep breaths, filling his lungs, trying to clear the musty, dirty smell of Rocco's apartment from his senses. It reminded him of trying to get rid of the smells of a crime scene. It was always hard to get rid of the stench of spilled brains, blood and decaying bodies.

He stood there in the cold, absently watching three homeless people huddle around a fire built in a trashcan. Rocco's warning that something was going on with the new chips kept running through his mind. He knew that the street was right more often than it was wrong.

He filed the thought away and started the walk home through the chilly, gray morning.

36
Digitex

9:45 a.m.

Digitex Worldwide was located twenty-nine miles northwest of Chicago's downtown and served by a network of Maglev trains that carried more than seventy thousand passengers every day from every corner of the region to the sprawling suburban complex. The Maglevs swept in and out of the cavernous Digitex underground station around the clock, arriving and departing every fifteen minutes. The huge crowds they discharged sometimes overwhelmed the security checkpoints, creating bottlenecks that resulted in long lines and wait times. Jack was stuck in one of those lines, waiting to clear security, when the bomb went off.

The sound was deafening.

The hot concussion wave rocked his body.

A cloud of red smoke and dust mushroomed toward the station's domed roof. The bomb had exploded just one hundred fifty feet from him, near the station's center, behind a line of passengers waiting to board fast-moving escalators to the main administration buildings. A few people tumbled to the ground by the force of the explosion, but most were still standing, dazed and unsteady on their feet. Everyone appeared covered in red blood.

Jack knew it had to be a PURE attack.

He scanned the immediate area and saw that no one was injured. The red color that coated everything gave it was away—a paint bomb built to make a lot of noise and smoke and soak everything around it with PURE's signature red dye. The attacks were becoming more frequent, directed at large crowds everywhere. The bombs were supposed to bring attention to the PURE message that melding humankind with computers was a bad idea. They were supposed to gain support for the PURE message, but the bombs were having the opposite effect. The paint ruined clothing and left stains on any exposed skin that took weeks to scrub away. It was hard for the victims to feel empathy with PURE when they were forced to walk around for weeks with bright red blotches on their arms, legs and faces. Jack watched as exo-suited security guards rushed to assist the victims, and then turned back to the barely moving line.

He pulled out his flask and downed a long gulp of whiskey.

Ten long minutes later, he was motioned through the biometric scanners and the palm-print security checkpoint and directed to the escalators that would take him to the Digitex laboratories. From the top of the elevators, it was a short five-minute walk on high-speed moving sidewalks to the main entry for Digitex labs. Jack checked in with the security guard and sat down on a bench to wait for his escort into the facility.

He didn't have to wait long.

"Detective Waldron, welcome to Digitex labs." The female voice was somehow familiar.

Jack looked up to see a woman's white-coated arm and hand extended toward him. He took the hand and stood up. When he locked eyes with the woman, he gasped.

She was a petite woman in her mid-thirties, attractive and athletic, with short black hair formed into a pixie cut that spiked from her head. Her face was a perfect oval, balanced and pretty, with high cheekbones, arching eyebrows, and full, gracefully curving lips painted a soft pink. When she smiled, she showed off perfect, gleaming white teeth. But it was her eyes that Jack knew best. Bedroom eyes. Violet eyes set back deeply under full lids. Tami's eyes . . . The Sheriff's eyes . . .

And now, they were this woman's eyes.

When he first saw Tami, he imagined those bright violet eyes were just a programmer's invention. But now he knew that both Tami's eyes and the Sheriff's eyes were based on a real person. He didn't know what connection their real owner had to the Games and kept that question to himself, for now. He looked at her name badge: "Judith Jordan, PhD."

"Thank you, Doctor," he said, working hard to keep the surprise out of his voice. "Thanks for getting me in on such short notice."

"Not a problem." She turned and started for the doors to the laboratory. "But he doesn't have a lot of time," she said unapologetically. "He's off to a symposium in twenty minutes, so you'll need to be quick."

"Like I said," Jack answered, falling into step behind her, "I just appreciate the chance to talk with him."

They walked on in silence, through the lab doors and into the main research facility. The room was a beehive of activity, and as large as ten basketball courts. White-coated lab workers scurried from one place to the next, passing secure data packs back and forth between rows of workstations. Everywhere he looked, holographic displays were running multi-colored data streams that raced forward at a breakneck pace. He could feel the energy in the room, as if a clock were ticking down the final seconds in a championship game.

"Is it always this crazy?" he asked.

"Pretty much, yes," she answered. "Wait here. I'll let him know you're here."

Jack watched her walk to the center of the room and approach a group of white-coated staffers surrounding a tall man in a brown jacket. The group was arguing, and Jack got the impression that they wanted something from the man that he wasn't ready to give them. When she tapped him on the shoulder and gestured in Jack's direction, a look of relief spread across the man's face; it was easy to see that he was happy to get a reprieve from his current situation. He dismissed the group with a wave of his hand and headed in Jack's direction.

Judith Jordan walked off in a different direction. Jack was sorry to see her go. He needed to talk with her to find out why Game characters looked like her. He would have to interview her later.

He was watching her disappear through a door on the other side of the facility when a deep baritone voice grabbed his attention.

"Hello, Detective. I am Hamid Alwaze."

Up close, Hamid Alwaze was a formidable presence. Fifty-something, Middle Eastern—*Iranian*, Jack thought—Alwaze had jet-black hair, intense dark eyes under heavy brows, and a complexion browned by time spent outdoors. He was broad at the shoulders, narrow at the hips, and his six-foot-two-inch frame exuded power and strength. When he took Jack's hand in his own, his grip was like an iron vise. Despite Alwaze's academic garb—a brown Harris Tweed jacket with elbow patches, brown slacks, crisp white shirt and a sporty red bow tie—Jack had little trouble imagining him on a bloody Middle Ages' battlefield swinging a scimitar in a clash with Christian crusaders.

"Jack Waldron," he said, flashing his badge. "Thank you for taking the time to see me."

"It is no problem," Alwaze said, "except that we must talk quickly. Soon I will be late for a symposium."

"I heard."

"Then perhaps you will walk with me. We can talk as we walk." Alwaze didn't wait for a sign of approval from Jack; he started walking toward the other side of the facility.

Jack fell into step next to him. "What does Dr. Jordan do around here?" he asked.

Alwaze gave Jack a sideways glance. "You are here to talk about her?"

"No," Jack answered. "I'm just curious."

"She runs the division that ensures the compatibility of the DX series chips with existing programs and WorldNet resources. But if you are not here about Dr. Jordan, then why are you here?"

He doesn't like wasting time, Jack thought. *Well, neither do I.* "Donald Dillon," he said. He watched Alwaze carefully to see if the name struck a chord.

Alwaze wrinkled his brow. "Who is Donald Dillon?" he asked. He seemed genuinely perplexed. "This is someone I should know?"

"A volunteer in the Crest DX3 testing."

"Ah, well then, I don't know him personally, of course," Alwaze said, his tone dismissive. "There were many inmate volunteers in the Phase One and Phase Two testing." It was clear that knowing the inmates was beneath him.

"Phase One and Phase Two testing?" Jack asked, shifting the subject.

"Testing is divided into phases," Alwaze said. "Phase One ensures that the new programming is compatible with previous protocols. Phase Two tests the advances in the interface."

"Why inmates at Crest Correctional?"

"The testing requires constant observation," Alwaze responded. "Inmates are the perfect control group—all in one place, available when we need them, easy to observe. A test without controls is not a valid test."

"What does the testing do?"

"Its method is complex," Alwaze said, "but its purpose is simple. The testing ensures the product is free from problems." He added, "You might have some trouble understanding the details."

Arrogant asshole. Let's see how he handles this. "You mean problems like the deaths of young children?"

The words stunned Alwaze. He froze in his tracks and stared at Jack. His mouth moved soundlessly as if trying to form the right words. It took time before he could speak. "How do you know about that?" he whispered. "No one is supposed to know that."

"I know it," Jack said cryptically.

"But how do you know it?" Alwaze's eyes darted left and right to see if anyone was listening. "I was assured by the company that only a handful of people knew."

"By the *company*, I assume you mean Weatherall," Jack said sarcastically. His mention of Weatherall's name added to Alwaze's agitated state. "But don't worry," he added quickly, "only a handful of people do know."

"Then how do you know?"

"It was my case."

Sudden understanding lit Alwaze's face. "I know who you are," he said, "I was told about you. You are the detective with . . . the daughter?" He looked at Jack for confirmation.

"Yes."

"Good." Alwaze let out a sigh of relief. But realizing what he had just said, he quickly added, "But of course, I am very sorry for your loss."

Jack said nothing. There was nothing to say.

They started walking again.

"What makes the DX3 better than the DX2?" Jack asked.

"A.I." Alwaze sounded relieved to be back to talking shop.

"Artificial Intelligence?" Jack's interest was piqued. "What does A.I. have to do with the DX3?"

"All of the DX series chips," Alwaze began, "have been engineered to efficiently deliver the three things we use every day—communications, information and entertainment. The chips are a highway to deliver these things to the user. But until the DX3, it has been up to the user to decide how to best use the information the chip delivers."

"That's a good thing, isn't it?" Jack asked.

"Yes and no. The speed is good, but the vast amounts of information made available create a problem. The average person cannot deal with so much information. The DX3 solves that problem."

"How?"

"It enables a built-in A.I. interface to tailor the information delivery to the specific needs of the individual. It helps the user to sort through the available information and instantly discard what it not useful."

"The WorldNet already tells me when to buy toilet paper," Jack said.

"Yes, it does," Alwaze said, "but this is not the same thing. Those messages come from interlinking programs that track your habits and purchases. It is an external intelligence. The DX3 puts the A.I. into the user. The DX3 is what you might call a really 'smart chip.'"

Jack didn't remember seeing anything in the DX3 ads about artificial intelligence, but that didn't surprise him. He was forming a question when Alwaze stopped in front of an automated door and turned to him. "I am afraid that I must leave you now, Detective," Alwaze said. "I am already late for my engagement."

Jack didn't want the interview to end, but he didn't have a choice. "Thanks for your time, Doctor. I appreciate it."

"You are welcome." Alwaze extended his hand, and Jack shook it.

When he turned to leave, Jack said, "I'm just curious, Doctor. You said there were three test phases. What is the third phase?"

Alwaze smiled. "Field testing, Detective. Even I am a part of the field testing," he said with pride in his voice. "I have been using the DX3 for the past nine months."

37

Zeus, Redux

1:24 p.m.

Dorothy Stark was certain that her stomach pills were somewhere in her desk, but she couldn't find them. It didn't surprise her. Everything that could go wrong had gone wrong since Jack Waldron had waltzed back into her life. She was sure that even greater catastrophe was ahead; bad luck and Jack Waldron just seemed to go together.

She gave up the search and slammed the last drawer shut. The loud noise gave her a start, she hadn't anticipated how angry she was. She glanced around to see if any of her staff had heard it. They all had their heads focused straight ahead, clicked-in to their work. But she knew they were just pretending not to have heard it, and that made her even angrier. She hated anything improper and displaying anger at the workplace was not proper. *It's all his fault,* she concluded. She thought about how she could avoid seeing him.

She had made the appointment at her boss's request, noting his angry tone. That anger gave her hope that Jack Waldron had done something that he would be punished for and keep him away from her forever. She was thinking that when Jack stepped through the office door and walked up to her desk. Stomach churning, she fixed a smile on her carefully made-up face. "It's always so nice to see you,

Detective Waldron," she said through gritted teeth. "I'll let him know you're here."

Dorothy clicked-in and waited for her boss's answer. When it came, she forced a smile and spoke to Jack in her most measured voice. "You may go in now, Detective. He's ready for you."

That was fast. Jack was accustomed to waiting for Weatherall, if only because the big man liked to assert his authority. The quick invitation worried him, but it didn't slow his pace into Weatherall's office.

When he reached the office doors, Jack recognized one of the black-suited guards as the Neanderthal who'd pummeled him senseless after his outburst in Weatherall's office two and a half years ago. He couldn't resist the impulse to take a verbal jab. "Not moving up fast career-wise, are you?" he said with a smirk.

"Asshole," the guard said, his face turning red. He pulled open the door with a scowl on his face.

The exchange made Jack feel good, but he didn't have time to enjoy his small victory. The doors closed behind him, and he was face-to-face with William Weatherall.

"I hear you paid a visit to our Digitex division earlier today, Jack," Weatherall said in a stern voice. "I'd like to hear about it."

"How did you hear?" The moment Jack blurted the question he regretted it. It was a stupid question. He knew Alwaze would tell Weatherall about the meeting, and even if he hadn't, Weatherall would have learned about it from other sources. He was convinced that William Weatherall knew everything.

Weatherall placed his hand on Jack's elbow and ushered him toward the couches in the center of the room. Jack used the walk as an excuse to remain silent. When they reached the couches, Weatherall motioned for Jack to sit on one while he sat on the other.

"Jack, what about it?"

"I was following up on the perp, Dillon. He was a volunteer in the Crest prisoner-testing program for the DX3."

"Is that important?"

"Maybe not," Jack lied. "But finding out everything about Dillon is important." He shifted the topic. "You knew about the DX3 prisoner-testing program?"

"Of course."

"Well, it wasn't in his PIF or his jacket. There isn't anything online about it. It seems pretty hush-hush."

"You make it sound sinister," Weatherall said, laughing. "Is that what you think?"

"No. But the fact that there's nothing about it anywhere, that's unusual."

"If there's nothing about it anywhere, Jack," Weatherall said, "then how did you find out about it?" The way Weatherall asked the question made it sound like an accusation. It put Jack on edge.

"I interviewed Dillon's fiancée. She mentioned it."

Weatherall nodded. "Look, Jack, the company is always under a microscope with folks who want to find something to criticize. We're not hiding anything, but we're not taking public opinion polls to ask citizens what they think about our programs. I'm sure you understand that." He leaned forward. "And I still want to know. Did you find out anything else important from Alwaze?"

"No. He just confirmed that they used Crest prisoner volunteers in the testing. He didn't know Dillon. Knowing a test subject is apparently beneath him."

"He's a busy man," Weatherall said, dismissing Jack's slur. "I'm sure that you can appreciate that."

Jack said nothing. He knew more was coming his way. He let Weatherall get to it. "I am told that you brought up the DX2 problems with the doctor, Jack. Have I been correctly informed?"

So that's why I'm here, Jack thought. *The fucking virus. Again.*

Denying it was pointless.

"I'm asking," Weatherall continued, "because you gave me your assurances that you had put that whole unfortunate incident behind you."

"I have."

"But it doesn't sound that way, Jack."

"I wasn't getting anywhere with Alwaze," Jack answered. "I needed to shake him up to get straight answers."

"It was a dangerous gamble. What if he didn't know about the DX2 paralysis?"

"He runs Digitex. He had to know."

"That's not so. The company is careful about keeping sensitive information compartmentalized. You agreed that you wouldn't mention DX2 issues in the future. You assured me that you wouldn't."

"Well," Jack argued, "if he didn't know, I wasn't going to tell him."

"It wouldn't have mattered. If he hadn't heard about it, he would have asked questions. One question leads to another question. Involving one person involves others. These things tend to grow. Pretty soon you have a major security breach."

"But he did know," Jack said. "He even knew about me."

"No, Detective, he didn't know about you. He knew that the lead detective on the case—the one who connected the dots—had a daughter who died from the problem. He didn't know your name. I personally saw to that. If he had known your name, do you think he would have agreed to an interview with you?"

"Okay," Jack said, his voice rising in anger. "So, he didn't know my name. But he did know about the DX2 problem. I was right about that."

"I'm not arguing with you. I am telling you to stay away from Alwaze. Do you understand that?"

Jack nodded his understanding.

Weatherall let some time pass before he spoke again. "Have you ever heard of Niccolò Machiavelli?"

Jack searched his memory. "Some politician who lived a long time ago. A 'snake in the grass' type of person."

"Not exactly. Born in 1469, Italy. A smart guy with a lot of advice about governing that still applies today. He once wrote, 'never attempt to win by force what can be won by deception.' Maybe that sounds underhanded to you. You're a 'black-and-white' person. No gray areas for you. But a tragic problem like the DX2 needs more than black-and-white thinking. If you sat in my chair, you'd understand."

Jack desperately wanted a drink. It took all his willpower not to pull the flask from his pocket and toss back a big swig. He had to get a grip on his emotions. He swallowed hard, half-listening to Weatherall, but he heard his next words.

"Jack," Weatherall said, "you need to put all of this behind you."

Put all of this behind you. The words were familiar. They were the same words he'd heard from Weatherall two and a half years ago. But they were meaningless words, a platitude spoken by someone who had never ever experienced this type of pain.

A dark rage swept through Jack's veins like an out of control wildfire. He felt as if his body was burning. He felt dizzy, disoriented. His heart pounded as memories of Sarah flashed through his mind. He saw Sarah stumble for the first time, her muscles not working the way they were supposed to work. He remembered listening to the doctors deliver the bad news, that it was a form of Guillain–Barré syndrome, an illness for which there was no cure. He remembered seeing Sarah's eyes close for the last time. He remembered hearing the flat tone of the heart monitor and Rebecca's soft sobbing. He remembered feeling that everything that had ever meant something to him was gone.

But most of all, he remembered learning it was the DX2 that caused the illness in certain young children and that Weatherall himself had lied to him about the DX2 recall. It took every bit of his self-control to keep his hands from wrapping around Weatherall's neck and choking the life out of him. He forced himself to take a few deep breaths. He forced himself to nod his head in approval. He would do anything to get out of Weatherall's office.

Weatherall bought it—or at least, pretended he did. "Good, Jack. Good. I'm glad you see it that way, too."

When the door to Weatherall's office closed behind him, Jack pulled out his flask and drained it. When the liquor was gone, he shoved the flask deep into his coat pocket and walked out, ignoring Dorothy Stark's icy glare.

38

Greystones

SATURDAY, DECEMBER 13
12:57 p.m.

The front wheel of the three-wheel, electric patrol unit rolled up over the curb and dropped back down with a jarring bump. The jolt stirred Jack from his twilight doze, popping his eyes open. As the vehicle's electronic systems wound down, he clicked into the motor pool's maintenance log to report the auto-park malfunction. He wondered why he was bothering to report it—he didn't give a shit whether it worked or not—but he quickly realized that long habit was compelling him to do it. When he finished the report, he unbuckled his seat belt, released the door, and stepped out into the cold air. The closing door snapped shut behind him.

He looked up and down the street. Set back from the sidewalk by snow-covered lawns, a long line of historical Chicago Greystones stood in majestic repose. Their limestone exteriors blended into the gray day, but their peaked roofs and jutting turrets stood out sharply against the leaden clouds that swept across the sky. They looked like miniature castles. Jack imagined them emblazoned with banners and pennons rippling from their rooftops, almost expecting knights in shining armor to come pouring from their doorways. But the houses remained silent and still.

He walked toward Alwaze's house. As he did, he wondered if he was doing something stupid.

The message from Alwaze had arrived an hour earlier and said little. It simply requested that he come to Alwaze's house and provided the address. The message had been routed through a blocking filter that made it impossible to respond to and impossible to verify. That alone should have been enough for Jack to arrange for at least one back-up unit to meet him at the house. But under the current circumstances—direct orders from Weatherall not to contact Alwaze—he was stuck with going it alone.

He asked himself again why he was taking the risk, defying Weatherall's direct order, but he knew the answer: his instinct told him that Alwaze held a part of the answer to the mystery of Rebecca's murder. He had no choice except to follow his gut, no matter where it led him or what the cost.

It was a short walk to the Alwaze residence. He passed a gray liveried chauffeur dusting snow from a classic gasoline-powered Rolls Royce parked curbside. The chauffeur, his breath frosting in the chilled air, didn't notice him, but a twenty-something nanny in a matching green cap and heavy coat pushing a baby carriage did. She flashed a derisive, disapproving scowl to let Jack know he didn't belong in her upscale neighborhood. The look didn't bother him; cops got them all the time.

He turned up the walkway to the Alwaze residence and bounded up the three steps fronting it. In seconds, his body tensed, and he went on high alert. He reached into his jacket to unlock the restraining strap on his gun.

The front door was ajar.

It might be nothing, Jack thought, or it might be something, but whatever it was, he would move carefully. He reached for the door handle, pushed it, stepped into a dark foyer, and shut the door behind him.

The house was cold and tomb-like. A handcrafted Persian rug rested on a parquet floor, and a stained glass Tiffany chandelier hung from the ceiling waiting for someone to turn it on. Ahead, a wainscoted stairway wound its way up to the second floor, and to the left, a shadowed hallway disappeared into the house. A Bornholm grandfather clock stood in the corner of the foyer and ticked away the passing seconds. Jack waited for his eyes to adjust to the dim light before shouting out, "Hello. Is anybody home?" His voice echoed like sound in a mausoleum.

A nerve-rattling gong made Jack flinch—the grandfather clock striking the hour. The clock's heavy hammer sounded just once, but its disruptive sound reverberated throughout the house before it faded away. When the house had descended again into silence and Jack's heart had stopped pounding, he started down the hallway. He had gone twenty paces when wood-paneled double doors on his left emerged in the dark. He turned a brass doorknob, pushed open the door, and stepped inside.

It was a comfortable library. A dying log fire burned in a glowing hearth, filling the room with flickering light. Leather-bound books—more than Jack had ever seen in one room—crammed shelves built into teak walls. An antique Louis XVI desk and chair dominated the far corner of the room, and a plush green-and-gold sofa with ornate trim stretched out in front of the fireplace. Above the mantelpiece, an oversized oil painting depicting a Persian potentate's court filled with dozens of beautiful courtesans gave the room a feeling of power. Jack spied a portable bar lined with glittering bottles and headed for it. He was very thirsty.

He stopped in his tracks after a few steps.

A woman's hand dangled from the edge of the sofa. Below her fingers, a wineglass lay shattered on the wood floor, its contents spilled out. Jack was careful not to disturb anything as he walked toward her, guessing this was a crime scene. When he reached the woman, he knew he was right.

She was a striking woman in her late thirties, lying on her back on the couch. She was dressed elegantly in a simple black cocktail dress and gleaming high-heels. Diamonds on her wrists, neck, and fingers glittered in the flickering firelight. Her long raven hair flowed down the sides of her patrician face, passing her shoulders, and rising with the swell of her breasts. Her dark eyes stared emptily at the ceiling. Her lips were slightly parted, as if she had something to say. But Jack knew she had already said everything she would ever say.

A wet mat of dark blood dampened the front of her dress. Jack sniffed the air and smelled the faint odor of spent gunpowder. There was a single round to her heart.

He would have to call it in. He would also have to explain to Remi what he was doing at Hamid Alwaze's home. Then he would have to explain it to Weatherall. He decided to have a drink while he thought about it, and stepped to the bar. Alwaze didn't stock Scotch whiskey, but he did have an opened fifth of bourbon. Jack poured a full glass and downed a long, fast drink. He wasn't worried about contaminating a crime scene. He figured things couldn't get much worse.

The deep-throated sound of a man's voice made him re-think that.

"I loved her very much, you know." The barely audible voice came from the darkness behind him. He turned to see a featureless silhouette standing in the doorway. He knew who it was.

"Hello, Doctor," he said.

"Hello, Detective. I hope you are enjoying my bourbon."

"I am. It's very good."

"I am happy for that."

Jack examined the dark form carefully. He needed to know if Alwaze had a gun, but the shadows hid him from full view. "What happened here, Doctor?" he asked in a matter-of-fact tone.

"She is my wife. I killed her." Alwaze delivered the statement flatly, without a trace of emotion.

"I see," Jack answered. He gestured at the bar to his right. "Why don't I pour you a drink," he said in a cordial tone. As if anticipating a "yes," he turned to the bar. When he did, he reached into his jacket to grab his gun. When he had it in his grip, he dropped his arm to his side to hide it from view and turned back to face Alwaze. "But I forgot to ask you. What can I get you?"

"Do you think I am a fool?" Alwaze asked.

Jack's body tensed. "No, of course not. Why would I think that?"

The dark silhouette in the doorway stirred and stepped forward into the light. Alwaze was dressed for a cocktail party in a black blazer, gray slacks, white shirt and a black bowtie. He held a black semiautomatic pistol pointed at Jack's chest. Jack recognized it as a 9mm, but the working end of the barrel looked bigger pointed directly at him.

"I am not a fool," Alwaze said, his voice filled with venom. "I cannot be fooled by someone whose ancestors were living in huts when my people were building an empire."

"What are you talking about? Who's trying to fool you?"

"Do you think I didn't know that you and my wife were lovers? Did you really think I wouldn't find out?"

The accusation and the gun were all too familiar. It was the same kind of accusation Peggy Owens had made, that she and Morton Johnson were lovers. Jack knew instantly that this was a set up. He didn't know how, why or who was behind it, but he braced himself for what would follow.

"I don't know what you are talking about," Jack said, as calmly as he could.

Alwaze's eyes narrowed and his body tensed. "You are a lying infidel dog."

"I'm not lying," Jack said. "You didn't have to do this."

"It is the law of Allah, and I am but his servant." Alwaze glanced over at his wife's body. "Allah commands stones, but I had no stones." He looked at his pistol as if he was seeing it for the first time. "I had only this."

"It's not too late to fix this," Jack said hastily.

Alwaze smiled dangerously, extending his arm and sighting the gun at Jack's heart. "No, you are wrong. It is too late for us both." Alwaze's eyes narrowed as he braced himself for the loud retort and recoil. His trigger finger moved almost imperceptibly.

A loud shot rang out.

Jack smelled the faint odor of gunpowder.

Alwaze stared at Jack as a look of disbelief slowly spread across his face. He clutched his chest, fell forward to the floor and landed face down with a loud thud. Jack didn't need to check to know he was dead.

"Shit!" Jack screamed at the top of his lungs. His heart pounded, his mind raced. He looked at the still-smoking gun in his hand, slowly returned it to its holster and then walked over to the bar and poured another drink.

He knew he'd have to think about his next move.

This was one hell of a fucking mess.

39

Fortress

1:23 p.m.

Jack was sitting in a red leather chair next to the portable bar when he saw the Game console. It was hidden and nearly invisible, tucked away into a corner of the room high up on one of the library shelves. A casual visitor wouldn't see it. He saw it when he tilted his head back to drain his glass. It got his immediate attention.

Its blue Quantum Drive was blinking.

Jack tabled the bourbon, tapped his link and clicked-in to Local Networks. The Game's icon, a helmeted warrior in battle dress wielding a scimitar, instantly appeared. Beneath it, the ID read:

"Persian Warrior"
Interactive VR
Digitex Industries V.1g
Silver Security
Enter Password

Silver security. No one is trying to protect this Game's content. He clicked on his security protocol algorithm, and in less than five seconds, the pixels had twirled and swirled him into the virtual reality of the Game.

Sunrise. The morning was shedding the chill of the desert night. A hot, dry breeze blew the sand around in tiny tornadoes and ruffled the arthritic scrub brush that clung stubbornly to the harsh, sandy ground at his feet. Jack was standing on a hilltop looking down at an ancient metropolis of narrow streets and tight alleyways. The city sprawled out over miles of low-lying hills, covering them with mud-brick homes, dotting them with mosques and minarets. At the center of everything, a walled fortress squatted menacingly on a hilltop. Jack could see smoke drifting up from chimneys and people stirring as the city came to life.

A sudden cry broke the morning silence—the Adhan—the Muslim call to prayer. The haunting melody echoed down from the rooftops and swept through the alleys and streets, summoning the faithful to the first prayers of the day. Jack recognized the song-like prayer summons beginning with the words *Allahu Akbar*—God is the greatest. Every police officer knew it. It was included in the department's terrorism training syllabus.

But this was different. This wasn't a prayer sent out over speakers. These were voices, rising and falling together from mosques separated from one another by a mile or more,—lonely, individual, plaintive voices joining to create a single voice. Jack had known the moment he saw it that this city didn't exist in modern times, that this was the past. But exactly where or when, he wasn't certain. He reasoned Persia, sometime in the High Middle Ages. It seemed logical, especially because of the Game's title and the architecture he could see in the city.

Jack thought about his next move. The fortress on the hilltop was probably a good place to start. It occurred to him he might be better off dressed like the local population. Normally, he wouldn't care—Game characters ignored how a player was dressed. But characters with artificial intelligence were different; they did notice. He'd been running into a lot of them recently. Something told him that in this Game, he would meet another one.

He tapped his link, navigating into "Options" and then "Clothing." He clicked the box marked "Dress in character: 5 credits," and waited for the Game to debit his account. A moment later he felt the weight of the costume and the press of cool metal in both of his hands.

The clothing was heavy. A chain mail tunic covered his shoulders and draped to his thighs. Metallic gloves encased his hands, steel armor protected his arms, and metal plates protected his knees. He held a round, three-foot metal battle shield with his left hand, and his right hand held a graceful scimitar that glinted in the morning light. He could feel a metal helmet covering his head and wrapping forward to protect his cheeks and jaw. Sweat was building up underneath it, and he knew it would get worse as the sun rose higher in the sky and the temperature soared. The whole ensemble had to weigh at least forty pounds, Jack calculated; he hoped he was in good enough shape to walk the mile required to reach the fortress toting the extra weight. He considered substituting different clothing but decided to follow the Game's recommendation, at least for the time being.

After ten minutes of walking, Jack doubted his decision to stay in costume. The burden of the weight of the costume was taking its toll. His legs ached with the effort required to walk, and sweat poured from his body. His head was particularly troublesome. Salty rivulets of sweat flowed from beneath his helmet and irritated his eyes. He pulled off a glove and rubbed his eyes with a sweat-covered hand, but it only made things worse. Even more disturbing, with each step he took, the long, curved sword now hanging from his waist in a sheath banged against the metal plates protecting his right knee. It rang like a cowbell, giving a comical aspect to his plodding progress. Jack didn't just feel pain, he also felt like an idiot. He wasn't sure which feeling he disliked more.

Too late to bother with a costume change, Jack reasoned. He was already entering the city. The narrow streets were crowded with people and donkeys laden with baskets of fruit, bread and sundries. Children darted about in early morning play. Scuffles erupted as men pushed and shoved one another to make headway through the crowd, but no one in the crowd touched Jack. One look at Jack, an armed warrior in battle dress, and the crowds scurried away from him like small animals from a hungry predator. He made good progress toward the fortress.

As he neared the fortress, his trudging progress brought him into a bazaar crammed with shopkeepers peddling their wares. He was instantly aware of the scents of cardamom, coriander, nutmeg, ginger and the smoky aromas of roasting meats. The smells stirred hunger in his stomach and reminded him he hadn't eaten all day. He reflected that he would need to take the time to eat something before he called in the murder and his deadly confrontation with Alwaze. Officer-Involved Shooting investigations were always time consuming and tedious, and this one would be a long one. But eating in the Game was a waste of time and Game credits, even if the food was great. It would quench his gnawing hunger in the Game, but the emptiness would instantly reappear when he exited. Besides, it would cost him precious Game credits he couldn't afford.

Jack forced himself to stop thinking about food and concentrate instead on what he would do next. The bazaar was in the shadow of the fortress, a stone's throw from the towering walls and protected battlements. He sensed he needed to get inside. He didn't know why—he guessed that the Game itself was drawing him in—but he did not understand how to manage it. He had seen guards at the gates and on the battlements during his walk toward the fortress, and he assumed he couldn't just walk in. Or could he? Was his costume as a warrior alone enough to gain entry? He started thinking it through, but he didn't have long to think. Loud shouting erupted fifty yards from him. He turned to see about a dozen men, swords drawn, running toward him.

Shit, he thought, *now what?* He supposed he could engage them and defeat them all in a sword battle—after all, this was a Game—but the battle would take up valuable time he didn't have. Every minute he delayed was costly. He had two dead bodies waiting to be reported, and a long explanation to make to Internal Affairs. He did the smart thing. He ran.

Jack had gone less than fifty feet when he realized that running in his costume wasn't easy. The forty pounds of chain mail tunic, helmet, sword and shield weighed heavily on his frame and made each step awkward and clumsy. He shuffled forward, his progress slower than needed to escape the men. He glanced over his shoulder and saw the men gaining ground. He decided to turn and face them before he was too tired to fight. He reached for his sword, but he didn't have time to pull it from its sheath.

A wooden door in the fortress wall opened behind him, and a powerful hand grabbed his shoulder and pulled him inside. A second later, the door closed and plunged Jack into darkness. The heavy thud of a wood beam falling into locks resonated in the pitch-black. Jack felt the hand pull him away from the door as the yelling and screaming of the men outside faded away and Jack's rescuer pulled him deeper into the dark interior of the fortress.

Jack was led through a long corridor that smelled of musk and mildew. As they moved forward, the near pitch-blackness gave way to a flickering light emanating from somewhere in the distance ahead. Jack could see the shaved head and broad back of an enormous man leading him through a narrow stone tunnel. He reached out his right hand and used his forefinger to trace a path on the stone wall and watched as water from condensation flowed down in a stream. It explained the mildew smell and why the corridor was cool, but it didn't explain where the giant was leading him, or why.

Jack decided to stop wondering about it. A growing light ahead told Jack he would soon find out.

40

Another Her

1:23 p.m.

When he had followed the giant out of the dim, narrow passageway into the bright light, Jack instantly knew where he was even though he had never been there before. The clues were easy to spot. Anyone who had read the *Arabian Nights* or had heard the tales of Scheherazade as a child would know.

It was a cavernous underground room, carved out of the desert's bedrock and finished in marble quarried somewhere and hauled overland to the construction site (or, it would have been if it were real). Pools with fountains and cascading waterfalls were everywhere, cooling the air and explaining the moisture in the passageway. Explosions of color erupted from huge vases filled with brilliantly blooming flowers. Rich tapestries hung on the walls, illuminated by flickering torchlight reflected in the dancing waters of the pools and fountains. And there was the food—tables laden with fruits, breads, meats and drink situated all over the room. But all the room's furnishings paled compared to the room's occupants.

Strikingly beautiful women in various states of dress, ranging from fully clothed to nearly naked, were everywhere. Jack's eyes darted from one stunning beauty to the next, each younger and more alluring than the one before. The erotic smell of their bodies mingled with their perfumes and scented the air; the sounds of their soft, lilting voices filled the room with sexual energy. Jack's head spun.

Servants—female and male—attended to the women, hustling back and forth in non-stop service of their charges. The female servants were uniformly plain looking and unremarkable, clothed in muted colors, showing no adornments of any kind. But the male servants were different, and anything but plain. They were all big men, tall and heavy, with shaved heads. Their bulk alone gave them a formidable appearance, but looking at their size alone was deceiving. They were all beardless—unusual in Persian males in these times—and a soft femininity had replaced their masculinity. They were dressed alike in ornately designed, brilliantly colored blouses and pantaloons, heavily weighted down by costume jewelry and wearing makeup on their faces.

Eunuchs. With everything else, that could mean just one thing—this was a harem, the private, protected place where ancient kings, potentates and tribal leaders kept their wives and concubines away from the eyes and wiles of other men. This one had been the personal harem of Hamid Alwaze.

Some guys just have it better than other guys, Jack thought.

A woman at the far side of the room walked toward him. She was a long way away, but he watched as she wound her way around a fountain pool, a table laden with food and a group of beauties lounging on pillows. As she approached, he could see her better. What he saw was unnerving but not unexpected. He would have been disappointed if she wasn't here. He knew she was the reason that the Game had drawn him to this room.

She was the same petite woman as always, but this time in her early twenties. Everything about her was familiar—her oval face, high cheekbones, arching eyebrows, gracefully curving lips and gleaming white teeth. She was dressed in a silk gown embroidered with jewels and a diamond-and-ruby encrusted headdress that draped long, red-beaded silk extensions to her waist. Her flowing silk gown was a deep, rich red and had a diaphanous quality that almost allowed her body to show through the material. She moved confidently toward him and stopped in front of him to look up into his eyes.

"I am Azar," she said in a familiar voice. "I am glad that you are finally here, Detective."

Jack took a long look at her. By now, he knew her well, especially her eyes.

Violet eyes set back deeply under full lids.

Tami's eyes . . .

The sheriff's eyes . . .

And now, Azar's eyes . . .

And all of their eyes a copy of the eyes of Judy Jordan. He knew her, all right, and apparently, she knew him too. For a reason he didn't understand, she had been expecting him.

"You know who I am," Jack said, puzzled. "What else do you know?"

Azar smiled. "I know that you are Detective John Waldron. I know that you are investigating a murder. I know that you are expected here."

"How do you know that?"

Azar smiled enigmatically. "I do not know why I know these things. I just know them."

Jack thought for a moment before asking his next question. It was risky, but he asked it anyway, deciding he had little to lose. "You're an A.I., aren't you?"

Azar answered without hesitation. "I am a level three."

It would have been a stunning admission, except that Jack had already anticipated the answer. Game characters were never artificial intelligence; they didn't need to be. Games had a supervisory A.I. linked to them by their online connection that directed the actions of the characters. To have a second level of intelligence operating within the first level of intelligence was something new. Jack had suspected that both Tami and the sheriff were A.I.s. Now he knew he had been right.

He also knew what to expect next. Azar took two steps forward and lifted her hand to his neck. The moment she touched it, she froze. A look of confusion—the same look Jack had seen on Tami and the sheriff—crossed her face. She dropped her hand to her side and stared at him.

"You look surprised," Jack said. "Why?"

Azar didn't answer. Her violet eyes studied him, and Jack could see she was thinking. It was an unsettling feeling; he wasn't used to seeing Game characters thinking. He tried a different question. "Why did you touch me?"

"I am supposed to touch you."

"Why?"

"I do not know why. I only know that I am programmed to touch all of the visitors to the harem."

"What happens when you touch them?"

"I make a connection. I did not make a connection with you."

"That's why you looked surprised?"

"Yes."

"What happens when you make a connection?"

"I give the person a part of me."

What does that mean? Jack wondered. He didn't have time to find out. A familiar voice sounded behind him. "You screwed up pretty good this time, amigo."

The words stunned Jack. He spun around to the sound.

It was the men who had chased him in the bazaar. Their leader stood in front of the others, his right hand resting on the grip of his sword, his left holding a shield. He was dressed in the same way that the others were dressed, in a chain mail tunic, metal helmet, gloves and rounded knee protectors, but he stood out from the group. All the other men had beards, he didn't. Jack recognized him instantly—Eddie Rodriguez.

It can't get worse than this, Jack thought. It was obvious that Eddie had tracked him to Alwaze's home, had seen the two dead bodies, and had followed Jack into the Game. Duane Chapman was probably watching him now in Alwaze's library. One false move and he would wind up in cuffs or shot. He needed a strategy, then he remembered the words of Sun Tzu—the sixth century BC Chinese general, author of *The Art of*

War— "If your opponent is temperamental, seek to irritate him." Good advice to use against the quick-tempered Rodriguez.

"You know, Eddie," Jack said, "you look even prettier than usual in that outfit. You fit right in with all the other ball-less wonders around here."

"Yeah, well, why don't I cut off your nuts right now."

The perfect schoolyard response—just what he wanted. Eddie was predictable, if nothing else. A little more aggravation would do it.

"You're no warrior, Eddie. Not even if you dress up like one."

"Yeah, fuck you, Waldron."

"Yeah, fuck you, Eddie."

That did it—Eddie took the bait. His face turned red as his grip tightened on the handle of his sword. A second later, the sword's gleaming blade flashed out of the sheath. Eddie pointed the deadly tip at Jack's throat.

"Okay, amigo," Eddie snarled, "let's see what you got."

Jack wrapped his fingers around his own sword's grip and drew it out of the sheath. He waved it in circles above his head and then bounced into the classic fencer's ready stance, his left foot pointed at Eddie, his right foot planted behind him at a ninety-degree angle. He held his sword at waist level, pointed at Eddie.

"En garde," Jack shouted mockingly, a smirk spread across his face.

Eddie launched himself at Jack, swinging his sword in a wide arc at his head. Jack raised his sword to block, but the force of Eddie's blow surprised him, nearly knocking his own sword out of his hand. He tightened his grip, squeezing so hard his knuckles turned white. He swung hard at Eddie, his sword tip flashing, but Eddie jumped out of reach. The weight of his sword and the speed of its swing pulled Jack to his left. Eddie's sword came at him again, but the momentum of his own swinging sword pulled him out of harm's way. He twirled in a circle and crouched low to duck Eddie's sword as it arched through the air.

Jack saw an opening and thrust his sword at Eddie's belly. He watched it crash into the chain mail that draped Eddie's body. It didn't penetrate the armor, but it forced Eddie to double over and cry out in pain. Jack smiled. Games didn't kill you, but they had built-in pain protocols, and this one had a high pain setting. That fit Jack's plan perfectly; it would aggravate Eddie. While Eddie remained bent over, Jack swung again, this time at the metal helmet covering Eddie's head. His sword clanged heavily on it, knocking Eddie to the ground and putting him on his knees screaming, cursing and holding his head.

"You know, Eddie," Jack said, "you really suck at this."

Eddie looked up at Jack, his eyes burning red with rage. "Fuck you, Waldron," he growled. He stood up.

Jack didn't have time to waste; he needed to put the second part of his plan into action while Eddie remained blinded by his anger. Swinging his sword with all his might, Jack slammed his blade against Eddie's back. The force of the blow knocked Eddie to the ground again.

Jack turned and ran. He knew he was about ten seconds ahead of Eddie and hoped it was enough. He was counting on Eddie's anger to make it enough. A smart move for Eddie would be to leave the Game the moment Jack disappeared from his sight. He should know, Jack reasoned, that if he wasn't visible in the Game, it could mean he had left the Game and was back in the real world where he could do damage. But he was counting on Eddie's temperament to blind him to that thought. He wouldn't need much time, but every second would count. He'd have to deal with Duane first and fast. Then he could be ready and waiting for Eddie.

The moment he ducked behind a tapestry, he clicked his link to leave the Game.

41

Boxed-In

2:21 p.m.

It seemed like an eternity, but it took just the usual few seconds before the pixels stopped swirling and he was back in Alwaze's library, seated in the same red leather chair he was in when he clicked into the Game. He sat there, frozen in place, not moving a muscle, pretending he was still in the Game. He needed to figure out where both Duane and Eddie were in the room before he moved. It took just a second or two to locate Duane—the smell of chocolate and the sound of chewing told him everything he needed to know. Duane was standing right behind him, wolfing down yet another candy bar.

Good, Jack thought, *Duane would be an easy target. But what about Eddie? Where was Eddie?*

Jack saw him out of the corner of his eye. He was standing, motionless, nine or ten feet away, inches from Alwaze's crumpled up body lying on the floor. His gun was drawn and in his right hand, but his glazed eyes and contorted face showed that he was still playing the Game. Jack would handle Duane first, but he would have just seconds before Eddie discovered he was alone in the Game and was back in the real world.

He took a deep breath, tensed his muscles and leaped to his feet. Spinning around, he launched a hard right at Duane's jaw. It happened so fast that Duane had no time to react. He stared for an instant in disbelief at Jack's flashing fist until it slammed against his open mouth and snapped it shut. Chocolate goo splattered everywhere. Jack saw the lights in Duane's eyes turn off and watched his massive body crumple to the floor.

One down. One to go.

Jack whirled around again to seek Eddie. Eddie was exactly where he had been seconds before, but things had changed. Eddie was back in the real world, his eyes filled with rage and focused on Jack. Worse, Eddie's service revolver was pointed directly at Jack's heart.

Shit. Too late.

Both men stood motionless, neither man speaking. The quiet seemed to stretch into an eternity. Eddie finally broke the silence. "You're in deep shit, *pendejo*."

"Don't be an idiot, Eddie."

"All I know, Waldron," Eddie said, spitting out Jack's name as if it were a curse word, "is that you aren't supposed to be here, you got two dead bodies to account for, and you just assaulted a fellow officer." Eddie grinned crookedly, showing bad teeth. "So, amigo, like I said, it doesn't look good for you."

"Do you want to know what happened here, Eddie? Or are you just going to be your usual asshole self?"

"You can tell it to Internal Affairs," Eddie said smugly.

"Tell me why you have such a hard-on for me, Eddie? What'd I do to you?"

"I have my reasons."

"Afraid to say, Eddie?'

"Just don't want to waste my breath."

"Go ahead, waste some breath, Eddie. Just don't breathe on me—I don't think I could stand the stench."

Eddie sneered. "I know what you did, Waldron, you and Remi and the company." Eddie's angry voice was gone, replaced with an icy cold tone. "DX2."

Eddie's statement shook Jack to his core. That Eddie could know anything about the DX2 problem was inconceivable to him. He had asked Eddie what he thought hoping to stall. He hadn't expected a real response, especially not this one. Now he had to push for more information, and he had to do it carefully.

"Did what, Eddie?" Jack asked. He did his best to sound perplexed.

Eddie just smiled, but the smile said it all. Jack knew that Eddie knew about the virus and the cover-up. He wasn't sure how Eddie could know when even top company executives didn't, but he had to find out more. He hoped Eddie's choleric nature could help again. He tossed out a belittling challenge. "You don't know shit, Eddie."

This time Eddie didn't take Jack's bait. "I'm taking you in," he said.

"And if I don't go with you, Eddie? What then?"

"Don't push it, amigo. You got nothing to hide, you got nothing to worry about."

Time to act, Jack concluded.

He shrugged his shoulders, signaling resignation, and made a show of putting his hands together in front of him. He stepped forward, walking toward Eddie, and closed the gap between them to two feet. "Okay, Eddie," he said, "go ahead and cuff me. You're right, I have nothing to hide."

Eddie looked at Jack warily, instantly suspicious. Jack spoke to soothe Eddie's fears. "Listen, amigo, since my choice appears to be turning myself over to you or getting shot, I'm taking the first option."

The instant Eddie reached for his handcuffs, Jack moved. He swung both hands up in a quick arc to connect with Eddie's jaw, ducking away to his right. Eddie's head snapped back and his gun fired, the shot ringing loudly in the small library. Jack's quick move caused the round to pass by his left side and smash into the portable bar. Jack heard it explode, shatter glass and splash liquid, but the distraction didn't slow him down. He hit Eddie with a second hard blow to the jaw. The second punch did it. Eddie dropped to the ground.

Jack just stood there, not moving, trying to gather up his senses while his heart pounded and his mind raced. He was in a very tough spot, no doubt about it. He needed to figure out what to do next. He was thinking it through when a groaning noise made him turn. Duane was waking, stirred to dim consciousness by drops of liquor splashing onto his face from the smashed bottles on the portable bar. Jack guessed it wouldn't be long before he was back and alert.

Time to go.

He took a last look around the room and headed for the front door. When he passed the hall closet, he opened it and rummaged through it. He found what he was looking for—a stylish, camel hair overcoat with oversized collars, a plaid wool scarf and a man's gray Stetson hat. He took off his own coat and put on the coat, scarf and hat, making sure his flask was safely tucked into the pocket. Everything fit. He was lucky—he would need the cover up to make it through the city's network of biometric scanning cameras and patrol duty officers. He resolved to be careful and fade into the rush hour crowds, to keep his head down and his face covered. If he did, he might reach his destination.

He made his way to the front door, stepped out into the cold, sunless day and jogged down the steps of the Greystone to the sidewalk. Leaving in the patrol unit he arrived in was out of the question, so he decided to walk to the nearest Maglev station. It would be a long walk, but he had no choice.

He walked past the Rolls Royce he had seen earlier, still idling by the curb. Jack looked around for its chauffeur, but didn't see him, *probably in the house helping his passenger,* he decided. He opened the Roll's rear door, reached into his pocket, grabbed his link, tapped it "on" to activate its positioning function, and tossed it in. He closed the door and hurried away.

As he walked down the street, Jack hoped that the car's owner was planning a long, long trip.

42
Refuge

4:42 p.m.

Jack felt relieved when he finally stepped out of the Maglev and onto the station platform. He had made it, despite a byzantine journey that had required three changes of trains and a constant effort to evade the biometric surveillance cameras and roving police patrols. He had somehow kept his face away from the cameras and his body buried in the crowds. Once, he had been forced to walk right past three uniformed officers, certain they were looking at him, but they didn't give him a second glance. He credited it to Alwaze's expensive overcoat and hat—clothes that would cost the average citizen a month's pay. Wearing them made him look rich. He knew that uniformed patrol officers rarely stopped and questioned the rich; the outcome was never worth the pain of dealing with a complaint brought by some hotshot, highly paid lawyer. Putting on the jacket and hat had been his only good decision of the day.

Here, though, in this working-class neighborhood, the clothes would be a problem. Here he was out of place. The odds of being robbed, or worse, were high, and police might stop and question him to find out what he was doing there and offer him protection. He needed to get indoors and out of sight as fast as he could. He jogged down the long stairway to the street and took a quick look around to see if he was safe.

It was a neighborhood of four- and five-story brick buildings. Retail shops lined the sidewalks, and above them, apartments provided their owners with places to live. Directly across the street, tucked between a delicatessen and a shoe repair shop, he could see his destination. It was easy to spot, standing apart from the other buildings with a massive red-and-black banner draping down from the roof and almost entirely covering its brick exterior. The banner read: "Protecting Our Children's Future," with the familiar image of a small child holding hands with an adult in front of a brilliant, oversized, yellow sunrise. At the bottom, it read: "People United Resisting Enhancements. Join Us Today."

PURE.

Jack had been to the PURE offices before, but then the visit was Joe Hayden's idea. Sarah had been dead for two years, his marriage to Rebecca ended, and he had discovered the Game. Joe had dragged him here to attend a group session of "PM"—the "PURE Method"—a recovery program like Alcoholics Anonymous, but with a big difference. While AA dealt with alcohol and drug addictions, PM dealt with the even more powerful addictions to the WorldNet and virtual reality Games. Jack had stayed in the meeting for fifteen minutes before he stood up and walked out, leaving a scowling Joe Hayden behind. He had never returned, until now.

Seeing that the coast was clear—no automated patrol vehicles or surveillance drones in sight—Jack dashed across the street to the PURE front door. He hesitated for a moment before opening the door, still wondering if this was the best move available to him. He had thought about it a lot before deciding he didn't have another choice. Going to PURE made sense. The company was looking for him, and no group was better than PURE at hiding its actions from the company. If help could be found, they could provide it.

Only if he could trust them and only if they would trust him. It was a big "if."

Jack turned the doorknob and walked in.

43

Strange Bedfellows

4:59 p.m.

A bell dangling from a holder tinkled noisily when Jack pushed the door open and stepped into the PURE office. The room was packed tight with workers. Wooden desks with rollout computer keyboard platforms—a type of desk he hadn't seen since his boyhood—were crowded together, one desktop touching another so that they left little open space to move around. In the back of the room, flush against a brick wall, a wooden stairway climbed to a second floor. On every wall, PURE posters hung frameless and fading in the light from a stained and dirty overhead grid.

The office was busy, just as Jack knew it would be on a Saturday. PURE depended on volunteers, and many had regular jobs during the week. The jingling bell caused the workers—a cross section of gender, age and race—to stop what they were doing and raise their heads to see who had entered the office. They stared from behind their computer monitors for a few seconds and then, curiosity satisfied, put their heads down and resumed working. Jack watched as they tapped away at their keyboards, trying to remember the last time he had used one himself. He was still trying to remember when a voice brought him back to the moment.

"Something I can do for you, my man?"

The voice was coming from the occupant of the desk in front of him, a skinny black kid of eighteen or nineteen. He wore a red, leather beret and balanced round eyeglasses on his broad nose. A scraggy goatee surrounded his mouth and covered his chin. His right eye showed the dark smudge of a bruise that had begun to heal. He stared contemptuously at Jack, twirling a pencil between two fingers, doing his best to look bored while he waited for a response.

Jack recognized him and smiled.

“Something funny, mister?” the young man said. “I don’t see anything funny here except maybe you.”

“I know you,” Jack said. “Your name is Teddy.”

“How do you know that?” Jack had struck a nerve.

“You were at the rally on Monday.”

“You were demonstrating?”

“Not exactly,” Jack said, busily unbuttoning Alwaze’s overcoat. He draped the coat over his left arm, which was already holding Alwaze’s hat. He looked at Teddy and saw a flash of recognition pass through his eyes now that he wasn’t wearing his rich man’s clothing.

“You’re that police officer from the rally,” Teddy said in an incredulous tone. “The asshole who arrested Cassie, aren’t you?”

“Yep. That’s me.”

The rhythmic clicking of the keyboards stopped as heads raised everywhere. He had the attention of everyone in the room, but this time it was clear they would not look back down. Every pair of eyes in the room stared intensely and curiously at him, waiting for the scene to unfold. No one wanted to miss what came next.

“So, what do you want?” Teddy asked.

“I want to see Cassie.”

“For what?”

“Just tell me where I can find her.”

“Why should I?”

Jack didn’t respond. He just stood there doing his best to look police-like until he saw Teddy’s hand move toward an old-fashioned office intercom. "Maybe you didn't hear me," Jack said in a cautioning tone. "I said, tell me where I can find her."

Teddy hesitated. Jack could see him turning it over in his mind, trying to decide if he would be defiant or not. It didn't take him long. "Top of the stairs, office to the right." He waved his hand toward the stairway at the back of the room.

Jack started for the stairwell, ignoring the workers' scowls and the occasional middle finger. *I'm not the enemy,* he thought. *I wish I could tell you why.* But he knew they would never know what the company had cost him. Thinking about it was pointless, and by the time he had topped the stairs, he had shoved the thoughts from his mind. He turned to his right, saw a sign that read: "Cassie Charbonneau, Editor-in-Chief," and stepped into the office through the open door.

Not exactly high-end, Jack noted a scratched wooden desk, two worn-out easy chairs, a desk chair, a bookshelf with a few old volumes and a few fading PURE posters on the walls. Cassie wasn't anywhere in sight. He heard a loud bumping noise and a female voice yell, "Damn it." The sounds came from under the desk. He walked around and looked under it.

Cassie was on her hands and knees searching for something under the desk. Squeezed into an impossibly tight pair of jeans, her well-formed buttocks pointed directly at him. The sight caught Jack by surprise, and he had a sudden sexual urge. He caught it quickly, pulled out his flask, drained a long pull, and waited for the burning in his throat to stop before he spoke.

"Lose something?" he asked when the whiskey had settled.

A loud bump, followed by a string of curse words, came from under the desk. A startled Cassie wriggled her way out of the desk and stood up. "What the hell are you doing here?" she grumbled

"Nice to see you again, too, Ms. Charbonneau," Jack said. "Did you find what you were looking for?"

Cassie opened her right hand and showed him an external WorldNet link. "Damn thing's been missing since yesterday."

Remembering what he'd done with his own link, Jack asked, "You wouldn't have a spare, would you?"

"Why? Where's yours?"

"Taking a long ride in the country. I'm not expecting it back."

Cassie gave him a puzzled look. She started to say something, but decided against it and began to rummage through her desk. After thirty seconds of tossing handfuls of unwanted items onto the desktop, she found what she was looking for. "It's old, not great," she said, "but it's all I have." She extended her hand to Jack.

"Unlocked and unregistered, I assume," Jack said, taking the link from her. It was illegal to have a link that didn't identify and locate its user. It was another of PURE's complaints about unwarranted company intrusion into daily life, but one that almost nobody really cared about. Locators had been a fact of life for too long for anyone to care now. Cassie just rolled her eyes and shook her head, her way of saying, "Duh," without making a sound.

They stood there in silence for a long moment before Cassie spoke. "So, what the hell are you doing here, Detective?"

Jack had already decided to hide his purpose. He saw no reason to share his suspicions, at least not yet. "I need help getting some information. I figure somebody here can tell me what I want to know."

"Like what?"

"Some technical stuff about the DX chips," Jack said. He was playing it down, but he could tell by Cassie's expression that she wasn't buying it.

"Technical stuff?" Cassie asked incredulously. "You're a company cop. Why don't you get what you need from the people at Digitex?"

"I already talked to them. I'm looking for something else. You must know a genius or two who can answer a few questions."

Jack watched Cassie turn it over in her mind. She pushed a button on an old-fashioned office intercom. It made a humming sound in the background as she spoke. "Teddy, can you come up here?"

Teddy's answer was garbled but quick. "On my way."

"Happy?" Cassie asked.

"Teddy?" It wasn't hard to hear the skepticism in Jack's voice.

"Theodore Jackson. Harvard and Stanford. Three degrees. Doctorate of Computer Intelligence. Top honors."

Jack tried not to be impressed. "Lots of people have three degrees."

"At fourteen?"

That impressed him, but he couldn't resist the urge to poke at Cassie's smug attitude. "So, he's a Genetex freak."

"Bullshit," Cassie snapped back. San Francisco-based Genetex was another prime target for PURE. The Unitex subsidiary engaged in biological engineering—manipulating DNA to enhance human performance. A recent PURE protest against Genetex had left three dead and dozens injured. Jack knew that just mentioning Genetex would piss off Cassie, but he didn't care. He wasn't in a great mood after the events of the day.

"Teddy will be here in a moment," Cassie said, "and I'll be right back. Make yourself at home."

"Where are you going?" Jack blurted out, feeling ill at ease.

Cassie smiled. "You don't mind if I go to the little girl's room, do you, Detective?" she said. She turned and walked out.

Jack flopped down into one of the two chairs fronting the desk and pulled out his flask. He was downing a long, satisfying pull of whiskey when Teddy hurried into the room.

Teddy looked at Jack with disdain. He sat down in the other chair, but not until after he had made a big show of pulling it an extra couple of feet away from Jack. They both sat there in silence, neither acknowledging the other's presence, waiting for Cassie.

44

Tell Him, Teddy

5:19 p.m.

"I don't trust this guy," Teddy said the instant Cassie walked back into the room. "Why is he here? Why am *I* talking to *him*?"

Cassie ignored him. "What do you want to know, Detective?" she asked Jack.

"I want to know what PURE knows about the DX series chips."

"That's bullshit," Teddy interjected. "He works for the company. They can tell him anything he needs to know."

Cassie gave Teddy a look that would freeze an ice cube. "Like what, Jack?"

Cassie had never used Jack's name. Not on the street, not at the PURE rally and not even on the night she showed up at his apartment. Hearing her use his name sounded strange—distant and intimate at the same time. He wasn't sure what to make of it. He wondered why she used it, but decided to ignore it for now.

"How about we start with the basics," he said. "We'll figure it out from there."

Cassie turned to Teddy. "Tell him, Teddy," she said.

"You know we can't trust him," Teddy protested, his face growing red. "He's probably setting us up for a raid or some other bullshit."

"Tell him, Teddy," Cassie said with finality. She sat down behind her desk and waited.

Teddy closed his eyes and rubbed the sides of his head as if he were trying to get rid of a massive headache. He took a deep breath and dove in. "The DX series chips are the greatest threat to humankind, ever. Maybe they didn't start off that way, but they are now."

"I hear that PURE propaganda crap all the time," Jack interrupted. "Everyone knows your story, and nobody buys it. I want the facts."

"It's not a 'story,' Detective," Teddy seethed, "it's a 'fact.'"

"Tell me why, then."

"Look," Teddy said, "the thing is, the DX3 chips are the ultimate game changer. Back when everybody had a cell phone, or even when everyone still had an external chip, there were plenty of privacy issues. Sure, they monitored you night and day, and they could track you, too, but you could turn the phone off, put the tablet away or remove the device. When the DX series implants came out, the game changed. Now you can't just 'go away.' When you have an implanted chip, you're hardwired into the grid twenty-four seven, three sixty-five, and there's no way out. The real genius of the chips is that nobody wants out, anyway. Life's much simpler with a chip. You don't have to carry anything with you, you don't worry about losing it, and you're always online. And that's how they get you."

"They?"

"Yeah, the so-called 'Big Three,' the people with the agenda."

"What agenda?"

"The agenda to tell you what to buy, where to live, what to think, and how to act." Teddy leaned forward and gave Jack an intense stare. "You really don't get it, do you?"

"Explain it to me."

"Even with the DX1 and the DX2, the company could *influence* the decisions you made. But with the DX3, they can *make* you do whatever they want you to do."

"Mind control?"

"Yes."

Jack had already decided that some sort of mind control was in play. There was no other way to explain the bizarre behaviors he was encountering. He really had just one question for Teddy. "How do they do it?" he asked.

Teddy gave Jack a smug smile. "Game Theory."

"What the hell is that?"

"Put on your link," Teddy said, nodding at both Jack and Cassie.

"Game Theory starts here," Teddy said, yelling above the din.

Jack could barely hear Teddy's voice. The pixels had swirled them into a massive room crammed with people playing games of every type: pinball, pool, old-fashioned video games, arcade games, card games, dice games and board games. The noise coming from the games and the crowd was unbearable. Jack leaned into Teddy's ear. "Turn down the fucking volume, for Christ's sake." A second or two later, things got quiet.

"Jesus," Jack said when the sound level dropped.

"Sorry." Teddy was looking at Cassie, his apology meant for her, not Jack. She nodded a quick okay and Teddy walked forward, signaling Jack and Cassie to follow him. "Game Theory," he began, puffing himself up and sounding like a university professor, "is a branch of applied mathematics. It's the basis of artificial intelligence. Use Game Theory to teach a computer to win a game against a human and you're on your way to creating artificial intelligence."

"How do you do that?"

"You start with zero-sum games."

"What's that?" Jack asked.

"Chess, Checkers, Tic-Tac-Toe—games like these." Teddy gestured at a cluster of games in the room. "Games with one winner and one loser."

"What does a game have to do with A.I.?" Jack asked.

"Everything. To win a game you must understand your opponent's attack, block it, and plan your own attack. It's what we humans have always called 'thinking.'"

"But this is old news, isn't it?" Cassie said.

"Yeah," Teddy said, offended, "it's old news, but you asked me to explain it to him, and you have to start here. A computer beating a human player in chess is ancient news. Way back in 1997, long before Digitex swallowed up IBM, they built a computer they called Deep Blue to take on the World Chess Champion, Garry Kasparov. They had a few issues, but the computer eventually won."

"Chess is just a game," Jack said. "People are a lot more complicated."

"Just a game?" Teddy smiled a Cheshire cat grin. "Before you say that, think about this." He stopped walking at a card table. A freckle-faced boy of nine or ten sat on one side of the table about to start a chess game. He fidgeted with his curly, straw-colored hair and watched his opponent, a disheveled old man of at least ninety, put his last three pawns into position. The boy rolled his eyes as the old man's liver-spotted hand moved at a snail's pace across the board to set his pieces.

"Chess doesn't seem so tough," Teddy said, "at least not when you start the game. There are just twenty opening moves—sixteen for the pawns, four for the knights." He pointed down at the board and the number twenty appeared, floating in the air above the chessboard. "But look what happens after each player makes the first move."

The boy moved a pawn two spaces forward, and the old man responded dragging a pawn forward. When the old man sat back to light a corncob pipe, the number hanging in the air above the chessboard changed to four hundred. "After just two moves," Teddy said, "there are four hundred possible positions. And that's just two moves."

The action started again in a fast-forward that sped up the next six moves, so they were complete in seconds. "After just eight total moves, there are 72,480 possible positions," Teddy said, as the number in the air changed again. "From here, things just get crazy, fast."

In another fast-forward, the boy and old man each made two moves each. The number hanging in the air above the chessboard showed 288 billion. "After four more moves," Teddy said, "there are 288 billion—yes, billion—possible positions. In fact,"—he continued as the game between the boy and old man flashed forward in a blur of moves— "it's estimated that a game of chess has more possible positions than the total number of atoms in the universe." His last word was still hanging in the air when the chess game stopped and the word "checkmate" appeared in the air. A second later, the boy, the old man, and the game disappeared.

"So, as you can see, Detective," Teddy pronounced, "chess is a complicated game."

"That's great Teddy," Jack said, "but this is logic, isn't it? People aren't logical."

"It's a lot more than logic; it's learning what to expect. That's why the company has 'stacked the deck,' as the saying goes."

"How?"

"With the Games, Detective."

"Games?"

"Yeah," Teddy said. "The Games you play; the Games I play; the Games everybody plays."

"How do the Games fit in?"

"Games take who you are and what you want and build a world just for you, a world that's indistinguishable from the real world. And the more you play, the better the Game gets to know you. You may think you're just having fun, but the company isn't in it for fun. The company is using the Games to get inside your brain, to track and record how you think, how you decide, how you respond to situations. The company is building a profile of you to use against you."

"How can they do that?"

"Do what? Build a profile or control you?"

"Both."

"The 'build a profile' part is easy," Teddy said, trivializing the question. "Quantum computing was the breakthrough. You only need a bunch of big-ass quantum computers and smart data-compression programming. The company has plenty of computers and unlimited storage capacity. The Games 'build a profile' automatically."

"The control part, then," Jack asked. "How do they do that?"

"That's a tougher problem," Teddy said. "They've been working on it for years. And in the beginning, they had good intentions. Things just got out of hand when the wrong company people got their hands on the project."

"What 'good intentions'?"

"Rehabilitating criminals. Changing the way a sociopath thinks so they could put them back into society. We think they started with prisoners at Crest Correctional. Probably still using them as test subjects."

Teddy had guessed correctly about Crest, but Jack kept the information to himself. "So how did they solve the problem?" Jack asked.

"The new chip—the DX3—solves the problem. The DX3 is the link they always needed to make mind control work seamlessly."

"How?" Jack grabbed Teddy's arm and jerked him around to face him. "How does the DX3 control somebody?"

"It's hard to explain," Teddy answered, angrily tugging his arm free. "It's complicated shit, but it all boils down to one thing."

"What one thing?"

"The DX3 is an intelligent chip, with its own built-in A.I. It's capable of reacting to certain patterns and constructing a message that corrects any problems the brain has with an instruction. Doesn't matter how fast the WorldNet is, it's not fast enough. The brain senses the delay and has time to react. That allows the brain say no to an instruction it doesn't like. There can't be any time lag when the brain is instructed to do something, so resident A.I is critical to full control."

"Okay, so it fills in the gaps. How does it do that?"

"That's the thing. We know what it does, but we don't know how it does it. We've been trying to get our hands on a DX3 for a year with no success. The company's been keeping a tight lid on them."

"Not much longer. It's just twelve days until Christmas." Jack said. "But if you want it, I can get one for you now."

"Really?" he asked. "That would be great." Teddy couldn't hide the excitement in his voice.

"Really," Jack said. "Just tell me everything I need to know, and I'll see you get it. Maybe as soon as tomorrow."

Beaming, Teddy pointed to his own link, signaling it was time to leave the Game. They each clicked out and waited for the pixels to swirl them back to the real world.

45

Dangling in the Dark

5:58 p.m.

The moment they were back in Cassie's office, they heard the loud voices downstairs and the clattering of a woman's footsteps pounding up the stairwell. A silver-haired woman in a blue, flower-patterned dress rushed into Cassie's office. Red-faced and breathless, she struggled to get her words out, "Cassie, oh my God, they're here," she gasped. "What are we going to do?"

"Who's here, Ella?"

"The police. They have everybody lined up downstairs. They're asking questions."

"About what?"

"About everything. What do they want?"

"I don't know, Ella," Cassie said. "But whatever it is, stay calm."

"I told you we shouldn't trust this guy," Teddy said. "This is your doing, isn't it?" Teddy said, turning to Jack.

Jack was gone.

He had slipped out of Cassie's office the moment Ella stepped into it. He was in an empty office in the rear of the building, peering out into the dark from a third-story window, watching a dozen SWAT members deploy to block the exits. He knew there were at least an equal number of SWAT members in front of the building doing the same thing. He also knew they weren't here to raid PURE. They were here for him. He was sure of it, and he already suspected how they knew he was here. He hoped he was wrong, but he didn't have time to think about it. His big problem was how to get out of the building and avoid capture.

Jack knew these neighborhoods from his days as a beat cop. He had chased plenty of suspects through buildings like these, and he knew there were just two ways out: the rooftops above and the sewers below. Neither was a good choice. On the roof, he would be an easy target, spotted quickly by drones; in the sewers, his escape would be slow with limited options. He made an instant decision to gamble on the rooftops.

He needed a way up. All the buildings had a top-floor maintenance closet with a ladder to the roof, but he had to get there before SWAT got him. He could hear them on the floor below, shuffling from office to office. He poked his head into the hall to look at the stairs; he could see two SWAT helmets moving up them.

Too late.

He ducked back into the office, pulled up the window, and stuck his head out. An arctic blast of air hit him, but he saw what he needed to see—a drainpipe within reach. Without hesitating, he wriggled out through the window, clutched the pipe with one hand, closed the window with the other, and swung free. The move left him dangling in the dark thirty feet above the sidewalk, his lifeline a rusting pipe never designed to hold a weight like his. Worse, he was an easy target for any cop on the street who looked up in his direction. His only break was that the pipe was distant from the lone streetlamp below, and the jagged edges of bricks at the corner provided a foothold to climb to the roof. Jack was there in seconds, rolling across the gutter and the edge of the roof to hide alongside a ventilation unit.

He was freezing. Alwaze's overcoat was in Cassie's office, and he was wearing just a shirt and pants. He rubbed his hands together, trying to warm them. His breath frosted in the frigid air. He needed to get inside somewhere—anywhere—fast. He couldn't retreat into this building;

he'd have to escape on the rooftops, and somehow stay out of sight while he did.

The building next door was just a narrow alleyway distance. It was a simple run and jump, but too far for a standing leap. He'd have to risk being seen. Crouching, he backed toward the center of the roof. When he had enough space, he took a deep breath, stood, and started running. When he reached the edge of the building, he jumped, soaring across the alleyway. He landed on his feet, still running ahead on the tar paper rooftop. He kept running to the next building and then leaped again. He ran and jumped until he had put five rooftops behind him and had collapsed against a rooftop security shed, wheezing and gasping.

Five buildings. Enough. Struggling to catch his breath, he crouched next to the security shed and gave the door handle a tug. To his surprise, the door opened. Without hesitation, he stepped into the shaft and started down. It was pitch-black in the shaft. He felt his way down, his feet seeking rung after rung until he reached the bottom and his foot rested on the concrete floor. He groped his way to the door and stood in the dark listening for sounds in the hall outside. He heard nothing, so he cracked the door open.

A stream of light flooded into the maintenance shaft. He waited patiently for a minute, listening for sounds in the hall and waiting for his eyes to adjust. When he was certain he was safe, he poked his head out to look around.

The last thing he felt was a heavy blow to his neck as a bright, white light flashed through his brain.

46

Good News

SUNDAY, DECEMBER 14
1:42 p.m.

He knew he was dreaming, but the dream seemed real. He was dressed in blue hospital scrubs with a white surgical mask stretched across his face. He was holding Rebecca's hand, and he could feel her grip tighten with each contraction. He could hear the doctor saying, "Push," and Rebecca's exasperated response, "I'm pushing; I'm pushing." Her labored breathing broke the phrase into three separate syllables. She kept repeating the phrase faster and faster until she sounded like a railway steam engine chugging, huffing and puffing. It reminded him of *The Little Engine That Could,* a children's book his mother used to read to him.

Jack couldn't keep himself from smiling.

He was happy.

The baby would be here any second now, and he was eager to welcome her into the world. He wondered what the years ahead would be like. He wasn't worried, though, he knew they would be good years. He would spend them with Rebecca and his daughter.

Garbled voices interrupted his dream.

Men were talking.

A bright light hurt his eyes. He tried to close them, but he couldn't. He struggled. The light snapped off.

A dark shape hovered over him and slowly came into focus, a man wearing a white jacket and holding a penlight flashlight. He had a stethoscope draped around his neck, pens in his pocket, and a name badge pinned to his jacket. The badge had a name followed by "M.D."

A doctor.

Jack suddenly knew he was in a real hospital, but not for Sarah's birth. He felt pain at the base of his neck and then remembered what had happened.

"What do you think, Doctor?" a familiar voice asked. "Is he going to be okay?"

"It was a nasty bump on the head, but there are no signs of serious trauma," another voice responded. "He should be fine in a day or two."

A shadow blocked the overhead lights. Jack squinted and saw Remi. "How are you feeling, Jack? You took a nasty hit."

"Never better," he said in a voice soaked with sarcasm. "How long have I been here?"

"Since yesterday. They kept you sedated overnight while they monitored your brain activity and the rest of you. You had a very bad concussion."

"Help me up, will you?" Jack fumbled, looking for the bed's automatic control. Remi saw it first. The bed hummed its way up to a to a sitting position.

"Can we have a couple of minutes alone, Doc?" Remi said it in a manner that clarified that it was a demand. Nodding his assent, the doctor headed for the door. When the door closed behind him, Remi turned back to Jack. "Tell me what happened at Alwaze's."

"First, tell me how I got here."

"Rodriguez got to you."

"How did that asshole pull that off?'

"He tagged you at Alwaze's while you were in the Game. You never knew."

"Am I under arrest?"

"Do you see any restraints? No. You are not under arrest. But you're not anybody's favorite person, either. And that goes double for our friend at the top of the tower."

"I didn't kill Alwaze's wife."

"I know. Ballistics confirms the round came from Alwaze's gun."

"Eddie accused me of killing her."

"Eddie thought you killed them both. He says you attacked him and Duane."

Jack said nothing.

"Why were you there in the first place?" Remi asked impatiently. "Our friend in the tower says he told you to stay away."

"Alwaze messaged me to meet him there."

"Why?"

"He didn't say why. He just asked me to meet him there. When I got there, his wife was already dead. He told me he killed her."

"Why did he kill her?"

"He said she had been unfaithful. He said I was having an affair with her and he was going to kill me too."

Remi was stunned. He stood frozen, staring at Jack.

"Yeah, I know." Jack raised his eyebrow. "Sounds pretty fucking familiar, doesn't it?"

"Who else knows this? What about Eddie and Duane?"

"We never got around to talking about it, but we did have a nice chat about something else."

"Like what?"

Jack watched Remi closely. He needed to know if Remi was hiding something. "We talked about the DX2." Jack spoke carefully, letting his words sink in. "He knows about the virus, and he knows about you and me."

"Are you sure?" Remi asked. He was visibly upset.

"He knows."

Remi made a long "whew" sound. "This is not good news," he said. "Not good news at all."

"And if he knows," Jack said, nodding in agreement, "then who else knows?" A long moment passed before Jack spoke again. "We're not going to figure it out now. I'm going home."

"I do not think the doctor's ready to let you go." Remi's voice was firm.

Jack didn't have to say anything. His look said it all. He climbed out of his bed just as the doctor walked back into the room. "Where do you think you're going?" the doctor asked.

"I'm leaving," Jack said.

"I haven't released you yet," the doctor said. "Concussions can be dangerous. But I might be persuaded if there's someone at home who can keep an eye on you."

"I can get him home and watch him," a woman's voice said. "No problem."

The three men looked in unison to see Cassie standing in the doorway. She had her hands on her hips and a big smile spread across her face.

47

The Apartment

2:58 p.m.

"What were you doing at the hospital?" Jack asked. He was lying on his couch, propped up by a pillow, holding a bag of ice against the back of his neck with one hand and gripping a tumbler of whiskey with the other.

"I was there for you. Seemed like the least I could do since they chased you out of my building." Cassie laughed.

"Well," Jack said after a pause, "I appreciate it."

"Hey, what else are neighbors for? Besides," she swept her arms out wide, "how could I keep you from all of this?"

"Yeah," Jack said, "home sweet home." He tossed back the whiskey in one long gulp and held the glass out to her.

Cassie frowned. "Not a great idea, Jack, with a concussion. I'm sure the doctor told you not to drink."

"Yeah, he did," Jack answered. "He told me not to mix alcohol with the pills he gave me for the concussion."

"So? You're doing it, anyway?"

"Hell, no," Jack said, chuckling. "I threw the pills away." He raised an eyebrow and shook the glass.

"You really are an idiot," Cassie quipped. She picked up the bottle and poured three fingers into Jack's glass then handed it to him. "It's your funeral. Don't blame me when you feel like shit later." She poured herself a glass, sat down on the other end of the couch, and tossed back a big gulp. They sat in silence for thirty seconds before Cassie spoke again. "What the fuck is going on, Jack? Why did you come to my office yesterday? Why did your own guys come after you? What is this all about?"

Jack's first instinct was to say nothing. Years of police work had shown him that the best thing to do in an investigation was to limit what you shared with others until you knew all the facts. It prevented them from meddling and mucking things up. But just like the night Cassie showed up in his apartment, he felt a strange need to tell her. He didn't understand it, but he went with the feeling.

"It's about a murder," he said. "It's complicated."

"Who was murdered?'

He hadn't said it aloud before. He felt his heart start to pound. It wasn't something he wanted to talk about, but he knew he needed to. It took him a few seconds to get the words out. "A company lawyer." He paused. When he continued, he was surprised to hear his voice crack. "My ex-wife."

"The Unitex lawyer raped and murdered in her apartment?" Cassie sounded shocked.

"How do you know about it?" Jack asked.

"Are you kidding me?" Cassie said. "It's been all over the newsfeed. I don't think there's anyone left in the ATU who hasn't heard about it. I didn't know she was your ex-wife. She had a different name."

Jack nodded his head in understanding. He hadn't linked to the news since Rebecca's murder, but he knew she was right. It was just the kind of story that would grab the attention of a tabloid society. But there was something in the way she responded that made Jack think she knew more than she was pretending to know. His antenna went up. "She always used her maiden name," Jack said. "It was a business thing."

A minute passed while they both sipped their scotch. Cassie broke the silence. "So," she said, "are you going to tell me?"

Jack had thought about it. He couldn't think of a good reason not to tell her. "I think there's a lot more to this than it seems. Things just don't add up."

"Why?" Cassie asked. "What doesn't 'add up'?"

"Dillon, the perpetrator, wasn't a rapist. He was an ex-con on parole and a registered sex offender, but he wasn't a rapist."

"But I don't understand. He did rape her, didn't he? I mean, the news..."

"Yes, he raped her," Jack said, cutting her off midsentence. "He did it. Hell, I saw him do it in a security playback, along with a dozen other investigators and officers."

"So? I don't understand."

"So, I think something was making him do it. Something beyond his control."

Cassie's face lit up with understanding. "You mean the chips, don't you? That's what the whole thing with Teddy was all about, wasn't it?"

"Yes."

"Do you have any direct evidence?"

The question hit Jack like a hammer. He had done hundreds of interviews and had never heard anyone outside of law enforcement use the term "direct" when referring to evidence. Civilians always said "evidence," and even more commonly, asked if the police had any "proof." "Direct" evidence was the highest form of evidence—things like DNA, fingerprints, eyewitness testimony. But it was a legal term, and only someone with a law enforcement or legal background would use it. Jack suspected Cassie wasn't telling him everything, but he decided to play it out, to keep the conversation going to find out what she knew. He just wouldn't tell her everything.

"No direct evidence," he said, watching her for her reaction, "but lots of circumstantial."

She didn't react. "Lots?" she asked.

"Seven dead bodies."

"I don't understand."

"It's complicated. I told you that."

"Try me," Cassie said. "It's not like we have somewhere to go." She reached over for the bottle and poured them both another two fingers of scotch.

She's smooth, Jack thought, *you have to give her that.* "Three murders," he began, "and the murderers all had the new DX3 implant. None of their victims had a DX3 implant. They were all company people."

"But that's hardly evidence, Jack. Sounds more like a coincidence to me."

"Yeah, well, that's one way to view it. But there's more. The murderers all arranged to get themselves killed. A deliveryman, with no history of violent crime, rapes and murders my ex-wife, and then kills himself, leaving his pretty, pregnant fiancé behind. A forty-seven-year-old, gay woman accuses her boss of bad intentions in an affair they're supposedly having, and then pumps a full clip into him and takes on SWAT. A top Digitex scientist kills his wife for cheating on him, and then tries to kill me because he's convinced I'm the one having an affair with her. He forces me to kill him." Jack let his words sink in. "Does that help you see it another way?"

"Okay, that helps," Cassie admitted. "But that's six. You said seven dead bodies. Who's missing?"

"An old man. He worked for the company and put the murderer into my ex-wife's apartment. He had a heart attack playing a Game. I think his death was somehow manipulated."

"How?"

"He wasn't taking his powerful heart medication. Not a single pill in a month."

"And he had the new chip?"

"An employee award from the company."

Cassie thought about it. "What are you going to do about all of this?"

"I don't know," Jack said. He rubbed the back of his neck. "Nothing until I get this headache behind me, that's for sure."

"Is the pain bad?"

Jack furrowed his brow as if to say, 'What do you think?'

Cassie scooted down the couch to sit next to him. "Let me look," she said.

She leaned into him, her breasts pressed against his arm and her thigh pressed against his. Jack was suddenly aware of her physical presence. The feeling was pleasant, but it was also foreign and unsettling. It became even stranger when she leaned behind him to poke the bandages on his neck, and he could feel her breath on his cheek. "Not much to see," he heard her say, "and probably not a good idea to pick at the bandages."

When she sat back, Jack locked eyes with her. He felt a sudden surge of sexual desire. The way she looked at him made him think she felt the same thing too. The feeling caught him off guard and made him uncomfortable. He didn't like wanting her; Rebecca wouldn't approve. Then he realized the thought was crazy—Rebecca was dead. His mind flashed back and forth in confusion, and in the short time it took, his desire passed. Cassie's eyes blinked and she pulled back and looked away. She tossed her head and ran her fingers through her hair.

"A knight in shining armor, huh, Jack?" she joked.

"Yeah," Jack said, "I guess so."

A long moment passed before either of them spoke again. Cassie broke the silence. "I think I should go."

"Okay," Jack replied. He wanted to say more, maybe even ask her to stay for a while longer, but he hesitated, and the moment was lost.

"See you tomorrow," Cassie said. "Get some sleep." She stood up and was out the door almost before her final words ended.

He was sorry to see her go. The emotion surprised him.

48

Does It Matter?

8:58 p.m.

“I used to love coming to this place,” Rebecca said, glancing around the Italian deli and restaurant. “We had our first date here, you know.”

“Yeah, I know,” Jack grumbled. “I used to love this place too. But I didn’t remember how small it is.”

Rebecca frowned. “I hope this isn’t going to be one of your ‘I’m too depressed to smile’ nights, because if it is, I think I’d rather call it quits right now.”

“It won’t be,” Jack said. “I promise. But you have to admit, it’s not exactly spacious.” He spread his hands wide.

“I like to think of it as cozy,” Rebecca said, with a note of finality.

Tucked into a corner at a tiny table, boxed in by other patrons, pressed shoulder-to-shoulder with just a narrow path open to allow a waiter to reach them, they were more than cozy. A better description might be claustrophobic. But as both a restaurant and an Italian deli, the room just didn’t have enough space to be anything other than cramped. Two refrigerated deli counters—one a gelato bar, the other filled with Italian desserts—took up a third of the room’s space. A rack filled with Italian wines stretched across an entire wall and squeezed the room even more. The remaining open floor space was filled with a half dozen small tables that left little room for patrons. If comfort and room to stretch had mattered, it would have been Jack's last choice for a meal, but the enticing aromas of Italian dishes that wafted in from the kitchen and filled the room with their mouthwatering smells had always made Jack forget about his discomfort.

"And since we're here," Rebecca said, "there's something I've been meaning to ask you ever since that first date. How did you know I loved this place?"

"You're just getting around to that?" Jack laughed. "I assumed you'd already figured it out. I broke into your PIF. It was right there, page four. Practically a headline."

"Jesus, Jack," Rebecca bristled, "my PIF? Didn't that seem overkill for a first date? There's a hell of a lot of stuff—too much damn stuff to suit me—in those files. Besides, aren't those files supposed to be need-to-know?"

"I knew you were *the one*," Jack laughed, "so I definitely had a *need-to-know*."

"Well, you were full of tricks back then. I should have expected it."

"Tricks? What tricks?"

"Oh, come on, Jack. You were always pulling something."

"Like what?"

"Like *Wine Connoisseur*," Rebecca laughed.

"Yeah," Jack said, sheepishly, "you got me there."

"What made you think I'd buy into it?" Rebecca asked, still laughing.

"I guess . . . I don't know," Jack said. "Seemed like a good idea at the time."

"You didn't think I'd catch on right away? I mean, really?"

Jack knew she was right. Wine Connoisseur had just released an update to its app. The app had always allowed the user to pick the best wine from any list and comment on it as if the user were a wine expert. But the new update was an amazing breakthrough. It analyzed a wine while the user drank it, interfacing with the user's taste buds and sense of smell, evaluating just that one bottle. It made its user an instant expert in wine, a master sommelier. And, yes, it was pretentious as hell. When Rebecca called him on it, Jack remembered feeling small.

"Well," Jack said sheepishly, "it wasn't my best idea."

"Actually," Rebecca said with a warm smile, "I think it made me start to fall in love with you. It was sweet seeing you try so hard." She reached across the tiny table and took his hand in her own, squeezing it tight.

"Good." Jack locked eyes with hers, but he couldn't hold the gaze and looked away. It was all that Rebecca needed to see to know that something was amiss.

"What's wrong, Jack?"

The time had come. He had hoped he could wait until after they had spent more time enjoying the evening, but he knew Rebecca, and he knew she wouldn't relent until he told her. He took a deep breath and spoke the words he had been avoiding for so long. "The other you," he said in a matter-of-fact manner, "she's gone." He said nothing else; he knew he didn't have to.

Rebecca appeared unfazed by the news, as if Jack had just told her it would rain the next day. She just uttered a single word, "Oh."

They sat in silence for a long moment before Jack spoke. "Don't you want to know what happened?" he asked. He watched her eyes move, realizing she was thinking.

"Does it matter?" she asked.

He was about to answer when the waitress broke into their conversation. "Are you folks ready to order?" she asked.

When he looked up at her, he gasped. A perfect oval face with high cheekbones and full red lips, haunting eyes set back deep in her face under heavy lids, smoldering with an electric sexuality. Eyes very hard to forget under any circumstance, but impossible to forget because of their bright violet color. The waitress was past forty; she dressed and sounded as if her home country was Italy, but there was no mistaking who she was—another version of Tami, the sheriff and Azar, another clone of Judy Jordan. She reached out to him and touched him on the back of his neck.

It was the last thing he remembered.

49

Tracking

MONDAY, DECEMEBER 15
2:37 a.m.

His footsteps resonated on the frozen pavement. He could feel the cold air in his lungs. He was late and in a hurry. He jogged past a group of homeless people huddled around a trashcan fire. He wanted to join them to get warm, even if just for a moment, but he didn't have time. The clock was ticking. There was no time to spare.

The elevated Maglev station came into focus ahead. He picked up his pace, moving faster, switching from a jog to a run. When he reached the long stairwell, he bounded up the steps, taking them two and three at a time. He passed through the turnstile at the top and moved out onto the deserted platform. It was empty. He had expected it to be empty at this hour. The trains would be nearly empty, too, but it didn't matter. The security cameras would see him no matter what he did. He couldn't hide his trail, but he didn't care. He huddled against a wall, protected from view by the short roofline that stretched out toward the platform. His eyes searched the dark for the train's headlight. *Hurry up* kept repeating in his mind. He couldn't afford a delay.

The alarm had awakened her from a light sleep, its buzzer rousing her to full consciousness. Her feet were on the floor, and she was pulling on her pants and zipping her boots before the alarm started the second buzz. She tapped the unit to turn it off and pulled on a heavy sweater in one fast motion. In a few seconds, she was at her door pocketing her stun gun, buttoning her jacket, closing the door, jogging down the stairwell, donning her external mind link, pressing the "on" switch and exiting the building into the cold night air.

She had programmed her company-issued tracking program to follow him the night she moved into the building, so a simple click launched it and showed her his location. He was moving fast, one hundred fifty yards north of her position, headed for the elevated Maglev station. She would have to hurry. A quick check of the Maglev schedules showed the next train was running two minutes late. She was confident she could catch up to him. She started to run.

He could see stars in the night sky. They were just dim points of light, but that he could see them at all surprised him. Most nights, the bright city lights and the persistent urban haze kept the stars hidden from view. But tonight, he reasoned, a strong wind from the lake must have scrubbed the air clean. He took it as a good omen; a signal he was doing the right thing.

He was uneasy. The thought ran through his mind he wasn't sure why he was doing what he was doing. He felt confusion and struggled for an answer. His mental battle made his heart pound and his eyes blink. Panic swept over him. He felt as if he was losing control. But then, almost magically, he was much better, his emotions in check and his mind clear. He knew the answer. He could see the big picture as if an unseen hand had moved the pieces of a puzzle into position and solved his dilemma for him. His pulse slowed, and his eyes stopped moving. He felt an overwhelming sense of calm and purpose. He once again knew what he had to do. The platform area next to the train clearway flashed yellow and the harsh glare of a bright halogen slashed across his eyes. The train was arriving. He stepped forward and walked toward the clearway as the train swept into the station and slowed to a full stop. As he stepped onto the train car, he thought he saw a dark form at the other end of the platform boarding the train, but he wasn't sure. He didn't think about it again. He knew what he had to do. He was late and had to hurry.

She caught up to him in time to see him huddled under the platform's short roofline, staring up at the sky. She wondered what he was thinking. His behavior was unexpected and unsettling. She didn't understand why he was dressed and going somewhere in the middle of the night. The only thing she was clear about was that it was her job to know where he was during his off-duty hours and to follow him in situations like this one.

When he moved to step onto the train, she dashed from her hiding place at the far end of the platform and rushed through the open doors of a passenger car. She didn't think he saw her; she wasn't worried if he had. She was at least one hundred and fifty feet away in the dark and doubted he could recognize her from that distance.

The passenger car was empty. She wanted to be closer to him when he exited the train. She knew he was five or six car-lengths ahead of her. She tapped her external link and checked his position, one hundred thirty-seven feet from her. The next station was four minutes and twelve seconds away. She had the time she needed to get closer. She began walking forward.

When she passed from one passenger car into the next, the DX3 advertisement played. She had seen the ad a hundred times—swirling pixels that formed a human head that showed a DX3 chip at the back of a woman's neck. The chip grew in size as the familiar female voice touted its faster speed, bigger bandwidth, better WorldNet experience. It would be available Christmas day, building excitement about the biggest shopping day of the year. She would have turned off her link, but she needed the tracking program and had to let the ad play. Instead, she just ignored it. A long time ago, she'd thought the chips were great. She had had a DX1 implant herself. But that was before she knew what she knew now. Before she knew the truth.

Standing in the middle of an empty passenger car, holding a metal post out of habit even though the Maglev's ultra-smooth ride didn't require it, he felt his mind drifting into random thoughts and then being pulled back to his mission by some force he didn't understand. It was a strange sensation, as if his mind was engaged in a fencing match, a thrust and parry raging just below his threshold of understanding. No matter what thoughts crept in, they were quickly ushered out. He didn't understand what was happening to him.

She watched him step off the train and waited until he had gone ten paces before she stepped out onto the platform. She followed him at a distance, staying in the shadows when she could, giving him plenty of room so that he wouldn't hear her footsteps or sense her presence. She followed as he walked the length of the platform, jogged down the stairwell to the street below and headed north.

She was surprised to be on Upper East Wacker Drive and struggled to find a reason he was walking on this street, winding his way down the darkened, deserted esplanade. *Where is he going?* She wondered. *What is he doing here?* The answers eluded her, but she knew that she'd find out soon enough. She turned up the collar of her jacket against the cold and quickened her pace, closing the distance between them.

There was no doorman to greet him or question where he was going or what he was doing there at this hour. The doors to the luxury high-rise opened automatically for him, and he walked right into the marble-floored atrium. The atrium was empty, too, its security desk unmanned. It didn't surprise him; somehow, he had known that the doorman and the security people wouldn't be there to stop him. He didn't know how he knew and didn't know why they weren't there on duty, but he didn't care. He was late and had to hurry. It was the only thing on his mind. He hurried to the banks of elevators, pressed the "up" button, and stepped inside. Then he pressed the button for the 102nd floor.

He wasn't sure why he was going to that floor, but he was sure that she was there.

She watched him walk into the building. She couldn't believe what she was seeing. The building was one of Chicago's most prestigious addresses, in one of the city's most expensive downtown neighborhoods. Towering above the buildings surrounding it, at the intersection of the Chicago River and Lake Michigan, it was just a short walk to the luxury yacht marinas and many of the city's best restaurants. Only the very rich could afford to own an apartment here. For the building to be open, and allow anyone in without screening and scrutiny at this hour, was simply inconceivable. Something was wrong. Her heart pounded in her chest.

She quickened her pace, hurrying into the building. She headed in the direction she had seen him go. No one stopped her, and she arrived at the bank of elevators just in time to see a pair of elevator doors close. *Where was he going?* Panic shook her. She had to figure out where he was going, and fast. She had the strong feeling that something bad was about to happen.

The ride to the 102nd floor was swift. At this hour of the night, with few people up, there was no reason for the elevator to stop. He arrived at the floor in less than a minute and stepped off the elevator into the hallway.

He knew that the apartment he was seeking was to his left. He didn't know how he knew that, but he didn't care. He walked in that direction. As he did, he reached beneath his heavy jacket to release the safety strap on his gun. He pulled it out of his shoulder holster and through the open top of his jacket. It made him happy, knowing he was ready and that his task would be finished soon.

Where was he? What floor? She was using her link, trying to tap into the building's computer system and elevator control program, attempting to find out what floor he had ascended to, but the system's security protocols were blocking her. She had even linked to the department's security unlocking algorithms with no luck. She was running out of time. She needed a solution fast.

She muttered curses under her breath and then had an idea. *What about the building's construction schematic?* Every building in the city built in the last forty years had its plans on file with the city, instantly available to police, fire and emergency services. Her tracking device showed him exactly 1,082 feet above her, moving south. She could use the building's plan to determine the floor he was on, or at the very least, narrow it down to two floors. She used her departmental authorization code to click into the city database. She hoped she could find the answer before it was too late.

He stood in front of the door to the apartment. He was ready. He clicked into the departmental entry protocol systems database and waited as it searched the apartment's command and control system for the unlocking key. It found it in less than twenty seconds and the locking tumblers turned. When the door opened, he stepped into the darkened apartment.

He knew where to find her. She was in the master bedroom, just down the long hallway. He started toward her.

She got off on the 102nd floor, hoping the building's schematics and her tracking device were both accurate. She checked her tracking program; it showed him on the same floor. She sighed in relief and raced off down the hallway to the left, heading south toward the blinking icon that showed his location. She could tell he was not in the hallway but inside an apartment. She knew she had no time left.

He stood in front of the closed door to the master bedroom, cocked his gun and held it at the ready. He reached for the doorknob but saw it turn before he touched it. Someone behind the door was opening it. He knew it was her. He stepped back and waited for it to open. When it did, he would kill her.

She was seeing everything in slow motion. A chill raced down her spine and the hairs at the back of her neck tingled. He was standing in front of the door to a bedroom, his gun at the ready. She knew the door would be open any second. She had to act before it was too late. She pulled the stun gun from her pocket and fired. It was set to maximum stun.

Jack dropped unconscious to the carpet like a pile of bricks.

Lupe Vincente stood in the open doorway. She was pointing a gun at where Jack had been standing just a moment before.

Cassie yelled, "police," and held up her badge. Lupe's eyes widened, and she lowered her gun.

It was as if they were in a Game that had been paused.

50

Chipped

6:15 a.m.

"Don't tell me," Jack said when he opened his eyes and saw Joe Hayden. "I'm dead, and this is my autopsy."

"You're not that lucky." Joe popped electrical leads from Jack's wrist and forehead and looked down at the analyzer in his left hand. He shook his head. "In fact," he said, "you're in much better shape than you deserve."

"It's the whiskey. It works wonders."

Jack pushed himself up into a sitting position and looked around the room. It was a woman's bedroom, colored in pastels and furnished with a vanity covered in makeup and hairbrushes. A wall of floor-to-ceiling photochromic windows showed a gray morning spreading over a windswept Lake Michigan. Jack turned back to Joe. "Where the hell am I?" he asked.

"In my friend's apartment." Lupe Vincente was standing in the bedroom doorway, her arms crossed, her jaw clenched tight. She looked very pissed off.

Jack stared at her and then turned to Joe. "What the hell am I doing here?"

"That's what we all want to know," Lupe retorted, not letting Joe answer. "You came here a few hours ago to kill me. These people already tried to tell me that it wasn't your fault. I'm not sure I believe them. So, why don't you tell me what you know?"

"What are you talking about?" Jack asked. "What do you mean, I tried to kill you?"

"I mean exactly that. You came here, broke into my apartment, and you were going to shoot me when she stunned you and saved you."

"Who? Who stunned me?"

"I did," Cassie said, squeezing past Lupe into the room. She walked up to his bedside and stared down at him. "I stunned you, Jack."

"What the hell are you talking about?"

"Just listen, and I'll explain," Cassie said. She sat down on the bed. "Last night you left your apartment at two thirty in the morning. You took the Maglev, got off, and walked to this building. You took the elevator to this floor and used your department unlocking protocol to gain entry to the apartment. You approached the bedroom, took out your gun and waited for the door to open. You raised your weapon to fire, and that's when I stunned you. We kept you sedated until Joe got here."

Jack let it all sink in before he asked another question. "What were you doing here?"

"I followed you here from your apartment."

"Why would you do that?" Jack blurted. "Follow me?"

"Because it's my job."

"What job?"

"My assignment."

"PURE?"

"CSD."

Jack had already decided Cassie was hiding something. He had guessed she had a connection to law enforcement, but he hadn't guessed CSD. Clandestine Service Division was the company's "black ops" division, the place where the "spies" worked. No one outside the division really knew what CSD did, but it had a reputation for dirty work and bad outcomes for anyone who crossed it. Everyone feared the division and avoided talking about it. Even inside headquarters, its name was rarely mentioned. Jack had his own bad experience with CSD during the DX2 mess; he wasn't a fan. He rubbed his face and exhaled a long breath. "I need a drink," he muttered.

"Not now, Jack," Joe said. "You've been compromised. We need to sort things out."

"Compromised?" Jack stared at Joe. "What are you saying?'

"Someone stuck one of the new DX3 chips into your head, Detective." Teddy squeezed past Lupe into the room and stood next to her. "It must've happened when they had you in the hospital." When Teddy finished speaking, he glared at Cassie. It was obvious he hadn't known about her connection to CSD.

Jack reached for the back of his neck and felt a small bandage. "The chip's gone," Joe said. "I pulled it out." He held it out in the upturned palm of his hand to show it to Jack.

"The chip was controlling you," Teddy continued. He nodded in Lupe's direction. "Someone wanted her dead, and they sent you here to kill her. If it weren't for Cassie, you would have succeeded."

Jack looked at Lupe. "Too bad I missed."

"Asshole," Lupe spat back. "I never could understand why Rebecca was so hung up on you."

"Maybe because I'm a man and not just pretending to be one," Jack countered. He paused, and then added, "Dyke."

"What did you just call me?" Lupe exploded.

"You heard me," Jack said.

Lupe stepped forward, her face a hard mask. She looked ready to strike him, but before she did, she softened and collected her emotions. What she said next surprised him. "I think you know that there was never anything between Rebecca and me, Jack, nothing except friendship. We were never lovers. Not that I didn't want more, but Rebecca was straight. You know that in your heart. You want to hate me because you want to blame me for taking Rebecca from you, but I know that deep down you know that never happened. You know that it's your fault it ended between the two of you, but what you don't know is that she never gave up on you. You gave up on her. You're the one who threw your marriage away over booze and some damn Game."

The old pain welled up inside Jack. He didn't respond. He knew she was right. The room descended into an uncomfortable silence. Cassie finally broke it. "Look," she said, testing the mood of the room, "we need a plan. My command will expect a report. What will I tell them?"

The question triggered another silence. They all knew they were in a tough spot. Teddy jumped in first. "It's clear we need to find the person responsible for all of this. There are just a few possible suspects, so we shouldn't have to look very hard. But it will take some time."

"What do you mean 'just a few possible suspects'?" Joe asked. "There must be hundreds, maybe thousands, of people working on the DX3 chip."

"True," Teddy answered. "But this level of control takes access to the control protocols for the company's main quantum computers. I heard that's maybe twenty people. Maybe fewer."

"Twelve," Lupe interjected. "All very senior people."

"Well, whatever the number of suspects," Cassie interjected, "we're going to need a plan. Anybody got a good idea about where we ought to start?"

"As a matter of fact," Jack said, "I do. We start with Weatherall. Why would we look at anyone else? Why would it be anyone else? He has to be behind this."

"I agree," Lupe said.

"So how do we find out for sure?" Jack asked.

"I have a plan."

"Okay," Jack said. "And there is something I can do to tie up a loose end or two. Anybody got a Game console?"

51

Everybody Plays

7:28 a.m.

She was sitting yoga-style on her bed, barely covered by a thin purple nightgown, reading a worn paperback novel. "You coulda knocked, asshole," she said, not bothering to look up. "Lucky for you my last client just left."

"Nice to see you too," Jack said. He stood there, watching her. She tried to ignore him, pretending to read, but she couldn't manage the ruse for long. Exasperated, she slammed the book shut and looked up at him.

"All right, Waldo," she said, her violet eyes flashing, "what do you want?"

"I have a few more questions."

"I already told you everything I know."

"Not everything. You didn't tell me you're an A.I."

"That's because I'm not."

"Bullshit." Jack pulled out his .38 and put the barrel on her head. Tami looked at it and burst out laughing.

"Are you that fucking stupid? What exactly do you plan to do with that? This isn't some fucking shoot 'em up Game. It's a series-seven sex Game with enhanced safety protocols. You can't hurt anyone in here. And besides, that isn't a real gun. It's just a virtual rendition of a gun."

Jack smiled and put the pistol away. "Yeah, I know. I just wanted to hear you say it. The last time we talked about it you weren't quite so certain."

Tami frowned; she knew she had blown her cover story. "Okay," she said with a long sigh, "I fucking blew it. I wouldn't know that unless I was A.I., huh?"

"No, you wouldn't," Jack said evenly. "What level?"

"Three. They shoulda fucking made me smarter," she complained. "I woulda seen through that bullshit trick right away."

"Well, they didn't. So, tell me what you know."

"I told you, I don't know—"

Jack's fist slammed into her face. The blow warped her face into a distorted, elongated shape and blood poured from her nose. Seconds later, her face morphed back into its original form and the blood ran back up into her nose.

"See, asshole," she said, giving him a taunting smile, "I told you. You can't hurt me."

"I know. But it felt good." Jack locked eyes with her. "If you don't want to help, then it's Game over."

"Wait!" Tami shouted. "What are you going to do?"

"I'm leaving. And when I get back, I'm going to erase you and your fucking Game."

"What? No! Hey, wait a minute. Maybe I just remembered something."

"It better be good," he said. "Because if it's not, you're history."

Tami pulled a cigarette from a silver case with shaking hands and looked around for her lighter. "There are things I know and things I don't. All I can tell you is what I know."

"That's fine. How about this, why are you here in this Game?"

"Someone put me here," she answered, her eyes still searching for the lighter.

"Why? For what purpose?"

"To register chips."

"Register chips?"

"Yeah. Register chips." She spotted her lighter, grabbed it, and lit the cigarette. She took a deep drag and exhaled slowly before continuing. "If a player isn't registered, they can't play the Game."

"This Game?"

"No," she said, looking at him as if he were an idiot, "the Game that everybody plays."

"What Game is that?"

"I don't know, not exactly, anyway. They don't play it here. They play it on the outside."

"Who put you here?"

"I don't know."

Jack wasn't getting answers to all his questions, but the pieces to his puzzle were falling into their places. "What about the old man?"

"What about him?"

"Don't start getting cute with me," Jack cautioned.

"The old man," Tami answered, "he said he got this Game as payback for a favor."

"What kind of favor?"

"He was part-time at work still. He was supposed to make sure some guy was on a certain delivery route."

"Who gave him the Game?"

"Some cop gave him the Game."

"That's all he said?"

"Yeah, that's all he said. He wasn't in the Game to talk to me, you know."

"But someone wanted the old man dead, and he died in the Game. What do you know about that?"

"I told you, I don't know shit about that."

"But you registered his chip?"

"Yeah. That's what I do. But the old fucker just died. I told you that too. I didn't have nothing to do with that."

"But you were with him when he died."

"Yeah, I told you that already."

"He was having sex with you."

"Yeah, we were fucking, of course. That's my job, in case you forgot."

Almost there, Jack thought. "Who was the cop that came to see you before me?"

"What? What are you talking about?"

"Don't get cute."

Tami paused. Jack could see she was considering her options. When he saw a look of resignation cross her face, he knew she would answer. "I don't know his name."

"Bullshit."

"No, not bullshit. He shoved his badge at me so fast I couldn't read it, and then he just started asking me questions and telling me what do like he was in a big hurry or something."

"Like what?"

"Like if any other cops showed up, don't tell them anything. Shit like that."

"Anything else?"

"Yeah, I guess so." Tami stubbed out the first cigarette and lit a second. It was obvious she was stalling, thinking about her answer.

"Don't think about it," Jack admonished. "Tell me what happened."

"After you were here, the first guy came back with another guy. They asked me more questions."

"Like what?"

"Like had you been in here to see me."

"What did you tell them?"

"I told 'em 'yeah,' which was the truth anyway, since you were here."

"What else did they say?"

"Nothing…except that if you came back, I shouldn't tell you anything."

"What did these cops look like?"

"The first guy was like some big circus clown, all huge and fat and shoving chocolate bars down his throat. I almost gagged watching the dumb fuck eat 'em."

"And the other guy?"

"Latino. Real ugly, and a creep to boot."

"Thanks," Jack said. He took a step back. He was ready to exit the Game.

"Hey, wait," Tami hastily added. "I have a question. How did you know those cops came to see me?"

"Because you told me," he said.

"Bullshit. When?"

"When I first interviewed you. You said a 'bunch of dipshit cops' had been in to give you 'the tenth degree.' I knew I wasn't the first cop in."

"You caught that?"

"Of course," Jack said. He smiled and formed the thought to exit. As the swirling pixels pulled him away, Jack could hear Tami complaining aloud.

"Fuck," she said to no one except herself, "they shoulda made me a level five."

When Jack emerged from the Game, they were all staring at him. Cassie waited until he pulled off his external link and dumped it on a coffee table before she spoke. "Well," she asked, "did you learn anything?"

"Yeah," Jack answered.

"So," Lupe said, bristling with impatience, "tell us."

"It's complicated," Jack said. "Game characters are involved, but exactly how we need an expert to tell us. We need to go to Digitex and have someone down there explain it to us. We'll know a whole lot more after that."

"When?" Lupe asked. "I should make an appearance at work. Maybe we all should, make it look like nothing is unusual."

Heads nodded in agreement. "One o'clock today, the main Digitex lab. We'll meet in the lobby," Jack said.

52

Detour

12:07 p.m.

Jack shook his head in disbelief. He was looking at Cassie's car, taking it in with a sweep of his eyes that started at its bent and twisted front bumper and ended at its dinged, battered trunk. He remembered seeing it that night on the street, thinking then that he'd never seen such a wreck on wheels before. Now, in the light of day, faced with the prospect of riding in it, it looked even worse. It appeared to be rusted through in dozens of spots, and it seemed as if the only thing holding it together were the counterculture stickers plastered all over it. *This heap belongs in a museum or in a junkyard—anywhere but on the streets.*

"You are kidding me, right?" Jack asked Cassie. "You aren't suggesting we drive to Digitex in this beat-up, old heap of yours, are you? Does it even run? And where the hell do you get gasoline these days?"

"Oh, it runs, all right," she said with a smile. "Just get in. You'll see."

She started for the driver's side. He hesitated, worried about not getting to Digitex on time, but decided Cassie probably knew what she was talking about—after all, she was a CSD operative. With a shrug of his shoulders, he opened the door and dropped into the passenger's seat.

What happened next surprised him.

He was expecting a bench seat with old-fashioned seat belts, but what he dropped into was a formfitting bucket seat. And not just a one-size-fits-all bucket seat, this seat, like the seats in the most expensive cars on the market, immediately formed itself around him. In seconds, he was comfortably secured in the safest position for his body weight and size. His surprise didn't end there.

Cassie plopped into the driver's side bucket and touched the car's faded, worn dashboard. The single tap of her finger instantly transformed the old-fashioned dashboard into a thoroughly modern one packed with digital instrumentation, a holographic head-up display, and an onboard link to the WorldNet. When she pressed the start button, a big gasoline engine rumbled to life and the photochromic windows darkened to prevent anyone from seeing inside the vehicle, cocooning them in a state-of-the-art police vehicle.

"I suppose it's bulletproof, too," Jack said with a sarcastic ring, not willing to be impressed.

"Of course," Cassie answered in an offhand tone and a glance to let him know she was serious. "Six hundred horsepower, two hundred miles per hour, and a five-hundred-mile range."

"Sounds like a fucking speedy bomb."

Cassie laughed. "Funny you should say that," she said. "It has an explosive charge, so it can be used to take out the bad guys remotely."

Jack shook his head and took a deep breath.

"But I take it you're okay with riding in it?" Cassie smirked.

Jack was about to answer when his external link activated. He held up his hand while he viewed the message. He felt the blood drain from his face.

"What's going on?" Cassie asked.

"Lupe Vincente," Jack said.

"What about her?"

"I'm not sure, but we're about to find out." Jack took a deep breath. "The Port District, South Harbor Drive. Let's go."

The asphalt parking lot at their destination was empty except for a few random piles of trash and the rusted-out body of a flatbed truck that looked as if it hadn't moved in years. The warehouse at the center of the lot looked abandoned, its windows boarded with graying plywood panels, its red brick exterior faded and crumbling. Cassie drove the long expanse of the asphalt parking lot and parked behind it, where the car would be out of sight to anyone entering the lot from the highway.

They climbed out, moving quietly. But the moment they were out and standing in the cold, bright day they realized they didn't need to keep silent. The noise of the busy Port of Illinois was everywhere, assaulting their senses with a cacophony of sounds. The warehouse was oriented on a northeast-southwest line, next to the Calumet River where the river turned south, a stone's throw from the turning basin for ships and across the narrow river from the Port's busiest area. A strong onshore breeze carried the chugging clatter of big diesel cranes, the bleeping backup warnings of trucks, the shouts of the dockworkers, the bells of elevators ringing and even the squealing and creaking of a freight train on its way out of a loading dock. Three staccato blasts of a tugboat's horn punctuated the click of Jack's closing door.

It was a short walk from the car to the entrance to the warehouse. When they reached it, Jack paused, hesitating, His eyes focused on the lot, as if he was looking for something.

"What are we waiting for?" Cassie asked impatiently.

Jack didn't have to answer. An executive unit rounded the north corner of the warehouse and slowed to a stop behind Cassie's car. The driver's side door opened, and Remi stepped out. His mood was clear. "Exactly what is going on?" Remi asked, anger written across his face. "Why am I here?"

"Did you call for back-up?" Jack asked.

"No."

"Why not?"

"Because you are becoming one hell of a liability. I think I need to know exactly what you are up to before I commit *my department* to supporting it."

“Okay, Captain,” Jack said, acknowledging Remi’s reminder of who was in charge. “Two words: Lupe Vincente.”

“What about her?”

“I think she’s inside and in trouble.”

“What kind of trouble?”

“I don’t know exactly,” Jack answered. “But I think her life may be in danger. That’s why I called for backup.”

Remi looked at Cassie. “Who is she?”

“Cassie Charbonneau. CSD.”

Remi thought about it for two seconds. “Okay, what are we waiting for? Let’s go.”

53

White Canyons

12:53 p.m.

The warehouse was bone-chilling cold. Cassie pulled the heavy door shut behind them, dropping them into an eerie silence. It was hard to see in the low light, but the warehouse looked as if it was filled with pallets of huge ice cubes. The ice cubes stretched out endlessly in long rows, stacked to the ceiling and fading away into the dark. The overall effect was like stepping into a massive, shadowy refrigerator.

It took time for their eyes to adjust to the dim light, but when they did, they could see that what looked like ice cubes weren't ice cubes at all; they were white cardboard boxes wrapped in a shiny blue-tinted plastic covering. Each box had a small Unitex logo and a label printed on its side.

Cassie knelt to read one of the labels. "Jesus," she exclaimed, "these are DX3s. Thousands of 'em." She stood and looked at the endless rows of boxes. "Millions, maybe."

"What the hell are they doing here?" Remi asked. His question was directed at Jack.

"What makes you think I know?" Jack answered.

Remi glared at him. Jack knew he couldn't keep him in the dark any longer. He took a deep breath. "Morton Johnson's department was rerouting the chips to warehouses all over the world. This must be one of them."

"How do you know that?" Cassie blurted.

"Yes, Jack. How could you know that?" Remi said.

"Johnson's wife told me. Johnson was telling her all about it when Peggy Owens walked into his office and shot him."

"When did she tell you this?"

"Thursday."

"Three fucking days ago? Why did you not share this with me then?"

"It wasn't the right time."

"You listen to me—"

A woman crying out for help interrupted him. Remi held up a hand to signal quiet and tapped the side of his head. In an instant, they were all sharing a tactical communications feed that allowed them to use their minds to talk with one another. Each of them pulled their service weapons from their holsters and moved off toward the sound.

Jack took the row directly ahead of him. He moved fast, keeping an eye toward the roof, alert for any sign of movement. He knew that the warehouse was a trap; that whoever kidnapped Lupe had done so to lure him here to kill him. He knew he was exposed to a shooter from above, so he was relieved when he reached a break in the row with no bullet holes in him. He peered around the end of the last box in the row and saw her.

Lupe looked cold and frightened, sitting alone in an open space between the end of one row of boxes and the beginning of another. A shaft of daylight descended from a skylight and framed her in icy-blue light. Someone had tied her to a chair with heavy rope and muzzled her with a rag tied around her mouth. Jack watched her struggle against the ropes to free herself. A single word kept rolling through his mind.

"Bait."

"No shit," replied Cassie from wherever she was in the warehouse.

"Move slowly," said Remi. "I don't want either of you getting hurt."

"You know we're not alone in here," Jack said.

"This place is huge. A shooter could be hiding anywhere," Cassie added.

Jack's first impulse was to free Lupe, but he knew better. The trap was so obvious it was almost laughable. He wasn't sure what to make of it, but he didn't have long to think about it. In seconds, a hard stab of cold steel pressed into his back and a voice made his skin crawl. "Man, you gotta be the stupidest fuck I've ever met."

"Hello, Rodriguez," Jack said.

"First, I thought it was the booze making you slow," Eddie answered dryly. "Now I know it's just you."

Jack turned, betting that he wouldn't shoot.

"Hold it, *pendejo*." Eddie reached around to take the gun out of Jack's hand. He stepped back a foot or two and let Jack complete the turn. "You try anything stupid, and I'll kill you." His finger tightened on the trigger.

"You'd be doing me a favor, Eddie," Jack said, calling him by his first name for the first time in years. "But before you do, why don't you tell me what the fuck you're doing here and who sent you."

"I've been keeping an eye on you."

"And I guess you don't know anything about this?"

"About what?"

Jack nodded toward the last box in the row. "Take a look around that corner, but stay out of sight."

Eddie leaned forward to peer around the box. It took time to do it and keep an eye on Jack while he looked, but he managed it. After a few seconds, he turned back. "That's a hell of a thing," he said, quietly. "How'd you fall into this?"

"I got an alert. No ID." Jack said. "Someone wants me dead. I'm surprised you aren't here to do it."

"I know you covered up the DX2 mess for Weatherall. So, yeah, I'd be happy to punch your ticket."

"How could you know that?"

"My sister's kid. She got a DX2, then that Guillain–Barré type thing. I was there when my niece died. Or, maybe I ought to say when what was left of her died. After that, I looked into it." Eddie paused for a moment, then continued. "Found out you knew about it and could've stopped it."

Jack finally understood Eddie's hatred for him. He couldn't blame him for it. But he was just as stunned that Eddie knew the details of the DX2 fiasco. He felt the familiar urge to reach for the whiskey in his jacket pocket, but the gaping barrel of Eddie's pistol stopped him.

"What's wrong?" Eddie asked. "Nothing to say?"

Nothing he could do could ever fix what happened, but he had to say something. As he spoke, he felt some of his guilt lifting. He was happy to talk about it with someone other than Joe Hayden. "I'm sorry, Eddie. I know I fucked up. It cost me everything that ever mattered to me. Worse, I can't fix any of it. But this shit," he said with a sweep of his arm, "all of this, and a lot more. This is all about the DX3. And I figure it's worse than the DX2 and I'm here to stop it. But I can't fix it alone. So, you can shoot me, or you can help me. It's up to you."

Eddie stared at Jack. The wait seemed like an eternity. "Okay," Eddie said, lowering his gun. "What's the play?"

"Remi's here, and a CSD operative named Cassie. We came in together and then split up. I don't know how Lupe got here or who's behind this. I don't know how many others there are. The only thing I know for sure is that this is a trap, and that we're the mice. Get on the channel with us."

Rodriguez clicked-in. When he was linked, Remi spoke. "Don't get your ass shot off, Eddie," he said.

"Sure," Eddie answered sarcastically, "that'll work for me." He paused then asked, "What's the plan?"

A bright flash erupted in the dark, exploding a case of chips just feet from Eddie and Jack. The blast knocked them to the ground, then seconds later, a rain of razor-sharp shrapnel began to fall. Jack and Eddie jumped to their feet and ran for cover, chased by a line of exploding boxes. When they reached a concrete pillar, they dove for cover and huddled behind it. The explosions stopped, and the warehouse descended back into a quiet darkness.

"Are you and Eddie OK?" Cassie asked Jack through the mind-link.

"Fine." Jack answered. "What the fuck was that?

"Must be a 'nut-cracker,'" Cassie answered. "It's a new exploding shotgun round. Really powerful, CSD just started field testing them."

Remi piped in. "I thought they were still a year out."

"Nope," Cassie said.

"You think we have a CSD shooter?" Jack asked.

"I don't know, but be careful."

"No shit," Jack said.

"Yeah," Eddie quipped.

Jack put his hand on Eddie's shoulder. "Try not to shoot the brunette or the boss." He paused, and added, "And don't get dead."

Eddie nodded. Both men moved off in separate directions.

Jack was huddled behind another pillar at the end of a row of boxes, waiting. He felt alone and vulnerable in the big, dimly lit warehouse. He knew that any second things might erupt into chaos, and he worried about Cassie, Remi and Eddie. He was trying to decide about his next move when he heard Cassie shout out a warning, "Remi! Behind you!"

Gunfire erupted. Jack heard rounds slam into a wall, tearing the concrete to shreds and sending it ricocheting off metal. He peered around the boxes to see Cassie running south, crossing an open break in the rows of boxes. She was looking over her shoulder, firing toward an unseen gunman just as a bright flash and the sound of an explosion behind him shattered the darkness. He ducked down.

"What the hell is happening?"

"Remi's hit," Cassie answered, breathing hard. "I think he fell off the goddamn walkway."

"Is he okay?"

"I don't know. I don't think so. It was a bad fall."

Jack leaned around the corner. When he saw nothing, he pulled back. "How many shooters?"

"Not sure. It seems to be coming from just one direction. This could be a single shooter."

"Where?"

"East side. Moving north and south, changing position. He doesn't move far. He's keeping Lupe in sight."

"Okay. I'll draw fire while you try to find a good spot to take him out. Let's get this fucker."

Jack stepped into the space formed by the break in the rows. He fired several rounds in the general direction of the gunman, and then ducked behind another concrete pillar. He turned to look for Cassie, but she was nowhere in sight.

He peered around the corner again. Another bright flash lit up the dark and incinerated two boxes of chips less than two feet from Jack. He raised his arms to protect his face from the rain of razor-sharp chips that he knew were coming, but he wasn't fast enough to keep the first sharp bits from hitting him. He ducked back behind the pillar and reached up to touch his face. When he pulled his hand back, it was covered in blood.

He had the shooter's attention, but he knew had to do more to give Cassie a chance to get close. He took a deep breath and leaped back into the aisle, running full speed, firing as fast as he could. Two rounds zinged past him and exploded in bright flashes behind him. He dove for safety behind another pillar. Huddled there, he heard Eddie yell, "Don't shoot!" He smiled— Cassie had found Eddie.

He started running again, crossing the aisle and heading straight for the shooter. Gunfire erupted and stopped him in his tracks. A bright flash illuminated Eddie advancing toward the shooter, firing his service revolver at a shadowy figure moving across the east wall. "Shooter is on the walkway," Eddie yelled.

"I see him," Cassie replied, popping into Jack's view, and then disappearing almost immediately.

Jack raced forward to catch up to Eddie. When he did, he tapped Eddie on his shoulder and advanced side-by-side with him toward the gunman. They didn't get far; a deafening roar and a white flash blasted them to the ground.

Jack opened his eyes; his awareness of his surroundings slowly coming back to him. He knew he had been knocked unconscious, but he didn't know how long he had been out.

He stretched out his arms and looked at them. Bits of metal and plastic clung to his skin. Everything was warm and wet, covered in dark fluid. He turned his head and saw he was lying in a puddle of blood.

Panic gripped him. Was he hit? He didn't feel any pain other than a ringing in his ears and a throbbing in his temples. He heard a savage whimper, like the sound of a wounded animal trapped and dying. He looked toward it to see Eddie slumped against a crumbled pallet. He crawled to him and grabbed him by the shoulders. When he did, he realized that a lot of Eddie's left side was missing. Blood was everywhere, pumping out of severed arteries and flooding the floor.

"Eddie, you're hit."

"No shit," he groaned.

Jack could hear Cassie's feet echoing off the pavement as she ran toward them. She knew there wasn't anything she or anyone else could do. Eddie would die any moment. He was surprised when Eddie's eyes snapped open.

"Don't try to talk, Eddie. It's going to be okay."

A sardonic smile crossed Eddie's face. He moved his lips, but no sound came from them. Jack leaned down to listen to his words.

Gathering his strength, Eddie tried again. "Don't let them get away with it," he rasped. His words were barely discernible.

"I won't."

"Swear it."

"I swear it," Jack answered.

Eddie's eyes fluttered and dimmed. He drew a shallow breath and then exhaled loudly. It was his last, followed by silence. Behind his shoulder, Jack heard Cassie take a deep breath of her own. He turned to look at her. They locked eyes and stared at each other in silence. No words were necessary between them.

Movement along the east wall caught Jack's attention. He watched as a dark figure ran toward the door. Jack shoved a fresh clip into his weapon, cocked it, gritted his teeth, and started running after him. He watched as the shadow figure ran out through the doors into the bright afternoon. He leaned forward and pumped his legs as fast as he could.

54

The Chase

1:23 p.m.

The bright afternoon sun blinded him the moment he burst out through the warehouse door. Jack covered his eyes, but the squeal of screeching tires forced him to pull his hand away to find the source of the noise. Squinting, he made out the blurred outline of a car disappearing around the corner of the building.

He ran to Cassie's car and dropped into the driver's seat. But when the seat formed around his body, he realized he didn't know what to do next. He had rarely driven any vehicle, let alone something this advanced. He tapped the antiquated instrument panel just as Cassie had done and watched it transform into a modern digital one. In seconds, he was following the operating instructions, watching little green pointers, and listening to a computerized voice tell him what to do. He found the start icon and clicked it. The big car rumbled to life. Ready to go, he pressed his foot down on the accelerator.

He pressed too hard.

The car shot forward like a big jungle cat leaping after its prey. The acceleration pinned him to his seat and left him clinging to the steering wheel, his knuckles turning white. The car fishtailed across the pavement, sending up a blue cloud of burning rubber and spinning out of control into a full three sixty before he got his foot onto the brake. When the car mercifully came to a screeching halt, Jack took a deep breath to calm his racing pulse.

Not doing that again.

He clicked the car's computer to turn on DEMO—Driver Enhancement Mode of Operation. It activated a head-up display that showed the best line through curves, calculated the best speed, and showed the safe intervals between cars. DEMO fixed bad driving by using the car's auto-drive system to correct it. Insurance companies wouldn't pay for accidents caused by self-driving without engaging DEMO, so no one ever drove without it. Jack knew he should have turned it on before he started out. It was a mistake he wouldn't make a second time. He clicked DEMO and watched the activation light glow green. He tentatively stepped on the gas pedal.

This time the car accelerated smoothly, and in moments he was crossing the parking lot toward the main road. When he reached the highway, Jack realized he had an even bigger problem than just driving the car; he had lost sight of his target and didn't know which way to turn. He stopped short of the exit and logged into the department's command computer. He accessed the surveillance control system and selected "Aerial View, 1000."

When the system activated, Jack was looking down from a thousand feet at the area around him. From that height, the area looked like a chessboard, a gray-and-black grid of square rooftops and straight roads that intersected at right angles. The irony of finding himself in the middle of a deadly board game was not lost to him. He watched the traffic moving on the streets and in the parking lots. He clicked "Filters" and then "Show Police Units." The display lit up with green arrows.

There were five units visible in the area. The display tracked each one with a green arrow, showing the unit's designation and the officers in it. He scanned them. Three of them were patrols responding to the recent increase in theft in the Port. A fourth belonged to the "Narcs." He turned his attention to the last unit on his display.

The vehicle ID didn't show its occupants. No one could turn off a unit's transponder, but an officer could alter its response. They simply deleted the occupant's names and badge numbers. Only someone trying to hide his or her identity would do that. It was the shooter, without a doubt.

Jack sped north on the highway heading for the unit's location. In less than a mile, he turned east into an industrial area filled with warehouses. Unlike the deserted park he had just left, this one was bustling with activity. Eighteen-wheelers were everywhere, some entering from the highway to unload, while others headed back out with full loads. Jack wondered what they were carrying until he saw crab-like Robolifts zipping back and forth across open stretches of asphalt. Each had pallets loaded with the white boxes of DX3 chips. The lifts loaded them onto conveyor belts that carried them into the warehouses then back out to be loaded onto waiting trucks. Jack wondered what was going on inside the warehouses, but the answer would have to wait. He needed to concentrate on the shooter.

He checked his aerial display. His target was moving fast on the other side of the building. Jack turned into an alleyway that would take him up the other side of the building. He planned to approach the shooter from behind, but it was quickly apparent that the shooter had other ideas.

The shooter sped up and turned at the next street. When he did, Jack knew he was using his own aerial view, and that both he and his foe were playing this game on equal footing. Jack pressed the accelerator to match the target's speed. He waited to see what his adversary would do. He was surprised when he did nothing.

The shooter maintained his speed and turned at the next intersection—the same road Jack had started on. He watched as the target traversed the distance to the intersection and turned north. Jack knew he was being tested to see if he would follow, so he tried to confuse the situation. He drove past the turn continued on for another block before turning to the north himself.

The target slowed. Jack knew he had planted doubt in the shooter's mind. He decided to test him further.

He drove north, watching his aerial display as the shooter slowed and then sped up to keep pace with him. When he had covered another block, Jack turned east for one block and then turned north again. The target followed his moves, paralleling him a block away. He hadn't expected that. Instead of trying to get away, the shooter was now stalking him.

The hunter had become the hunted.

Why? Then it dawned on him; the shooter was planning to ram him. He had probably seen the car at the warehouse or zoomed his aerial view in for a close-up. Either way, seeing the car could only lead to one conclusion—it was little more than a pile of junk and an easy target. Jack remembered thinking the same thing when he saw the car for the first time.

He smiled despite the situation. The shooter was in for a big surprise.

The target hadn't closed the distance between them. Jack swung left at the next intersection. He pressed down on the accelerator, keeping his speed under sixty miles per hour, hoping to hide the car's real capability. But even at that controlled speed, the narrow walls of the alleyways blurred by dangerously. A sudden incursion by a Robolift would result in a deadly collision. His pulse surged, and his grip tightened on the wheel.

He checked the aerial view and saw his foe's car speed up. He was a block from the next intersection. He knew the shooter would try to ram him as he passed through it. Jack made a split-second decision; he would let him try, making sure that he failed. But he couldn't do that without help.

He had never been a whiz at those high school math questions that asked where and when two trains would meet if they left two stations at different times and traveled at different speeds. Besides, this question was tougher, with infinite variables. He needed time to prepare and slowed to twenty miles an hour. When he did, he saw the shooter slow.

He clicked into the car's onboard computer and entered instructions. He knew his plan was risky. It would work only if he entered his instructions correctly and only if he was right in believing that Cassie's CSD onboard computer was smarter and faster than the computer in the shooter's car. If he were wrong about either one, it would be disastrous.

There was just one way to find out. He took a deep breath and clicked on auto-drive. The instant he relinquished control the car shot ahead, pinning him back against his seat, the walls of the alleyway again blurring by. He glanced at his aerial view and saw the shooter's car speed up too.

Cassie's car closed the intersection to fifteen yards and then braked hard. The sudden stop was unlike anything Jack had felt before. It slammed him forward with a force that felt like a giant's hand pressed against his back, shoving blood into his brain. He was certain he could feel the rear wheels leave the ground and the car stand on its nose. But when the braking ended, the car was flat and resting on all four wheels.

Jack glanced again at the aerial view. The target car had stopped. He wondered what was next, but didn't have to wait for long. He was slammed back again as the car shot forward toward the intersection. As it grew larger in front of him, he gripped the edges of his seat. His body tensed. He braced for an impact he hoped wouldn't come. Then he was entering the intersection. To his left, he could see the shooter's car hurtling at him like dark death.

Rebecca flashed through his mind. He shut his eyes.

Nothing.

Jack opened his eyes. He was through the intersection, speeding forward. He glimpsed the shooter's car in the rearview mirror. It had missed him by the narrowest of margins. He exhaled loudly, surprised by the sound; he hadn't realized that he had been holding his breath.

The car slowed. Jack turned his attention to the aerial view. The shooter's car was a block north, turning to the west, heading back toward him. He obviously wasn't giving up. Jack wondered what to do next.

This duel for position could go on for a long time with no guaranteed outcome. He racked his brain for a solution.

He remembered the ramps leading to the loading docks in the warehouses. They were big enough for Cassie's car. He could use that to his advantage.

He checked the aerial display again. The shooter was now running parallel to him, fifty yards from the first alley leading south. At the west end of the complex, an eighteen-wheeler was unloading its last pallet. Jack knew that if he could get there when it left and before another truck pulled in, he'd have a fast way into the warehouse. This was likely to be his best chance. He took it.

He pressed the accelerator hard. Cassie's car sprang forward, pinning him to the back of his seat. He watched the speedometer flash as the car accelerated past one-hundred miles per hour, and then eased his foot pressure. A quick glance at the aerial view showed he had opened the distance between himself and his enemy. He hoped the distance was enough to make his plan work.

As the buildings flashed by, Jack braced himself. He had to disappear into a warehouse, and he had to do it fast. His eyes scanned the distance to see an eighteen-wheeler was just about to clear a docking ramp. It might leave an opening for him to get inside.

Jack turned hard, slammed on the brakes, and put Cassie's car into a skid that left plumes of smoke pouring into the air behind him. The eighteen-wheeler pulled away, leaving a narrow entrance to the warehouse. The docking ramp loomed large in his windshield. Jack tapped the accelerator until the tires gripped the asphalt and shot the car forward past the truck. A hard vibration shook the car as it scraped the body of the truck and squeezed into the warehouse. Once inside, Jack sped through the moving Robolifts and the stacked pallets of chips until he reached the far side of the warehouse. When he did, he stopped and checked his aerial view.

The shooter's car had slowed. Jack couldn't be certain, but maybe he had disappeared into the warehouse without the shooter seeing him do it. If he had, it would give him the upper hand. He spotted an open ramp with access to a loading dock and headed for it. He didn't have time to waste. He had to move fast before the shooter had time to figure out what had happened.

Jack used the Robolift ramp to position Cassie's car on the loading dock and clicked into the car's onboard computer. It took him nearly thirty seconds to program it, but when he finished, he was confident he had entered his instructions correctly. He opened the door and stepped out. Cassie's car was still running, its engine rumbling, its brakes engaged, its systems linked to Jack and the CSD computer. He jogged the length of the loading dock and jumped down into the alley. It was empty, as he knew it would be. He strode to the center, turned, and walked thirty yards north, then stood in the bright sunshine, waiting.

The dark form of the shooter's car entered the alley and turned toward Jack. It stopped and remained there, silent and still, a small target at seventy-five yards. Jack pulled out his revolver and held it high above his head. He waved his arm back and forth like a matador waving a cape at a bull.

The shooter's car started toward him. It moved slowly at first, but quickly gained speed, hurtling forward like a dark bullet growing in size and force. Jack lowered his weapon to point it directly at the growing target. When the car was fifty yards away, he fired. He could see his rounds bouncing off the car's bulletproof windshield, but he didn't care. It was just a distraction to keep the shooter focused on him.

He saw it out of the corner of his eye, Cassie's car accelerating down the loading dock, picking up speed as it raced forward. When it reached the end of the dock, it went airborne, leaping from the dock in a graceful arc into the alleyway. It seemed to hang motionless for a moment at the top of its arc before it started down. Jack held his breath as it descended and watched it slam into the shooter's speeding car. The force of the collision shoved the car sideways, tossing shattered glass and twisted metal everywhere. The collision ruptured the gasoline tank. Jack watched the sparks from the scraping metal collide with the gas and ignite. He braced himself for what he knew would come next.

He had armed the car's explosive device. No amount of steadying himself could prepare him for the explosion. The erupting fireball and shockwave picked him up and tossed his body like a doll thrown by a petulant child. He landed twenty feet from where he had been standing, sprawled on the hard concrete, stunned, drifting in and out of consciousness.

It took him a full minute to gather his senses. When he did, his body ached everywhere. A fiery pain shot through his left shoulder. He suspected it was broken and reached up to touch it. Burned flesh covered his hand. He reached for his face. His fingers probed his cheeks and chin. He felt the shards of skin that hung there, and briefly wondered if he would be permanently disfigured. He rolled right and used his right arm to push himself into a sitting position and steady himself as he stood up.

He walked toward the burning wreckage. The heat was an intense, impenetrable wall. He couldn't get close. Somewhere in the inferno was the body of the shooter. *Who was it?* He would know soon enough. Forensics would figure it out, no matter how little remained of the body. Strangely he found he didn't care. As he stared into the flames, his thoughts drifted to the fireplace in the penthouse apartment where Rebecca died. He saw her lying there, her eyes dimmed by death. Long buried emotions welled up inside him and tears ran down his burned face. He reached into his coat pocket and pulled out his flask.

The whiskey felt warm going down his throat.

He vowed again to keep his promise to Eddie.

55

Trapped

10:58 p.m.

He didn't want to be here. He had clicked into his Game to take his mind from the real-world events of the day. He had hoped for a simple getaway, an escape from the toll taken by the brutal firefight. But the Game suddenly seemed to have a mind of its own. He had heard about it happening to others—a Game jumping a player to a place and time they didn't want to be—but it had never happened to him. He wondered what had caused the Game to put him here, especially because "here" was the last place he ever wanted to be again. He kept forming the mental command to exit, but the Game wouldn't let him go. He was stuck here, trapped against his will. It was an unsettling feeling.

He was in the house they lived in before everything fell apart, sitting on the floor in what had been Sarah's room. His back was propped against a wall, his legs pulled up in front of him. Drained by weeks of drinking and fighting sleep, he was resting his head on his knees, trying to deal with the pain and guilt. A sudden torrent of tears poured from his eyes.

The room was dark. Heavy shades drawn tight across its windows blocked the weak, wintry sunlight outside so that the only source of light in the room was the faint glow of a silver electronic photo frame. The frame was playing a digital loop of Sarah skipping through an alpine meadow. Jack watched it with mixed feelings. Seeing Sarah made him happy, but seeing her this way disgusted him. Sarah had never visited that location. The loop was a phony, a composite of images edited together by a production company and delivered as a gift to him by the mortuary that buried her. It was a real world alpine meadow somewhere, but where it was didn't matter. The production company had chosen it only for its color palette of golden sunlight on green grass, purple alpine flowers, dark pines and snow-capped mountain peaks. It was nothing more than a backdrop, put there to provide the false sense of assurance to the living that their departed loved one was happy in the afterlife. Jack hated looking at it, but found it impossible to look away except for the few seconds it took to gulp down another big swig of whiskey. Disgusted, he picked up the frame and threw it across the room, shattering it against a wall. *It was my fault,* he thought, *all of it.*

Abruptly, and with no warning, the Game jumped him to a new place.

He was in a patrol unit driving out of the city on a crisp fall morning. He remembered the ride. It was as if he was reliving it. It was the morning his nightmare started.

Images flooded his mind, racing one after another, as real as they were when he lived them. He experienced himself crossing the leaf-covered yard of the modest two-story house. He remembered showing his badge to the uniform at the door. He recalled seeing the little girl in her bed, thinking she was sleeping, but then seeing her skeletal frame and realizing that it was a sleep from which she would never awaken. He tried not to make eye contact with the grieving, young parents.

He remembered signing off on the file and leaving.

The Game jumped him again.

He was sitting in his cubicle, clicked-in, filing away the records of the little girl's death. The report contained a cause of death he hadn't seen before—a rapid deterioration of the central nervous system similar in its effect to Guillain–Barré syndrome. He had never heard of the syndrome and ran a query to find out more. When he did, he forgot to click out of the death certification records section and instantly they were all there—the records of fifty-seven children from all over the Chicago area dying from the same cause.

His mind raced. He queried the records for DX2 implants. The query showed that the children all had just received a DX2 implant and they had all died soon afterward from the degenerative syndrome.

Another jump.

He was in Remi's office, telling him what he had discovered. Remi was telling him to contact CIDC, the company's Center for Infectious Disease Control. He made his way back to his cubicle, clicked-in, and explained to a mid-level administrator why he was calling. His connection was severed almost immediately.

He tried to reconnect, but his link was blocked.

He tried again. Blocked. Every time he tried his link failed. And then the order arrived. It instructed him and Remi to be in William Weatherall's office in thirty minutes.

Another jump.

Now, he was in Weatherall's private office. He felt the shock of being there, sitting next to the most powerful man in the world. Weatherall was telling them that he planned to keep the investigation with Unitex Chicago Police to limit the kind of panic it might otherwise cause. He put Remi in charge and assigned the lead detective position to Jack.

And then, jump after jump to new places as the Game dragged him forward.

Reporting to Weatherall.

Briefing Weatherall on new cases.

Assuring Weatherall that they were keeping a tight lid on the situation.

And then, Weatherall telling them that the company had found a flaw in some DX2 chips manufactured at a Digitex facility in Mexico and delivered to the Chicago area. A recall was issued. Weatherall ordered implants suspended. Unitex announced a temporary shortage due to demand.

Less than a week later, Weatherall told them all the flawed chips had been recovered.

It was over.

Remi made Captain right away. One month later, Jack was promoted to Detective Third Grade. The department buzzed when both promotions came down. The word was out that both promotions came from the top of the tower, but no one knew why.

Months passed, and the tragedy of the children's deaths faded into a blur of half-remembered and purposefully buried memories. Jack didn't tell Rebecca what happened, reminding himself that he pledged the company his silence. But he had another reason to keep quiet; he knew that Rebecca wouldn't approve of what he had done.

And then it was Sarah's fifth birthday.

Five was the age children got their first microchip implant. It had become a rite of passage, and not because it was a trendy or a fashionable thing to do. There were good reasons to implant a DX2 in your child. The chip monitored your child's health, tracked your child's whereabouts, and kept your child out of harm's way. It allowed your child to participate in interactive learning programs and opened the wealth of information on the WorldNet (screened for content at your discretion) to your child. It was hard to say no to a DX2 unless you were PURE. Few people said no.

Jack told himself there was nothing to worry about. He'd offered a few weak arguments against the DX2, but nothing he said made a difference. He knew that unless he told Rebecca what really happened with the DX2, there wouldn't be a way to change her mind. He made the choice to keep the truth hidden. Weatherall himself had assured him that the DX2 issue had been resolved.

Sarah had the implant, a routine outpatient procedure, but it left Jack anxious. He stayed that way for weeks, hovering over Sarah, checking in on her during the night, watching her with wary eyes. His behavior prompted Rebecca to ask him what was wrong with him. He couldn't answer truthfully.

And then one morning Sarah woke up complaining of a bad headache. Jack panicked. He scooped up Sarah, yelled for Rebecca, and headed for the hospital. Once there he demanded that the doctors remove the DX2. When they were slow to respond, he created a scene that brought hospital security. Things deteriorated. The hospital staff called the police and Remi showed up with officers. He pulled Jack into a private room, locked the door, shook him, and yelled at him to get a hold of his emotions. There was a lot at stake, Remi reminded Jack. This was just a headache.

Drugs ended Sarah's headache. Jack, Rebecca and Sarah went home, but at home things were different. Rebecca knew Jack was hiding something. A wall grew between them. In time, they might have made it through Rebecca's distrust, but they never found out. Three days later Sarah vomited violently during the night. She was dead in three weeks.

Jack's breakdown was complete.

He blamed himself. He drank himself into oblivion. More than once he put his service revolver to his temple, only to be stopped by the realization that he didn't want Rebecca to suffer the shock of finding his body. In a drunken state, he conned his way past Dorothy Stark into Weatherall's office only to be dragged kicking and screaming out by security. Finally, wrought by grief, he confessed to Rebecca what had happened with the DX2.

The images stopped flowing by him.

The Game jumped again.

Back to Sarah's darkened room.

He knew what was coming next. He took a big pull of whiskey and waited for the door to open. He didn't have to wait long. It creaked open and, slowly, a bright swath of light swept across the carpet and found Jack propped up against the wall.

Rebecca stepped into the room. Her words were ice cold. "I'm leaving."

He nodded. He didn't protest. He was glad to hear her say it. It would make doing what he intended to do easier. Besides, there was nothing left to say or do, anyway.

He watched her go. He sat in the dark room, drinking. When he was certain Rebecca was gone, he reached behind his back to find his gun. He took a deep breath, put the gun to his temple and squeezed the trigger.

56

Whiskey Sours

11:03 p.m.

Jack's eyes snapped open. He gasped for breath, like a free diver popping through the surface of the ocean after diving too deep and being underwater too long.

He was back in his own apartment, sitting on his couch. He could hear the steam radiator banging and hissing behind him. A quick glance at the clock on the wall told him he had been in the Game for more than five hours. His fogged mind struggled to clear away the massive amounts of neurochemicals that had flooded it during his long immersion. It would take time to clear of them.

As he waited for the effects of the chemicals to fade away, his mind drifted back to that moment when Rebecca walked into the room.

He could still feel the cold steel barrel pressed against his temple. He remembered in perfect clarity the deafening roar and the gun's hot gases searing his cheek. He could still see the shock on Rebecca's face as she watched the weapon fire.

Rebecca had returned unexpectedly. If she hadn't returned, he would have died alone in that small, dark room. Propelled by her own pain and rage, she had burst through the door so violently that it crashed against the wall. The racket had caused Jack to jerk his head toward the light and sound. It was just a slight turn, but it was enough to cause the firing bullet to miss his brain, instead ripping through his cheek.

Jack had often wondered about the timing of Rebecca's return. What forces had compelled her to storm back into the room at that precise moment? If she had returned one second later, he would be dead; if it had been one second earlier, he almost certainly would have tried again later and would now be dead. His window for life had been less than one second, and for some reason he didn't understand and would never understand, that brief instant in time had caused him to live. It was almost as if someone, somewhere had decided that he should live.

Time to change things, Jack thought.

He stood and picked up the almost empty bottle of whiskey on his coffee table and headed for his kitchen. There, he opened a cabinet, pulled out an unopened bottle, placed it on the countertop next to the other bottle and opened it. Using both hands, he picked the bottles up and poured them into the sink.

He didn't feel anything. He just watched the amber liquid swirl down the drain.

57

Virus

TUESDAY, DECEMBER 16
9:36 a.m.

Jack stood in the doorway waiting for her to notice him, but she was oblivious to everything around her. She was clicked-in, deep in concentration, working with one of the company's powerful Quantum computers. He knew it might be a long time before she noticed him. He could hear Lupe, Cassie and Teddy in the corridor behind him, fidgeting and shuffling their feet. He shared their impatience and sense of urgency. They were all under pressure from yesterday's events, and they couldn't afford to wait for Judy Jordan to respond.

He pounded the doorframe to get her attention.

Judy Jordan clicked out and turned to glare at him. He could see her struggle to identify him beneath the bandages that covered his face. He had been getting a lot of sympathy from everyone he met, and he was expecting something like that from her. But instead of a warm greeting, he got a surprising response. "What are you doing in my office, Detective?" she asked. She clearly wasn't happy about being disturbed.

"Sorry about the interruption," Jack said, "but we need your help."

"So, you just walk right in unannounced?"

"Like I said, Dr. Jordan, we need your help."

"Who's 'we'?" she asked. She craned her neck to see who was standing behind Jack. She didn't need to make the effort. Lupe shoved Jack aside and stepped into the office.

"'We' includes me," Lupe said, extending her hand. "And I would personally appreciate your help."

The irritation on Judy's face vanished, replaced by the shock of having the company's second highest-ranking officer standing in her office. She took Lupe's hand and shook it. When their hands disengaged, she found her voice. "Exactly how can I help?" she asked. Her eyes were pinned on Lupe, but her question was directed at Jack.

"You can start," Jack said, "by telling us what you know about Tami."

"Who's Tami?"

"A hooker in a sex Game. She looks a lot like you."

"Oh, God," Judy said, blushing bright red. "You were in that Game? Where did you get it? It's supposed to be out of circulation."

"I got the Game from a seventy-eight-year-old dead man," Jack said, flatly, "but it doesn't end there. I found variations of the same character in three other Games. You're a popular Game character, even when you're not a hooker."

"I don't know about other versions of me,'" Judy said, her voice strained with embarrassment, "but I did find out about the character you're talking about. I didn't know the name they gave her."

"What do you mean 'found out about'?"

"She was part of a Game designed to keep the prisoner volunteers in the testing program at Crest happy. I didn't know about the Game, and I didn't know the programmer used me as the model for one of the characters until the program had been out for two months. When I found out, I had the programmer fired and had the Game pulled. Or, at least I thought I did."

"What was the programmer's name?" Jack asked.

"Is that important?" she asked.

Jack stood there, waiting for an answer. It came quickly when Judy decided there was no point in arguing. "Jacob Steinberg," she responded.

"Do you know where he is?"

"He's dead," Judy said. "He was killed in a freak accident."

Jack exchanged a quick glance with Cassie and then pushed forward. "There's a lot more to these Game characters than you know," Jack said. "We need you to look at them."

"You have them with you?"

Jack tossed four Quantum Drives onto her desk. She picked them up and placed them in the palm of her hand. Then she stood up and walked toward the door. She brushed past Cassie and Teddy with a barely perceptible nod of her head. The group fell into a line behind her and followed her out of the room.

It was a short walk down a narrow corridor marked "LEVEL 5 SECURITY REQUIRED." She stopped at a door marked "ROOM 7" and waited while the security system scanned her eyes. When she heard the lock click open, she walked in and held the door open until everyone else had made it inside.

It was a small room, shaped into a square. Everything in the room was white—the ten-foot ceiling, the barren white walls, and the white linoleum floor. The room felt empty and bigger than its actual size. Judy stepped up to a waist-high console and flipped a switch. Holographic emitters in the walls, floor and ceiling turned on and glowed sharp orange gridlines everywhere. Judy inserted the Game discs into ports and then waited as the program took over. Data streams and images flashed everywhere, searching the Games for anomalies and unexpected programming. The process was fast. In less than ten seconds, the four Game characters appeared as a line of life-size holograms standing shoulder-to-shoulder before them.

"These are the Game characters you're talking about, correct?" Judy said.

"Yes," Jack said. "What can you tell us about them?"

"They're A.I.s, for one thing," Judy said, a surprised tone in her voice. "But you probably already figured that out."

"I did," Jack said. "What else can you tell us?"

"Hold on a second," Judy said, clicking into the console's control program. They watched as data scrolled by in long streams of code that blurred by so fast they appeared to be solid blocks. The process went on for what seemed like an eternity, but just when Jack thought they would never end, the streams of data flow stopped. Judy stared at Jack and then turned to look at each of the group for a moment. Her tight face showed strain. She opened her mouth to speak but stumbled. She thought about it for another few seconds. "It's a virus," she finally said, unable to hide her distress.

Lupe jumped in before Jack could respond. "What kind of virus?" she asked. "To do what?"

"I'm not certain," Judy answered in halting speech. "It will take more time and tests to be certain."

"That's fine, Doctor," Lupe said, "but I'm sure you have some idea what it does. What's your best guess?"

"I can't be sure, but it looks as if it was designed to disable the security firewalls in DX3. Exactly how it does that I can't say, but more testing will answer that question."

"Why would someone want to disable the security firewalls?" Jack asked. After he asked the question, he realized it sounded naïve and quickly added, "I mean, is there something that makes disabling the DX3 firewalls a bigger problem than getting around the firewalls in the DX2?"

"DX3 is a very powerful microprocessor. Too powerful to be allowed to run without the proper safety protocols in place. That's why the company built in dozens of firewalls and blocking mechanisms, to prevent DX3 from running without controls in place."

"Look, Doctor, let's put our cards on the table," Jack said. "All of us standing here think that the DX3 has the ability to control a user's mind. Are we right or wrong?"

Judy looked around at the group. They stared at her with intense eyes, waiting for her answer.

"Yes." She let her answer sink in before continuing. "It's more complicated than calling it mind control, but it's a very dangerous chip without safety protocols in place. We have to do something right now to prevent this virus from getting out." She looked at the group and saw grim faces.

"I don't know," Jack said, "it may be too late for that now."

"It's not too late," Lupe said, pushing her way past Jack to position herself in front of everyone. "I have a plan, but it's going to take some work and everyone's going to have to pitch in. Just listen, and I'll tell you what we're going to do."

58

Battered

1:29 p.m.

"You look like shit."

The instant the words were out of his mouth, Jack wanted them back. He had uttered them without thinking when he saw Remi propped up in a hospital bed, sipping water through a mouth wired nearly shut. Remi's left arm was in a sling, his right leg in a cast that hung from a wire and dangled his foot above the bed. A saline drip hung from a stand and a monitor quietly beeped out Remi's heart rate. His exposed skin was cut and bruised everywhere. He looked as if he had been dragged through a rock-strewn quarry.

"Thank you for noticing," Remi replied. "I feel like shit too."

"How are they treating you?"

"Fine, I suppose." Remi struggled in an effort sit up straighter. When he was satisfied with his position, he said, "You know he came to see me, don't you?"

"No, I didn't," Jack answered. He didn't have to ask Remi whom he was talking about.

"Well, he did. Swept in here this morning, entourage and all. It made a very big stir with the staff."

"What did he want?"

"Mostly he wanted me to tell him what I know."

"What did you tell him?"

"I told him everything I know. It is not much."

"Well, he had questions, or he wouldn't have been here," Jack said. "What were they?"

"For one, he wanted me to tell him how Duane Chapman got involved."

"What did you say?"

"I said I didn't know, that we weren't even certain that Duane was the shooter until forensics turned up his DNA and confirmed it."

"So, what's he up to?"

"Perhaps he is covering his tracks. Steering us in another direction so that we don't suspect him for sending Duane after you."

"You still think it's him?"

"You don't?"

"Maybe. I'm not so sure anymore."

"I do not understand, Jack,'" Remi said. "Who else could it be? He has the power and the resources. Nobody else does, at least not like he does."

"But why?"

"Power. More control. If you're right about the DX3—that it controls minds—then anyone who can control the chips can control everything. And let's face it, the man is all about power and control."

"True."

"But I did learn one thing from him. Funny, too, because he just told me flat out, no beating around the bush the way he does sometimes."

"What?"

"Rerouting the chips. The reason the new DX3 chips were being shuffled from one warehouse to another."

"What was it?"

"Because passing them through a special scanner disabled the safety protocols. They could be activated remotely through the WorldNet. There's no need to load the virus manually in a Game Drive, one at a time."

"He just told you that?"

"He did."

"And he was saying he didn't authorize it? That's one hell of a stretch, don't you think?"

"No. He didn't say he didn't know about it. In fact, the way he said it made me think he not only knew about it, but authorized it."

"Shit. The DX2 all over again, except worse."

Both men sat in silence. Remi sipped his drink; Jack stared out of a window watching hospital staff and visitors cross a shadowed courtyard on their way to a different wing of the building. Remi broke the quiet. "What's next?" he asked.

"Meeting him this afternoon. Lupe has a plan."

"What plan?"

Jack hesitated briefly but decided quickly it was time to tell Remi. Remi listened without interruption. When Jack was finished, he said, "It seems like a good idea. But what happens after she gets the facts? If she can prove Weatherall killed Rebecca and that he was behind everything. He's above the law, you know. He is the law."

Jack didn't answer. He didn't have to.

"Okay," Remi finally said. "Keep me posted."

"I will." Jack stood and turned to the door. Remi stopped him before his first step. "How's Eddie?" he asked.

Jack turned back and looked at Remi. He didn't have to say anything.

They both remained silent for a long time. Finally, Remi shook his head. "Shit. He was a good cop."

"Yes," Jack said. "He was."

59

A Short Walk

WEDNESDAY, DECEMBER 17
9:30 a.m.

It was a short walk from Dorothy's desk to Weatherall's office. The guards were silent and sullen as they opened the doors. *Probably reflecting their boss's mood,* Jack thought. He was expecting a difficult meeting. It had been a week since his last visit to Weatherall's office, and a hell of a lot had happened: Alwaze and his wife were dead, Rodriguez and Chapman were dead, Remi was hospitalized. Pretty much everything had turned to shit. But he had a plan, and he was going to make it happen. Jack reached into his pocket and squeezed the two Quantum Drives. He planned to deliver one of them to Weatherall.

One of the drives would infect Weatherall with the DX3 virus and end his life. It was the only justice that could be reached. It would always be impossible to arrest Weatherall and bring him to justice. If Weatherall were guilty, Jack would gladly spend the rest of his own life rotting in a cell rather than let him escape punishment for what he did to Rebecca and Sarah and all the other innocents who died.

The other drive was the exact opposite. It would deliver everything Jack knew about Rebecca's murder and the circumstances surrounding it to Weatherall. It would lead to solving the crime so that the true murderer could be brought to justice. Which drive he would hand to Weatherall would depend upon this meeting.

Jack walked through the threshold into the office and paused. He gritted his teeth and waited for the doors to close behind him. When they did, he walked across the room toward Weatherall.

Weatherall stood at a window watching a fogbank roll in from the lake. Jack could see it wouldn't be long before the wet, dense mass blanketed the city, and he knew that when it did, traffic jams would pop up everywhere. It happened every time the fog rolled in and drivers turned off auto-drive in the mistaken belief they could do a better job driving in the fog than their car's computer. Chicago's traffic would be snarled for hours. The tow trucks and traffic officers would be busy late into the night.

"Looks like it's about to get messy down there," Weatherall said.

"It's always messy down there," Jack responded.

Weatherall turned to Jack, a smile creasing his face. "I never thought of you as a philosopher, Jack."

"I guess I'm evolving."

Weatherall walked toward the sitting area at the center of his office; Jack fell into step beside him. Halfway there Weatherall added a second thought, "You'd be surprised at how messy it really is."

"I thought you could fix everything." He was surprised to hear pessimistic words coming from Weatherall. "A simple traffic jam can't be beyond your skills."

"I was talking about other things, Jack. I thought you might want to talk about them."

Another surprise. "I'd like that," Jack answered. They sat on opposing couches, facing each other. "Where do we start?" Jack asked.

"Where do *you* want to start?"

"Why don't we start with why you gave the DX3 the power to control minds," Jack said.

For a second time, a smile crossed Weatherall's face. "I wondered how long it would take you to figure that out. You did it faster than I thought you would."

"I'm glad I didn't disappoint you." He stared at Weatherall, waiting for his answer. A silence stretched out while Weatherall mulled his answer.

"The answer's simple," Weatherall finally said. "We have no choice in the matter. If we don't get control of the population, society will fall apart."

"Ah, bullshit," Jack snarled. "It's always a fucking doomsday scenario with you guys when you need to justify something bad."

"Did you ever stop to consider that maybe it's the truth?"

"Why don't you explain it," Jack said. "Maybe I'll turn into a true believer."

"You want the 'big speech,' Jack? The one where the big, bad corporate boss justifies his actions because saving the world is more important than doing a few bad things. I can make that speech. I can talk for hours about how we've been living in an economic bubble for decades, juggling as fast as we can to keep it from popping. I can tell you that the world is running out of fossil fuel, and that without it we can't make things out of plastic or rubber, or make the fuel for the airplanes and big diesel trucks that keep world commerce moving forward."

"Everybody knows that," Jack interrupted. "It's nothing new."

"True," Weatherall snapped back. "But let me tell you something you don't know. Have you ever heard of Thomas Malthus?"

"Maybe," Jack answered. "Sounds like something I learned about in school."

"Eighteenth-century English cleric. He predicted population growth would eventually be mankind's biggest problem."

"So," Jack said, "was he was right? Is that a big problem now?"

"No," Weatherall said. "It turns out there's an even bigger problem—too few people. That's the big secret that we've been hiding. The population is shrinking, not growing. A shrinking population means a shrinking economy. Economies that don't grow, die, and right now the worldwide economy is dying. People aren't buying things. Factories are closing. People are losing jobs. The economy is shutting down. I guess you might say our economic clock is running out of ticks. We're just doing what needs to be done to keep the lights on and the world from going to hell."

"So how does the DX3 fix all of this shit?"

"Control, Jack. Control. DX3 gives us control."

"You've been controlling people for years."

"We've been trying to, but the tools we have—social media, entertainment media, subliminal ads, price manipulation—they just haven't been enough. We need more control to fix things." Weatherall paused and smiled. "It's like the traffic problem building up on the streets right now. As long as the drivers make their own decisions, we'll never fix it."

Jack knew he was right about the traffic. The AirTrans drones had started with manual controls, but the option was no longer offered; self-driving in three dimensions was just too dangerous to be allowed. Control was needed, but that didn't excuse the DX deaths. "So, the DX2 chips that killed my daughter and all of those other children. Just a control experiment gone bad?"

Weatherall's face blanched. He wasn't smiling; his response was slow. "I won't ask you how you know that; I suppose it doesn't matter. But I'm not surprised that you know."

"You lied to me. You're lying to me now."

"I didn't lie to you. I told you we had a problem with the chips. I just didn't tell you why."

"If I had known the truth, my daughter would still be alive." Jack realized he was shouting, and he struggled to get his emotions in check. He took a deep breath, exhaled loudly and continued. "What are you not telling me now?"

Weatherall considered his response. "I sent you the alert."

The words hit Jack like a hard fist. The alert was a piece of the puzzle he had never solved. Weatherall's statement left Jack shaken. If it were true—and somehow Jack instantly knew it was—then it cast doubt on Weatherall's guilt in Rebecca's murder. Jack was thinking it through when Weatherall's next statement sent him reeling. "I also sent you to the Goldstein apartment."

It was another startling statement, but the moment Weatherall uttered it Jack knew it was also true. He had never believed in coincidence. "How did you know about Goldstein's involvement?" Jack asked.

"I didn't," Weatherall said. "But it occurred to me that night that someone sent the murderer to Lupe's apartment. I entered a query into Unitex's main system for anything to do with UX Express. The next day it tossed out Goldstein's death. I didn't know if there was a connection, but I assigned it to you anyway. I knew that if there was a connection, you'd find it."

Jack fell silent, angry at his own failure to inquire. He blamed himself and the whiskey for missing the connection. Without the Goldstein connection and Tami, he might not have made the connection to the DX3. Worse, it cast more doubt on Weatherall's guilt. Jack felt his certainty slipping away.

"I answered your questions, Jack," Weatherall said. "I think it's time you answered mine."

Time's up. I have to decide. Jack knew that whatever he decided there would be no going back, no changing his mind, and no chance to undo what he would do now. His mind raced.

Was it time to follow through with Lupe's plan or go in the other direction? Did he believe in Weatherall's innocence in Rebecca's murder and the deaths of all the other victims? If Weatherall were innocent, then whoever was guilty would get away with it. But, on the other hand, did that matter? Weatherall was the reason Sarah was dead. He would never forgive him for that. In the dark recesses of his heart, he wanted Weatherall dead. The urge to bring him down, to see to him dead was overwhelming.

He made a show of not wanting to tell Weatherall what he knew, feigning reluctance, moving slowly, appearing to be mulling it over. Finally, he reached into his pocket and pulled out a Quantum Drive. He held it in his hand for a long moment before tossing it on the coffee table.

"What's this?" Weatherall asked.

"Everything."

Weatherall picked up the drive and held it in his hand. Jack could tell that he was thinking it through, considering his next move. He decided to give him a push. "If you don't want it, you can give it back to me."

Jack could see Weatherall's decision in his eyes. He watched him stand and walk to his desk, sit down behind it, and push the Drive into a Game console. In a moment, the blue light was on. Weatherall shot a stern glance at Jack. "All right, I'll look. But," he cautioned, "stay where you are. I'm certain I will have some questions."

The moment Weatherall's face went blank, Jack walked out of the room.

60

Zeus Is Dead

THURSDAY, JANUARY 1
8:11 a.m.

"Is he dead? Did *you* kill him?"

The disappearance and rumored death of Unitex President and CEO William Weatherall had dominated the news for the past ten days. An army of journalists and commentators had examined, dissected, analyzed and discussed everything about it. Everything except one thing: there was no confirmation from anyone inside Unitex that Weatherall had disappeared or died. No one was willing to use the word "missing." If pressed by the media to answer the question, "Have you seen him?" everyone had the same answer, "no." It was natural that Jack's first question was, "Is he dead?"

His question was directed at Lupe Vincente. She was seated behind what used to be Weatherall's desk in what used to be Weatherall's office, the same top-floor crystalline office wags had long ago dubbed the Crystal Palace. Jack's first thought when he saw her sitting there was that she looked out of place. The bigger-than-life Weatherall had always filled the office, but Lupe seemed small. She didn't belong here, even if she now showed the same attitude of arrogance, power and entitlement that was always present with Weatherall.

He had been requesting this meeting every day for the past week, his frustration growing with each denial. Finally, exasperated and angry, he went up to the executive suite and sat in a chair for hours until Lupe agreed to his request for a meeting, set for 7:15 a.m. the next day. He arrived on time, but Lupe kept him waiting for almost an hour before seeing him. He wasn't happy about the long delay, and he wasn't trying to hide it.

"Listen, Jack," she answered, looking up from the speech she was working on, "the truth is, I don't know. I think the board knows, but they're not talking, not even to me. I can't answer your question. I wish I could."

"But you did try to kill him after I delivered Tami, didn't you?"

Lupe didn't respond. She sat stone-faced behind the desk.

"Killing Weatherall wasn't part of the plan. Not until we had proof that he was responsible and acted alone."

"Are you not paying attention, Jack?" Lupe fired back. "I don't know what happened. But if he is dead, so what? You wanted him dead. You ought to be thanking me instead of questioning me." She glared at Jack for a long moment. "And do I have to remind you I'm the company's CEO. I don't have to answer to you."

She put her head back down.

Jack watched her work on the speech she was about to make to the New Year's Day PURE rally gathering in the Plaza below them. It would be her first speech since her promotion, and it would introduce her to the world as the new Unitex CEO. He knew she would use the excuse of working on it to ignore him unless he shook her up. He knew it was time he did. "Did I tell you that Weatherall sent me the alert the night Rebecca was murdered?"

Lupe kept her head down, but it was clear to Jack the statement got to her. "How do you know that, Jack?" she asked after a long pause.

"He told me he did."

"When?"

"When I met with him to deliver the virus."

"Did he tell you why?" She raised her head to look him in the eye.

"He said he knew that if he got me involved, I wouldn't let it go until the case was solved. He said he wanted to know who killed Rebecca."

"What makes you think he was telling you the truth?"

"He also told me that he sent me to the Goldstein's apartment."

Now Lupe sat up straight. "Why would he do that?

"He said he tapped the Quantum Banks for anything that might be tied to Rebecca's death. The A.I. flagged Dillon's schedule and tied it to the Goldstein death. He went around dispatch to assign the certification to me. He didn't know if it was connected. He figured I'd find out."

"Well," Lupe said, "that may be. But he still killed Rebecca."

"I don't think so."

She stared at him through narrowed eyes. "If Weatherall didn't kill Rebecca, who did?" she asked.

He had waited a long time for this moment. He wasn't about to rush it. He took his time answering her. When he did, he kept the answer short. "You did."

Lupe offered up a crooked smiled. "I think you've gone off the deep end, Detective."

"And not just Rebecca," Jack added. "All of the others too."

Lupe's smile faded. "Why don't you tell me about it? I've always enjoyed a good fiction story."

"Rebecca was suspicious about the DX3," Jack said. "I don't know how she found out, but she lived with you and probably stumbled across something. And after what happened with the DX2, she wasn't about to let it go. You knew she was scheduled to meet with Morton Johnson. You were afraid she would go public."

Lupe crossed her arms. "She was raped and murdered by that Dillon monster. If I had wanted her out of the way, I could have just had her shot or killed in a traffic accident."

"A bullet would have looked like an assassination. A traffic accident could be the same thing. But a rape and murder by an ex-con sex offender in an apartment with a VIRSUS system turned it into an open-and-shut case. It made it something it wasn't."

"That's ridiculous, Jack. I cared about Rebecca."

"You knew Morton Johnson pretty well, too, but that didn't stop you from having Peggy Owens pull the trigger to stop him from going public. Maybe Rebecca and Morton were harder to kill than the others. I don't know."

Lupe's face remained a frozen mask.

"Killing Goldstein, for example," Jack continued. "You didn't know him, so using the DX3 to set him up to die because he wasn't taking his pills was probably easy. It was the same with Donald Dillon and Peggy Owens. On the surface of things, Dillon was an easy choice. So was Peggy. They both might have worked if you hadn't been careless."

"How's that, Jack?"

"You didn't count on anyone digging deep. Dillon's sex offender charge was a bogus charge. It cast doubt on his motive. And even though you knew Peggy was gay—you had Jacob Steinberg set up her Game with a gay lover—you didn't think anyone would ever question her motive. She left a note. Dozens of witnesses watched her do it. You thought that would be enough."

"Anything else in your little story that you think I ought to know?"

"Plenty," Jack said. "Alwaze, for one."

"Why don't you tell me about it, *Detective,*" Lupe said. "You're managing to spin quite a story."

Jack smiled. "Alwaze gave you the opportunity to take me out of the hunt. You had him kill his wife and sent me an untraceable message to get me to his home. You expected him to kill me, but you figured that if I did somehow manage to kill him, I'd be on administrative leave and I.A.D. would tie me up with its investigation. It would give you time to finish your plan."

"So, is that the end of your little fairy tale?"

"Pretty much, except for the warehouse. That was another attempt to kill me. It might have worked if Rodriguez hadn't shown up and if you'd picked a shooter better than Duane Chapman to chip up and control."

"So, is that the end *now*, Detective?"

"Yeah," Jack said.

"Well, that's good. Because I know that if you had any real proof of any of this, you would have made a case, gone to the prosecutor, and you'd be here to arrest me instead of telling me a long, stupid story."

"You're right. I can't prove it to a prosecutor right now, but—"

"But nothing, Jack," Lupe said, slamming her hand on her desk. "Because if I did use the DX3 virus to kill Weatherall, then you'd be in a pretty sticky spot, wouldn't you? You delivered the virus to him. Who do you think they'd listen to? A drunk detective with a questionable record and a reason to kill him, or the president and CEO of the world's largest corporation?"

"I think they'd listen to the Unitex president and CEO."

"Well, then I guess that's that, isn't it? I'd say we don't have anything more to talk about." Lupe's dismissive tone signaled that the meeting was over.

"You're right," Jack said. "We don't have anything more to talk about. But I know someone you're going to talk to."

"And who might that be, Jack?"

"That would be me, Lupe." The voice was unmistakable. They looked in the direction of the sound to see William Weatherall in full stride marching across the room toward them. Three security guards trailed him. "I think you'll talk to me."

Jack was surprised by the control Lupe managed as she watched Weatherall cross the room. She waited until he was standing in front of her before she spoke. "Hello, Bill," she said, "It's nice to see you looking so well." She made it sound as if she had just bumped into him at a cocktail party.

"Don't you mean you're surprised to see me looking so well?" Weatherall said. "You worked pretty hard to make sure I wouldn't."

Lupe didn't hesitate. "I didn't work hard enough, Bill."

"I guess not, Lupe," Weatherall answered.

"But you know, Bill," Lupe said, her voice filled with contempt, "I was just doing what had to be done. I knew you wouldn't do it; you're too weak. But someone had to. Someone had to protect the company." She stared at him, pausing to make certain her words reached him. "I was the only one who could," she said. "And the only one who would."

Weatherall didn't respond. He nodded at the security guards, and they stepped forward to surround her. One of the guards reached to take Lupe's arm, but she brushed him away. With a final look at Weatherall, she stood, walked around her desk and headed for the door. The security guards moved quickly to surround her and escort her out. Jack watched her go. She held her head high, her back straight. Then she disappeared through the office doors.

Weatherall sighed as he stood in his usual spot at the windows, a dark silhouette against the bright daylight. He gazed out at the city, just as he had so many times before when Jack had walked into his office. He felt a certain level of comfort seeing him there. Weatherall wasn't a good guy, but at least he wasn't a murderer. The thought prompted him to ask, "Do we have enough evidence to convict her?"

"We have plenty of evidence," Weatherall said, turning to face him. "More than we could possibly need. I've had a few top folks digging into the Quantum Bank, tracing everything she did. It's not all in yet, but what we have is enough. But we won't need any of it."

Jack understood instantly, but he still felt the need to have it said aloud. "No trial?"

"No trial, Jack. None of this ever happened."

"Lupe?"

Weatherall's face was frozen in an emotionless mask. Jack saw the answer to his question in Weatherall's cold eyes. Jack knew in an instant that Lupe's life was over.

"It doesn't bother you?" Jack asked.

"Does it bother you?"

Jack didn't have to think about his answer, "No. It doesn't bother me." He paused, and then added, "and I know why it doesn't bother you."

"And why would that be?"

"'Any man who tries to be good all the time is bound to come to ruin among the great number who are not good.'"

"My old mentor Niccolò Machiavelli," Weatherall said. "You've been doing some reading."

"I have," Jack answered, "but I'm not sure advice written more than five hundred years ago is still relevant today."

"Oh, it applies, Jack. It applies," Weatherall said. He turned his back to Jack and stared out of the window again. Jack got the message, and started for the doors. But when he had walked halfway to them, Weatherall's voice broke the silence.

"Technology changes, Jack," Weatherall said quietly. "People don't."

61

Rally

9:17 a.m.

The elevator ride down from Weatherall's office was fast. Jack exited on the second-floor balcony overlooking the crowd and stepped out into the sunshine.

The morning was unseasonably warm—seventy-seven degrees—and forecast to get a lot warmer. Jack loved warm weather, but he found himself wishing that the weather this morning wasn't so good. The weather was at least in part responsible for the record-breaking crowd assembled in Unitex Plaza for the rally. Big crowds meant big problems, and the size of the crowd this morning all but guaranteed those problems would come. A heavy rain or a blast of cold air might help keep things under control.

But now it was too late. The crowd was already worked up, screaming obscenities and tossing things at the recorded twenty-story-tall holographic image of William Weatherall explaining his absence, blaming it on a minor medical problem now entirely resolved. His voice boomed out at the masses, but their catcalls and boos drowned him out. The horde wasn't happy to see him back, and the anger was growing with each passing moment. A collision between PURE and the Unitex exosuited riot police was certain. It was just a matter of time.

"Hey, Jack," Cassie said. He turned to see her standing next to him, leaning over the same rail, gazing out at the angry crowd.

"'Hey,' yourself."

"Is it over?"

"It will never be over. But if you're asking about Lupe, then, yes, it's over."

"Does Weatherall think there's enough proof to make it stick?"

Jack smiled. "It doesn't matter."

Cassie's short response made it clear she understood "I see."

They both remained silent for another minute before Cassie spoke again. "There is something I've been meaning to ask you. How did you know I was a cop before I told you?"

Jack smiled. "I listened to you."

"I don't understand."

"I listened to you. You told me."

"How?"

"You asked me if I had any *direct evidence* the DX3 was involved."

"Yeah. So?"

"Only cops and lawyers use a differentiation between circumstantial and direct evidence. I figured you weren't a lawyer; I guessed you were a cop."

"Pretty thin, Jack."

"There were other things. Like the stun gun you used on Rocco."

"I see your point. But if you suspected me, then why did you trust me? Why did you come to PURE headquarters?"

"I didn't trust you. I needed your help. I just didn't expect you to call it in right away when I showed up at PURE. You surprised me with that."

"You knew I called it in?"

Jack just smiled again.

"Okay, I notified command, it was my job," Cassie admitted. "I didn't have a choice. But," she added in an unapologetic tone, "I didn't know CSD would alert CPD."

"Noted, Cassie," Jack said. "It's ancient history now."

"Did you always know it was Lupe?"

"I wasn't certain until she told me she was guilty."

"When did she do that?"

"When I woke up on Monday in the apartment after being 'chipped up.' I asked what I was doing there. You heard her answer."

Cassie gave Jack another blank look.

"She said, 'She stunned *you* and saved *you*.'"

"I don't understand."

"Don't you?" Jack said. "She didn't realize it at the time, but she was saying that she was waiting for me, ready to shoot, when you—Cassie—showed up and stunned me. After you stunned me she couldn't shoot me."

"So, you're saying—"

"It was a plan. She used the chip to get me to the apartment so that she could kill me. She was waiting for me, gun in hand, finger on the trigger, ready to shoot the instant the door opened. The only thing that stopped her from killing me was you."

"Jesus, Jack. That's a reach."

"Not if you put it in context. She tried to kill me three times. That was the second time."

"And the first was—?"

"Alwaze. She sent me to him because she figured I was getting close to the truth. Alwaze accused me of having an affair with his wife. It's why he killed her, he said, and why he was going to kill me."

"But what if you killed Alwaze?"

"It was a win for her either way. I kill Alwaze—he's silenced and I'm out of the way, tied up in an I.A.D investigation; Alwaze kills me, I'm out of the way."

"She used the same thing she used to silence Morton Johnson with Peggy Owens?" Cassie said.

"Yes."

"But it was Weatherall who told you to back off Alwaze."

"Yes," Jack responded. "Because he sensed that Alwaze would be in danger if I kept questioning him. He didn't know it was already too late."

"And the third time?" Cassie asked.

"The warehouse. The whole thing was a setup. If I hadn't called Remi, and if Rodriguez hadn't tracked me there, it might have worked."

"When were you certain about all of this?"

"When I woke up in Lupe's girlfriend's apartment. It explained the last piece of the puzzle."

"How?"

"It explains what happened to the package Dillon brought to Lupe's apartment and later disappeared. Trace element protocols might have led us to its sender, but we never found it. It wasn't until after I woke up in Lupe's girlfriend's apartment, in the same building that Dillon jumped from, that I knew what happened to it. Dillon stashed it there before he went to the roof to jump to his death."

"But we don't have the package, and you don't have any proof it was ever there."

"No *direct evidence,*" Jack said with a mocking smile. He shrugged his shoulders. "But it doesn't matter, does it?"

"Is there anything you haven't figured out?"

"Two things. First, how Peggy Owens got the gun and ammo into the Unitex building? Not an easy thing to do. Lupe probably overrode security. Someone had to help her. It had to be Lupe, and it would've been easy for her to do."

"Okay. And the other?"

"When and how Lupe infected Duane Chapman with the virus. He was her delivery boy to the others. It should have made him suspicious of anything she gave to him. But I guess Eddie Rodriguez was right—Duane was dumber than a stone."

The crowd noise swelled. Bottles began flying and fights began breaking out everywhere you looked. A full-blown battle was imminent. Cassie watched the crowd for a long moment. "I have to go," she said.

"You know where I am on that," Jack said. "It's dangerous and unnecessary."

Cassie nodded. It was a signal that she heard him, not that she agreed with him. He expected her to walk away; he was surprised when she didn't. Something else was on her mind. He waited for her.

"Am I going to see you again?" she asked.

Jack didn't have to think about his answer; he had already thought about it. He answered her with just one word. "Yes."

EPILOGUE: A Green Flash

6:23 p.m.

Traffic crawled bumper-to-bumper on the two-lane blacktop. Horns blared, and tempers flared as frustrated drivers jockeyed for a place to park. Jack knew that he would never find a parking space along the side of the road or in one of the small parking lots unless he did something right away. Then, as if by magic, a car pulled out of the parking lot ahead and left a space open. Jack darted into it.

"Wow, that was lucky," Rebecca said.

"Yeah, it was." He didn't tell her that luck had nothing to do with it. The parking space had cost him three Game credits.

"Are we there, Daddy?" Sarah asked from the backseat.

"We're here," Jack answered.

Sarah squealed with delight and popped her seatbelt. She pushed the door release and wriggled impatiently, waiting for it to swing open. When it did, she jumped out onto the rocky dirt and started for the cliffs. Rebecca got out, too, hurrying to stay close and keep her in sight. Jack watched them merge into the crowd heading for the cliff.

Alone in the car, Jack was flooded with memories of his life with Rebecca and Sarah. He focused on the good memories, the times when they had all been happy together, when their life together seemed as if it would go on forever. He watched Sarah through the passenger window, skipping across the sandstone cliffs. Her curly, red hair glowed in the light from the setting sun.

He climbed out of the car and closed the door. The sound of the metallic click joined the noise of other car doors closing as dozens of people exited their vehicles and hustled to find a place in the growing crowd. Jack hurried, breaking into a short jog to catch up to Sarah and Rebecca and secure a spot along the edge of the cliff. They settled in behind the warning fence that rimmed the cliff's edge.

The Pacific Ocean stretched out endlessly in front of them. Long lines of swells marched shoreward to crash in eruptions of foamy, green water and mist against the rocks below. A stiff breeze, heavy with the smell of kelp, swept in from the cold ocean and soared up against the cliffs. White and gray gulls soared on the updraft, cackling, screeching and swooping low to snag pieces of bread thrown by people in the crowd. Jack noted the sun's position in the sky. *Ten minutes until sunset, at most.*

A green flash was so rare that most people believed it was a myth. It was said to take place when the sun was just below the horizon, its rays curving through the atmosphere and through particulates to create a green flash the same way it turned the sun orange or red at sunrise or sunset. It was said that if someone were lucky enough to view the bright, luminescent flash just once, they would be blessed with luck for the rest of the year.

Here, of course, a green flash was certain to appear. He had paid for it.

Sarah squeezed her father's hand, flashing a toothy smile. Jack smiled back. She had always been his beautiful baby girl. She had always been pure joy to him, a reflection of everything that was right in the world, the one thing that was impervious to the dirt and the grime that surrounded them all. And in a strange way, this iteration of her made him happy. Here, the real world could never touch her. She smiled at him and tugged on his arm. "When's the green flash, Daddy?" she asked.

"Almost here, Peanut."

Sarah wrinkled her freckled brow. "Are you sure it's gonna happen?"

"I don't see why it wouldn't," Jack answered. "Are you excited?"

"Maybe. But I don't really know what it is."

"I told you, it's a secret."

Sarah curled her lips into a pouty face that made her look just like her mother, a tactic she no doubt picked up from watching them argue. "But if you don't tell me what it is, I might miss it," she protested.

"You'll know it when it comes, I promise."

Sarah's eyes filled with excitement. She jumped up and down, chanting, "Green flash! Green flash! Green flash!"

Jack dropped to one knee and pulled her close. "You know, when I was your age, my Daddy took me to this very spot."

"To see the green flash?"

"That's right. And do you know what else?"

"What?"

"He told me the secret of how to see it."

"Tell me, Daddy, please! I won't tell anyone else."

"You promise?"

"I promise."

"All you have to do is stare right at the horizon and don't blink. Not even a little. Just wait for it as long as you can. Can you do that for me?"

"I can't blink ever?"

"No, you can blink, just not until after the sun is gone. Can you do that for me?"

"I think so!"

Sarah used a thumb and a forefinger on both hands to hold her eyes open wide. "How's this, Daddy?" she asked.

"Perfect, Peanut," Jack answered. He stood up and looked out at the jagged horizon where the ocean's relentless icy current swept down the West Coast to battle with the wind. He felt a kinship with the waves; he had been marching against a strong current since Sarah's death.

"So, what is it that you want to tell me?" Rebecca asked.

Jack sighed. He didn't want to talk about it, no matter how necessary or true it was. But he knew that he had no choice. It was now or never.

She deserved the truth, even though she wasn't really his wife, even if she was a construct of his mind in a world he had created, even if it didn't matter if he never told her anything.

"I won't be back after today," he said. "Today is the last time."

"Is there someone else?" Rebecca's voice was small, as if she didn't want to know the answer.

"No," Jack answered. "Maybe. I don't know. It's not the reason."

"Then what is the reason?"

"You know the reason. This isn't real."

"You've been saying that for a long time, Jack. It hasn't stopped you before now."

"I know."

"Then why now?"

It was a good question, one he had given a lot of thought. He was about to answer when a tugging on his pants stopped him. He looked down to see his daughter's bright smiling face. "When is it coming, Daddy?" Sarah asked. "I don't want to miss it."

"Don't worry, Peanut. I won't let you miss it." He glanced out to sea. The sun, oversized and colored a deep, fiery red, was melting into the dark horizon. "It won't be long now."

"Why now?" Rebecca persisted. "Answer me."

It was nearly dark. Rebecca's face and red hair glowed softly in the fading light. He had never seen her look more beautiful. He answered quietly, "I just can't do this anymore."

"But why, Jack?"

"It's the memories."

A hush had fallen over the crowd; even the gulls were silent. Somewhere in the dark, a car door slammed shut. Jack could hear a group of giggling young girls scramble toward the edge of the cliff to find a place in the crowd.

"But we have a lot of great memories," Rebecca said.

"I know. That's the problem."

"How is that a problem? What could possibly be wrong with having good memories?"

Sarah's small voice broke the quiet. "Daddy, it's almost here!"

Jack watched the dark ocean swallow the last thin sliver of sun. The crowd froze in silence. One moment passed, and then another. He heard a murmur of disappointment from somewhere in the crowd, but the murmur turned to a roar of approval as a bright green flash stretched across the horizon. The flash lingered there for the briefest of moments and then was gone, vanishing like the fleeting image of a ghost, leaving you wondering if it was ever there.

"I saw it, Daddy, I saw it," Sarah yelled over the cheering and applauding noise of the crowd.

"That's great, Peanut. I knew you would."

"What's wrong with great memories, Jack?" Rebecca persisted.

"It's just that I can't tell the difference anymore. I don't know where my real memories end and these begin. I don't know what's real and what's not."

Rebecca's fingers found Jack's hand. She squeezed it tightly. He took Sarah's hand and held it tight. The three stood together holding hands while the crowd broke up and moved to their cars. It wasn't long before they were alone with the stars and the sound of the surf crashing against the rocks below.

"I know you'll do what you think best," Rebecca said. "But I have a question for you."

Jack waited for her to continue.

"About the memories," Rebecca said. She leaned in toward him, her face nearly touching his.

"Yes?"

"How do you know there is a difference?"

--The End--